INTERWOVEN ignited my imagination with its precise world building and sense of mystery. No one in this story has the benefit of the full picture, and the more they discover, the more questions arise. The result is a novel with enormous heart and a clear message for readers who are seeking to define their purpose and place in the world: If we really want to reach for the stars, we have to tell the truth about ourselves.

—**Nathan Alan Davis**, playwright and screenwriter. Mr. Davis's recognition includes Windham-Campbell Prize (2021), Steinberg Playwright Award (2020), Lorraine Hansberry Award (2013)

INTERWOVEN is a dramatic blend of human struggle and creative science speculation to tell the story of the first space mission to go beyond our solar system. Authors H.E. Wallace and Roi Qualls have given us a riveting peek into our future and left us with a lot to ponder. I recommend this book to anyone who is hopeful and/or concerned for human destiny.

—**Dr. Louis-Gregory (Lou) Strolger**, Observatory Scientist and Deputy Head of the Instruments Division at Space Telescope Science Institute

INTERWOVEN by H.E. Wallace & Roi Qualls, is a powerful blend of science fiction and social commentary set in a future that feels disturbingly close. Earth is dying from the impact of human greed, indifference and falsehoods. We experience this through the life of the main character as he wrestles with his past, confronts the present, and discards everything he thought he knew to find hope for a future. It grabbed me in from the beginning and held me to the end. This is a profound, and beautiful read. I highly recommend it.

—**Sharon Nesbit-Davis**, Author *INTENDED, a marriage in Black & White,* writing coach and facilitator for Creativity Recharge workshops. sharonnesbitdavis.com

A vividly imagined work, this impressive novel will take readers on a breathtaking adventure into the future. The compelling characters, the suspense filled plot, the scintillating dialogue, the rich, jaw dropping descriptions, and the issues explored all make for enjoyable, thought-provoking reading. I wish for this book's success; it deserves it.

—**Sidney Morrison**, author of *Frederick Douglass: A Novel*

If words were akin to wine, the beautifully detailed world of *INTERWOVEN* could be described as carrying the exquisitely crafted undertones of Octavia Butler, the rich imagination of Ray Bradbury, while evoking the moral complexity so prevalent in the work of Ta-Nehisi Coates.

Set in the not-so-distant future, the result of human made mischief has culminated in a distressing predicament – we must prevail with untested space exploration, or perish. Standing at humanity's helm is Dr. Tah Morant, whose critical mission is further complicated by personal tensions that scientific advancement has proved unable to mitigate – childhood trauma, fickle friendships, and brittle intimacies of marriage. To make matters even worse, Tah must steer clear of danger while navigating with a moral compass clouded by corporate bureaucracy and personal vendettas.

If humanity is to survive, it must do so at the hands of a man who is as brilliant as he is fragile, and for that reason *INTERWOVEN*'s dire dilemma and vividly imagined world feels not just theoretical, but deeply personal and surprisingly timely.

—**Kemba Saran Braynon**, Award-winning architect and writer, author of *To Dine with the Blameless Ethiopians,* and author of performing work *A Dress of Steel Mesh*

POINTS OF FAILURE VOL. 1

INTERWOVEN

A NOVEL BY H.E. WALLACE AND ROI QUALLS

eBook ISBN: 978-1-965761-55-7
Paperback ISBN: 978-1-965761-56-4
Hardcover ISBN: 978-1-965761-57-1
Ingram Spark Paperback ISBN: 978-1-965761-58-8
Ingram Spark Hardcover ISBN: 978-1-965761-59-5
Library of Congress Control Number: 2025914704

Editor: Brooke Bryan
Cover Illustration: Asiya Aidarkhan
Interior Design: Marigold2k
Publisher: Spotlight Publishing House™ https://spotlightpublishinghouse.com

Foreword

Points of Failure: *INTERWOVEN*, a bold and beautifully written debut set in 2275, imagines a fractured future shaped by the ethical failures we've long avoided—climate collapse, surveillance, social fragmentation, and a spiritual hunger that can't be filled by what we've created. Though the story is set 250 years ahead, the questions it raises feel uncomfortably present.

What moved me most was the emotional honesty of the writing. Tah, the central character, is not a distant hero. He's a young man burdened by early loss and betrayal, caught in systems that constantly test his values. The relationships he navigates—those that nourish him and those that devastate—reveal the fragile balance between survival and integrity, conscience and complicity.

The authors—H.E. Wallace, a millennial-generation Black woman with deep creative vision, and Roi Qualls, an older white male writer and recent retiree—bring a rare kind of collaboration to this work. Their partnership across racial, generational, and experiential lines adds weight to one of the book's core questions: Can we transform what's broken by facing truth together—with courage, imagination, and care?

This isn't a dystopian warning or a utopian escape. It's something more honest and more urgent. The story pulses with tension, but not without hope. It invites us to reflect on how we live, how we relate, and what it might take to build a more just future—from the inside out.

The first in the Knowetix series, INTERWOVEN, left me both unsettled and inspired. The characters stay with you. The questions keep working on you. And the deeper invitation—to change not only the world, but the way we move through it—feels timely, necessary, and real.

This is the kind of book that will ignite meaningful conversations in book groups and communities everywhere. It invites us to examine ourselves, the past we carry, and the patterns we repeat, often without even realizing it. Through Tah and the other vividly rendered characters, we're offered a mirror: How do we face struggle? How do we respond to betrayal, loss, or the slow erosion of truth? How do we find the courage to break cycles and participate in something more whole? INTERWOVEN doesn't just tell a powerful story—it asks us to examine our own, and to consider how the work of transformation, already begun by so many individuals and communities, might be reinvigorated and sustained with greater integrity, mutual support, and collective vision.

—**Kim Douglas**, Founder of Write to Unite, Author of *High Desert: A Journey of Survival and Hope*, Co-Author of *Arising*

As a special treat to our readers
we invite you to capture the spirit of this book.
We hope you will enjoy these special messages from
H.E. Wallace and Roi Qualls

Dedications

To my mother, the golden ray that let me bloom in my own time. You
saw the writer in me before I knew it to be true. How blessed am I?
~ H.E. Wallace

To Linden–my wife, partner, advisor, helpmate, friend
and companion in this life and beyond.
~ Roi Qualls

North America - 163 NC*

Russia

North Pole

Kalaallit Nunaat

Alaska

Dominion of Canada

Chicago ★

GFM ●

S-245 ●

● Jarret DC

Texas

Mexico

★ Dominion Capital
● Point of Interest

| 1,000 km |

Cuba

Republica Dominicana

*2275 OC (old calendar)

Part I

1

I found my father first. He was in the hallway, on the cold marble tile. A bullet wound between his eyes. Blood pooled, thick and shiny, around his head. His cherry-black skin was gray like a fog laid over him and sank into his pores. His lips sagged. His wide nostrils that usually flared in his sleep stayed perfectly round as he lay there staring straight ahead like he was coming to check on me.

I looked up. Saw my mother's feet. One with a slipper, the other without. Both right behind the loveseat in the reading room. I stopped breathing and stared. I waited for her to move. Then I was there. Seeing her. Her knees bent at crooked angles. Bullet wounds in the palms of her hands. She wore the gold bracelet I picked out for her. She liked something similar worn by a character in her favorite soap opera. But in the moonlight that crept through the windows and skylights, I saw the dark smattering. The soaked collar. I looked away. Gasped for air. And saw the upturned chairs. The broken glass. The stamped footprints across the room. Child sized. Smeared. Sticky. I looked down. Saw they led to where I stood. Saw my blood-stained feet. And screamed.

That's what woke me the morning of the Umoja-19 launch. Forty-eight years old and screaming like a baby in the black before dawn. My wife, Itzel, tried her best to console me. Used her softest voice to bring me out of the nightmare and into our bedroom. I wavered, back and forth, stuck between a gruesome reality and an anxious present. I twisted away from her and hit the floor. Pain coursed up my leg.

"You okay, Tah?"

I groaned, pushing myself up. "I'm alright, Izzie. Go back to bed."

I had to catch myself. Felt like the floor was wet. Like I'd stepped in something slick.

"Did you, Tah?"

"Did I what?" I croaked, still trying to figure out if there was blood on my foot.

"Did you have the dream again?"

I don't know why I snapped at her, but I did. "It's just a– it's just a dream, Itzel." I inadvertently told on myself, too.

I turned around to see her, half aglow in the amber light shining from the baseboards. The new haum update was a little too responsive and a little too nosy for my liking, but she looked beautiful, sitting there, glaring at me.

"I'm sorry, Izzie. I just—" I stopped, hung my head. I didn't have an excuse for being mad at her, but anger always hits first. It's always the loudest and dumbest one to speak. "I'm sorry."

She moved the covers aside and stood. I took a step back, not ready to be touched.

We stared at each other for a moment.

I looked down first and focused on the floor warming my feet. No moonlight or blood stains. Just the amber glow and our shadows.

She stepped toward me.

"I'm soaked, Itzel," I said, peeling my shirt from my stomach and motioning for her to see.

She stopped. The low amber light honeyed her red-brown cheeks and brow. Her face softened into a sad smile. "Okay, Tah."

She sat on the edge of the bed leaving space for me. She looked up with tired and patient eyes. Her black and gray fly-aways haloed her cherub cheeked face. Who was I to resist an Earth angel?

I took a breath and sank into the bed next to her, curled forward to rest my elbows on my knees. She leaned into me, slowly. Then gently placed a hand on my back. I didn't flinch or turn away. I leaned into her, relieved of some tension when I felt her softness against my ribs. She rested her cheek on my side and gently rocked the both of us.

"What's wrong, Tah?" she asked, in almost a whisper, pitched up with worry. I felt her breath warm and cool against my salt-slicked shirt.

She was right to worry. I hadn't had the nightmare in years. Seven years to be exact. It stopped when our daughter, Mai, was born. My screaming-self got distracted that day, intrigued by my daughter's first cry. I couldn't leave Mai's side after that. I became that parent who filled their office with framed stills and videos. I captured Mai's first time using a spoon correctly, her first time holding a cup on her own, her first time playing with my kinked-up hair and discovering her own tight curls. I felt cured of all that ailed me the day Mai came into our lives.

So why now? What set little-me screaming?

"I don't know, Izzie. Stress?"

She hummed, unimpressed. "You've been stressed all year, Tah."

The year had been stressful. Beau hen-pecked everyone on the Umoja team for nearly thirteen months. We all needed to order new uniforms, take new pictures, update our profiles, be more accessible to the media, on and on and on. All of that on top of fulfilling our actual job descriptions of ensuring the mission timeline was nailed down and that the damn engine worked. My engine. Well, the one I developed and engineered. That's how Beau and I came back into each other's lives. He was the Program Director for GEM's Umoja program. I was the Chief Scientist.

I told her I didn't know. She nudged for a better answer. I stopped rocking and told her I didn't have one. And I didn't want to figure it out. Not then. Not that morning. I had bigger things to worry about than my nightmares. She didn't push for anything more. She removed her hand from my back and sat up straight.

I looked over my shoulder at her. I saw the worry on her face. I wanted to apologize and assure her I was okay. I just didn't want to admit that I was terrified. And that I didn't know why.

"I need to head in soon," I said, glad for the excuse.

I stood, kissed her forehead and shuffled to the bathroom. I kept my eyes down and let the door slide shut, cutting us off from each other. In the brief darkness, I wish I had glanced back.

When the bathroom lights turned on, I didn't look in the mirror. I didn't want to see my father's face looking back at me.

I morphed into him over the years: wide nostrils, deep set eyes, gray at my temples and on the crown of my head. Even my body was his. Too tall to hide, too thin to blend in. My mother used to cheer me up when the neighborhood kids teased me for my height and weight. I'd come home crying, dragging my arms behind me. She'd lift my chin, smile sweetly and say, "It *is* a shame that mothers carry the babies for nearly ten months, only for the babies to look like their fathers." She'd wipe my tears and look me over. "Lucky for you, my sweet string bean, your father is so handsome! The handsomest man I know!"

"You appear dehydrated, Dr. Morant. May I recommend an electrolyte beverage? I can warm it to help you return to sleep."

The recent haum updates were as much a nuisance as a convenience. The lights turned on when we talked or walked into a room. Now the mirrors watched, recorded, and advised.

I sighed at its assessment and prescribed treatment. "No, thank you," I said, stripping off my sour smelling sleepwear and climbing into the shower.

I relaxed as the steam rose. My shoulders sagged under the hot stream as it rinsed the sweat off. I told myself I was okay and it'd been thirty-eight years since that night. I was fine. I reminded myself of the day's mission and that I needed to focus.

I stepped under the overhead spigot, and closed my eyes, sure the nightmare had left me.

Moonlight filled that darkness. It lit up a dark room. A room filled with books and upturned furniture. I looked down. Saw her legs. Her bracelet. Her locs tossed back. Red everywhere. Even on my feet.

I screamed. Slipped. Hit my head on the wall behind me.

Itzel barged in, yelling my name.

"I'm fine!" I barked— naked, ashamed, and terrified.

Seven years of normal dreaming. No phantoms lurking behind my eyes. Just normal nonsense, or nothing at all. It made me *feel* normal. It would have been normal to have a nightmare about the Dragon's Gate— the anomaly in Neptune's upper orbit. Plenty of ships and single cell organisms were lost and destroyed, or altered beyond recognition over the past thirty-some years of its investigation. Recovery missions brought back night terrors in petri dishes and bent and twisted metal. But somehow I escaped the haunting of the electromagnetic specter that swirled in the deep dark edges of our solar system.

Dr. Andres Dragonomassi, the astronomer who discovered the Gate, used the words "dumbfounding, awe-inspiring, spiritual" and "all at once terrifying in the most terrific way" in her personal journals. And I imagine it was; sitting in a small observation craft, all alone, drifting out to where the sun can't quite reach. It would have been like seeing the aurora borealis for the first time, alone in an endless black pit. How terrifying, indeed.

That's what GEM, or the Galaxy Exploration Mission was contracted to explore. That's what the Umoja-19 launch was all about. Sending four astronauts, the first humans ever, over four billion kilometers away from Earth, past the outer edge of the heliosphere, where the sun stops. All the way to the edge of our Oort cloud where the Dragon's Gate hides. And then sending them through it. If that's not worth a nightmare, I don't know what is.

2

Our move from the nation's capital to the southwest was hard for Itzel, but we didn't have much choice. Her ecology rehab organization ran out of funding and GEM paid well. GEM City provided everything we needed, more than what Chicago ever did. It was just so different.

Desert surrounded GEM City and the corresponding campus— its labs and launch site eighty kilometers west. At first I ignored it. I'd board the tram just after sunrise, flip through the palm projection glowing from my GEM wrist rello, and pay it no mind. I shut everything out. I'd tune out all the announcements from the tram's viztras, whether they were screens at the front of the cars or playing half-transparent at the windows. The global updates never improved. Somewhere a monsoon season drowned a couple hundred, or an unseasonable drought starved another thousand. Sometimes it was a fire that burned five-thousand kilometers, ruining crops and cities indiscriminately. On occasion, a disease, new or old, collapsed an industry. There was always something awful happening somewhere. I suppose it was necessary to know to keep us focused on our purpose and working toward the Common Goal. But after so many years, I didn't need reminding. We all knew Earth was dying and we needed a new home. For that first year, I used my commute as an additional thirty minutes to review and finalize reports before and after work. Outside the tram meant nothing.

A year after our arrival, GEM hosted an event for family and friends. A gala to show off and celebrate recent accomplishments and new recruits. Beau swatted me when I rolled my eyes, then told me it was mandatory. So Itzel and I got dressed up and boarded the tram with about ten other couples. She sat next to the window. I sat next to her and we both stared out at the neighborhoods. We passed the potted trees and the well-planned parks, the GEM sponsored shops and restaurants, all white with solar-capped roofs. We passed the identical condo buildings differentiated by large numbers stamped over their entrances—125, 127,

129, et cetera, et cetera. It was clean and orderly, a significant difference from our Chicago days, but I could tell she didn't like it.

It wasn't until we exited the city shield that Itzel sat up, excited. She drew me in as she whispered about the orange yellow that crested over the dusty purple silhouettes of distant mountains. She pointed out the complementing ruddy orange ground to the deepening blue sky behind us, and the pink, orange, and red sunset enveloping us.

She introduced me to a masterpiece during that ride. I found myself mesmerized by the desert after that night. I made an effort to get my work done before I left the office just so I could spot the subtle changes each day. Like the slopes of sand and where they'd shift with the wind. The shadows cast by the mountain range bordering GEM City became old friends, greeting me at sunrise and sunset. For years the desert comforted me. Until Beau's ambition cropped up.

It began with decorating GEM City as the Umoja-19 launch approached. The blue, black, and gold wreaths hung on every condo door; the animated posters cycling through GEM history day and night; the change from white to blue lighting of every tree and lamppost to match our new uniforms; the banners over the tramline; the viztra-synched windows and telecscreens playing adverts at every tram stop and cafe; the smiling faces of the mission's crew members plastered on every tram; the blue and yellow lights swooping back and forth at every city entrance and exit. The makeover was too much, but at least it was contained. Until it leached into the desert.

Eight months before the launch, construction crews appeared fifteen kilometers west of GEM City. Suddenly big, lumbering machinery was scattered along the route. For a week they sat and spoiled the view. Then one day, they came to life and ripped the desert apart.

The excavators clawed away the sand. The mixers poured and the rollers paved over all the slopes that rose and fell over the years. I didn't have time to grieve before the next phase began— when they snapped together prefabricated buildings over the paved site, obscuring the northern horizon. To the south was a man-made rock wall bordering Canada from Mexico and Texas. I felt trapped between the two.

Other GEM employees were impressed by the pace of alteration, claiming it was a better use of all that empty space between GEM City and Campus. "The cobalt blue really pops out there!" one engineer commented when the buildings were finished. I wondered if he knew anything about color theory like Itzel did, but didn't think so. He never mentioned the sky-ground combo that had been there the whole time.

After they finished the sprawling hundred-and-five hotels, lined up like giant, blue tombstones, they installed the water towers. Bulbous masses painted black and blue and capped in gold, like crowns on rotted teeth. Then came the underground parking garages. They weren't so bad except for the flashing signs giving away their locations. Then the RV parks, the billboards, and the new tramline. For eight months I rode past the mutilation of a friend that'd been loyal for sixteen years. At first I was angry. But what could I have done? I just stopped looking after a while.

Three weeks before the launch, GEM's executive board ceremoniously revealed a large, engraved, red stone, harvested from the insides of a mountain, reading:

Welcome to Umoja Village
Est. June 14, 163 NC

It sat front and center of the fifty-kilometer grave site, facing the GEM tramline. It was insulting.

Two weeks before the launch, the desert city officially opened. I caught the end of a news stream about it. I had to ask Beau "What the hell?!" when I saw all the amenities, the hotel staff, the souvenir shops.

"I thought this was a temporary thing, Beau?"

He waved me off. "It is! But we have to consider bigger possibilities!" He smirked when I frowned. "Preparedness is key for progress, Tah!"

I couldn't argue, but I felt like he missed the point.

***

That morning, I saw the to-and-fro lights before we reached the village. As we got closer, the kick up of red sand bloodied the sunrise. The billboards shot through the fading dark, rapid fire flashing the day's events: A benediction. A speech. The shuttle launch, accompanied by the Global Orchestra. A marching band. A film. A choir. A raffle with great prizes! The leap through the Dragon's Gate followed by fireworks and a DJ set.

For fuck's sake, I thought. *Beau brought the damn circus!*

While the other GEM employees marveled at the spectacle I distracted myself with old habits. I swiped through the palm projection for my protocols. I closed my eyes and ran through all of the redundancies, precautions, and scenarios, step-by-step. For a moment I felt relief. My heart rate slowed. My mind cleared.

Right as I felt refocused, I heard someone balk, "Aww shit! I was wondering about them!"

I peeked around. Everyone on the tram was looking out the window toward the eyesore of a city. I didn't want to know what they were looking at. So I closed my eyes again and restarted my review, but the tram's chatter soured.

"What's their problem?"

I turned and saw protestors. As we shuttled past, I watched them stab the ground and unfurl flags and banners. Written in angry, red letters, they read: TICK TOCK GOES THE DOOMSDAY CLOCK!

"I can't believe security let them come!"

"Freedom of speech at its worst, hey?"

"I hope they get run off!"

I looked around and saw a clump of new recruits two rows ahead of me. Had this been any other launch I would have ignored the protestors and the recruits. Both parties had their opinions and reasons for how they felt, and normally I wouldn't care. Launches required focus and both parties were distractions. But there was something about those protestors. I couldn't stop watching them. Until they were too small to see.

My throat tightened when we came to the mile marker, fifteen kilometers from GEM Campus. I hadn't noticed the changes until that morning. The sign had the new GEM logo, an elongated diamond with a crosshair in the center; the call and response mantra, *Forever Onward! Onward Toward the Goal!* in its usual place above everything, but with the addition of saluting civilians of all ages. Including children. As we passed it I felt pulled backward. Back before I found my parents. Back to a time when we tried all of this before.

3

Beau was in my office when I arrived. He was seated behind my desk, looking down at his palm. His light brown hair was slicked back. His sharp face rounded into a smile as he read a message. He didn't look like the 50-year-old man I'd known since neither of us had facial hair. He looked maybe in his forties. Late thirties even. Something was different. I thought maybe it was the angle of his head or possibly the lighting. It was bright inside the GEM campus building, brighter still in the offices. The white walls, mostly white furnishings, and white, glass touchdesk made the room too bright. Itzel did her best to bring color and warmth into my office. She picked out two, burnt orange chairs to sit across from the desk. We hung paintings of plants and landscapes, framed family photos and videos on the southern wall like a gallery. One I could admire from my chair. I put up shelves on the northern wall to display crafts from Mai's toddler years, her school photos, as well as some mementos from Chicago and Itzel's world travels. Behind my desk was the prototype schematic of the deuteron engine. It had its own lighting and neatly hung over whoever sat in my chair.

I coughed.

He looked up. His eyes got big and his smile vanished when he saw me. "You look like shit, Doc."

I shrugged. "Got a lot on my mind."

"Need a psych-sesh?" he asked.

"No," I said, rounding the corner of my desk. I saw his call log float above his palm. It looked like it had been a busy morning for him.

He stood and smiled when he caught me looking. "Been getting a lot of calls!"

I sighed and sat down. I could tell he wanted me to ask from whom, but I didn't feel like it. I wanted to be left alone. I needed time to focus.

"Just got off a call with Felix Santigo, herself! Doesn't get much bigger than that!"

I smiled weakly. She, like all tech giants, had been gushing their excitement for months. I was glad it was Beau receiving the calls and not me.

He leaned back on the edge of my desk and folded his arms. "Buck up, Doc! Everyone will be taking their cues from us today!" He patted my shoulder. "You go out there looking like this, they'll think something's wrong."

I scoffed and rocked back in my chair. The ceiling lights were too bright. Itzel had suggested warmer lighting or dimmers, but I had told her that was unnecessary. That morning, I wished I'd listened.

He sighed. "What is it, Tah?"

I huffed out a laugh. *Where do I start?* I thought.

"If you have something to say just get it out now," he said, impatiently.

I turned to him. I considered mentioning the nightmare but I didn't. I was more upset by everything I saw on the way to work.

"Fireworks and a DJ, Beau?"

He looked confused at first then rolled his eyes. "I know, I know. You hate it. But–"

"But what, Beau? Here we are racing against a clock on a mission that could go wrong thousands of ways, and you turn it into a spectacle?"

He straightened and turned completely toward me, ready to debate. "Look, Tah, we need the public's support. The launch and leap are huge events, but they're just the start. It's going to take a lot of support— financially, politically, and socially— to pull this off. We have to keep the momentum going. Any slowdown will look like stagnation."

I shook my head and turned away. I didn't want to hear the sales pitch he used on everyone else. I powered my desk on, tapped through the biometrics and waited for him to leave. But he just stood there.

"You need to get your head in the game, Tah."

I took a deep breath and closed my eyes.

"If you're nervous, don't be," he said, softer, like he was coaching his son through his first baseball tournament. "Today is really big, Tah. And I know all this attention makes you nervous. But today is also a day to celebrate all the hard work we've done— that you've done!" He motioned to the schematic behind us. "All the stuff out there is to celebrate you and your engine!" I heard the apology in his voice. "You *and* Itzel have sacrificed a lot! That should be honored and celebrated, too!"

I looked up at him. He smiled like he knew what he was talking about. I never told him the whole story about how or why I made the deuteron engine. It never felt right to share it with anyone. He just knew about my research and the prototype I developed. He didn't know what was lost in the process.

***

Itzel and I were in our mid-twenties, only two years married, cooped up in our little studio apartment on the west side of Chicago. All of Saskatchewan and Alberta were on fire that summer. The sky was a thick, curry yellow and the news was awful if it was anything. I remember watching replays of a mudslide wipe the face off a few mountains out west all while the south was holding its breath for hurricane season. In the Midwest, we were hoping for just rain but knew tornadoes were inevitable as July rolled into August. The year 138 was turning out to be just as bad as the last.

Itzel came out of the bathroom, one hand behind her back, the other over her mouth. I sat up trying to figure out if I should be excited or worried based on the faces she made. When she handed the digitest to me, I froze. All I could think about was how much our living-costs would increase. We didn't have any savings and applying for additional aid was its own battle. I was years away from finishing my doctorate and she was on an unpaid internship. Our studio was a room with a bed, a bathroom, and a few shelves.

Then I looked up at her and saw pure joy. She laughed a laugh I wish I could have bottled and saved for my darkest times. I opened my arms and she fell into them, giggling and wide-eyed. We got wrapped up in how to tell her parents and what we'd name the baby and which of us the baby would favor. I hoped for an exact duplicate of her. Frown lines and all. She laughed big at that and let me know I was the source of a few. I kissed where she pointed.

Beneath her laugh and our hugs and kissing, beneath our hopes and dreams, was the number of homes, schools, businesses, and lives lost in the fires that day. I knew I couldn't doom a child to this world if I didn't try my hardest to find a solution to the Common Goal. Earth was tired of us and I was more convinced than ever that collectively we needed to find a new home.

Like most of my PhD cohort, I assumed GEM would figure out the Dragon's Gate sooner than later. But suddenly, our "later" was due in eight or nine months. If the Dragon was the only way out, I was determined to get my family off this planet as fast as possible. I put my PhD on hold and dove into anything I could find about the Dragon's Gate. I devoured the GEM abstracts and articles. Each one announced that they'd failed again but next time! It became apparent that "next time" meant *we don't know what we're doing*. According to the Doomsdayers, GEM was just wasting time and money.

It took about four months before I submitted my proposal based on the interplanetary orbital resonance between Neptune, its moons, and the Dragon's cycle. I found that in the right configuration of the celestial bodies, the Dragon's Gate opened for a short period of time. After my proposal got accepted, GEM started basing their mission timelines on my predictions. When I got the news from my advisors, I nearly passed out. I called Itzel and left a message that I was definitely on to something and that I'd be home in an hour.

I picked up some dinner to celebrate, using money we didn't really have. I burst through the door, chest first, proud as could be only to find Itzel hunched over, moaning and holding her rounded belly.

She miscarried, for the first time, that night.

When we got back from med, I just held her. Three days. Maybe five. She cried herself dry then disappeared into half days of sleep. Even then, she'd thrash and let out guttural moans as if she was fighting against whatever took our baby. After some weeks, crying became something else. Something almost violent. She'd turn herself inside out looking for the little life that had started and vanished inside of her. Then she'd recoil so deep, I had to check if she was breathing even if her eyes were open.

I hated seeing her like that, set adrift in an ocean of grief with no way to reach her and pull her back in. Her emotions tossed her around and left her to float somewhere far away even when she was sitting right next to me. Her big, dark, brown eyes turned fever-red then glazed over and she'd drift to a corner of the room where I wasn't and stay that way for hours.

Her parents told me to give her time but I couldn't sit and watch. I needed to do something. So I dove into my work. I got up early, made enough food for the day, kissed her hollowing face, told her I loved her and headed to the quantum studies lab. In the afternoon, I hitched a ride home on the trolley to make sure she'd eaten, then leave again. I'd ask a neighbor to check on her in the evening so I could get a little more work done. Night after night, I stumbled my way home around midnight, bleary eyed and aching all over. I slept in intervals to check her breathing, then got up a few hours later, and did it all over again.

What started off as a means to create a better future for a child I'd never know, turned into a life raft to keep from sinking into my own grief. I barely slept for the eighteen months it took to develop the engine. My research advisors voiced their concerns about my lack of sleep, weight loss, and apparent decline in hygiene, but I assured them I was fine. Just focused. So focused I lost about 20 kilos and ended up in med in a state of delirium. But I did it. I built the prototype and submitted it to the Global Contributors Committee. I developed the first engine to enable faster-than-light travel.

From my hospital bed, I watched Itzel accept the award on my behalf.

Five years passed before Beau convinced the board they needed me, as well as my engine, at GEM. Five years and another miscarriage.

After our second loss, she turned to me, eyes full of grief, and asked, "Why haven't you cried?"

I didn't say it, but I couldn't. Not in front of her or anyone.

When I didn't answer, I saw something inside of her retract. Something that needed to be unburdened. It pulled away from me and never came back. I didn't seek it out. I just focused on my engine.

4

Beau nudged me. "You still in there?"

I let out a long breath and nodded. "Yeah."

"Good!" he said. He slapped my shoulder and made his way to my office door. "You've got an interview in," he checked his rello, "ten minutes!"

I sat up. "Wait, what?"

"Remember? We talked about this! Global News Network wants an exposé on you. Family man, Chief Scientist Dr. Tah Morant takes us to the heart of the galaxy!"

"I don't think that's a good idea, Beau," I pleaded.

He turned back to me. "Too late, buddy. She's already here!"

"Who?" I asked.

He smiled, like a mischievous child. "Tessa Laine!"

Her name shot through me.

"Breathe, Tah. She's just interested in the man behind the machine."

I'd witnessed what Tessa Laine was capable of. I'd recently watched her Metalynx exposé with Itzel. It was unsettling. Ms. Laine clenched the CEO in a lie, and just dug in. She ripped her apart on camera, leaving scraps of who she pretended to be. It was a prime-time blood bath while Itzel cooked dinner and I folded laundry. Tessa Laine was as terrifying as she was award winning.

"The board thinks it'll help with GEM's public image," Beau said.

I thought about those protestors. A pole piercing the ground. A flag unfurling. I let out a sigh thinking how they'd love to see my public slaughter.

"Just make sure you highlight the good work we're doing, and all the benefits of Umoja-19. And future missions!"

I rolled my eyes. "Anything else?"

"Smile. You got this, Doc!" He slapped the doorframe and left.

I don't think ten minutes passed before she was at my door. I flinched at her voice, and was taken aback by her look. Her rust-colored hair was gathered into a bushel of frizz behind her sharp angled face. Her eyes were large and piercing. She extended a hand, tipped with red, pointy nails. Then she smiled and to my surprise the sharpness softened. "Tessa Laine, with Global News. Director Soncal said you'd be ready for me."

I stood, surprised by how tall she was.

"Ah, yes, Ms. Laine, thank you— er— welcome," I stumbled, warm in the face and neck as I shook her hand, surprised by her firm grip. "Uh— please have a seat. Can I get you anything?" I offered.

"I have what I need," she said, gesturing to an autocart blinking by her feet. "I know today is a busy day for you and everyone at GEM. I'm so grateful they gave me a little time with you." She paused and looked me over.

I suddenly felt self-conscious and regretted not taking a moment to brush my hair, shave, or practice a smile.

She let out a breathy laugh and said, "I can come back a little later if you'd rather. I have plenty of b-roll to record."

I considered her offer for a moment. I still had system checks to finalize. But I figured it was best to get it over with.

"Now is fine," I said, sitting back down.

She thanked me and went about setting up her floater. It'd hover just behind her shoulder, recording our exchange. Its chameleon-eye lenses, independent of each other, tracked us both.

"This won't take long at all," she said, miking herself. "I just want to get to know you and how you came to work for GEM."

She swooped around my desk, floater in tow, and went about attaching a microphone to my uniform. She grinned at me while she fiddled with it. I looked away. Her brown skin was pore less and tight like she had a few modifications— beauty treatments Itzel had mentioned in passing over the years. I never paid much attention but seeing the results up close made me grateful for Itzel's tiny flaws. I glanced down just as Ms. Laine's red nails flit around and snapped the small apparatus into place.

"You've got a lovely daughter," she cooed, pointing to my collection of videos and stills of Mai.

"She's my everything," I said.

And just like that, she had me.

I showed off Mai's class photos and some of her crafts. "I know this doesn't look like a buffalo, but I promise that it is," I said about the brown and black roundness mounted on a small green base.

"No, I can see it," Ms. Laine said, using her red nails to point out the horns and raised hump.

"She was two when she made this," I bragged.

"An eye for detail! Does she get it from you, or the other Dr. Morant?"

I chuckled. "Definitely her mother, the original Dr. Morant."

"Ahhhh, I see! Well, she takes after her in a lot of ways then. She's beautiful."

It felt good to not think about the nightmare or the mess in the desert, to take a break from the stress of the day. It felt good to talk about the people I loved.

"They are the most beautiful people I know," I said, unwilling to look away from a candid picture of Itzel and Mai chopping carrots. Mai was a lean four-year-old in the picture, excitedly holding up a dirty, thin carrot. Its green tendrils flopped over her small hand. Her smile took over her entire face. Her hair was pineappled on top of her head, spirals going in every direction.

Ms. Laine picked up a framed-still and said softly, almost to herself, "You look so happy in this one."

It was our wedding photo and the only one in my office featuring me. I wore a gray-blue kaftan with matching pants and stood half a meter taller than Itzel, dressed in a matching blue dress. She held a small bouquet of flowers she'd grown, clipped, and arranged for our day. Just as we left the temple, the wind kicked up and whipped her hair all around. We both laughed as the strands tickled and stung my cheeks. When we got the stills back, I looked at that one and thought if God and I ever spoke, I'd have to ask what I did to deserve her.

I looked over Ms. Laine's shoulder and said, "My family is the reason I'm here."

She hummed as she placed the frame where she found it. She glanced at her rello then lowered herself into the chair across from my desk.

I glanced at my rello. Ten minutes had passed and she hadn't asked me anything about the mission.

"I'm sorry, Ms. Laine, I didn't mean to take up so much time." I quickly sat and prepared myself.

"Oh, not a problem, Dr. Morant. This is excellent footage. People love a family-oriented angle," she said knowingly. "Most people say your friendship with Director Soncal is the reason you're here."

That caught me off guard. I heard more than what she said in how she said it. Like it was almost a question of me and not about me.

I replied cautiously, "Objectively speaking, yes. He did recommend my recruitment."

She raised her hands. "I mean no offense, I just heard you've known each other for a long time, and he saw the value of *you* being at GEM. Not just your engine."

"Are we starting?" I asked, waiting for a question.

She looked pleased and shrugged. "Why not? I think that's an excellent place to start. The dynamics of your friendship seem to culminate in today's events. Why not start there?" She leaned back into the chair and waited.

I'd never thought about it that way. Never considered the timeline of our friendship leading to an eventuality of something, but I liked her assessment and relaxed again.

"Alright. Sure. We met in prep-school."

I told her the easy stories. The safe ones. The ones I knew couldn't be switched around on me. I peppered in stories about some pranks Beau and I pulled on staff and upperclassmen. How I spent most of my holiday breaks with Beau's family in the Alps. I even told her about the one time his father took me hunting but I didn't have it in me to shoot. I carved around certain memories like Beau taught me to ski. Lean a little and tuck around the hazards.

"It was always an adventure with the Soncals! They treated me like family. Still do," I boasted.

"And today, you said your wife and daughter are the real reason you're here?"

"That's right," I said, smiling.

"I imagine they're very proud," she said, sweetly.

I blushed. "I'd like to think they are. All of this work is done with future generations in mind and that's something we should all be proud of."

She hummed and leaned forward. Cocked her head to the side and said, "I have one more question, Dr. Morant."

Now if I had watched more of her interviews, studied them like Itzel did, I would have known to end it then. She'd asked all the right questions. Sent me down memories free of thorny bushes and old pines. Leading me up to the one I didn't see coming. Smacked me hard and fast.

"What about your parents?"

5

That question broke a dam. I didn't think about the camera or Ms. Laine. I couldn't stop myself. I heaved down the hall. Slammed into the bathroom stall just in time to pitch everything I couldn't say.

Beau tapped on the door, "You okay, Tah?"

The way he said my name, not Doc, took me back to high school. He asked like if I wasn't okay we'd both get in trouble and his father was coming to visit. There was a consequence on the other side of that question mark.

"Yeah. Sure," I said, spitting and flushing it all down.

I stepped out of the stall. He puffed up his cheeks and blew out the air when he saw me. He called me a sagging willow tree in a rain storm once and I felt like it, thrashed around by everything. I arched over the sink and rinsed my mouth out.

"What happened in there?" he asked.

I didn't answer. I just wanted to get past all the drudged-up memories, lay the dead bodies to rest, and focus on something outside of me. "How long until the launch?" I asked.

He checked his rello. "Forty-five—"

"Good." I spat again and set the water temperature to hot.

I felt Beau watch me as my palms burned red. I met his gaze in the mirror.

"I'll see you in Command," he said and backed away.

I let out a silent scream when I was alone.

***

What I didn't tell Ms. Laine about Beau and me was the truth of how our friendship started. It wasn't a boyhood adventure or some wholesome schoolyard playtime. It was me knocking the shit out of him.

It was four weeks into my first semester at Great Lakes Academy, the "elite school for elite learners." A cute tag line to give some parents a sense of pride about their mostly shameful children.

Beau, or Aristide 'Beau' Soncal, was a short, stocky kid advertised to be friendly and kind by the admissions officer. She painted him to be the perfect roommate for little orphaned me. That he'd show me the ropes and help me make friends.

Either she lied or he was defective because he was outright nasty to me. Within the first week, he told everyone about my screaming night terrors. So much so, the other kids kept their distance, but whispered loud enough to let me know what they thought. That I was some psycho in the making. A mental case let out too soon. I tried to ignore them. Tried to stay focused on my studies like my grandmother encouraged me to do.

She sent me videos upon my departure, seasoned with my mother's affections and my father's admonitions. When she'd say, "I love you, Tolulopé!" I'd swear it was my mother. I'd break apart and spill everywhere when she signed off. Her voice became my security blanket. I'd wake up to her smile and fall asleep with her words in my ears. I'd sneak between classes and skip meals to watch her videos.

But one evening, Aristide came back early from the dining hall. Caught me with my face pressed against my viztra and crying. It was the last video she ever sent.

"What a fucking baby!" He said it like it was funny. Like he couldn't see there was something seriously wrong with me, an eleven-year-old child.

I fumbled, trying to stop the video and hide my shame but he kept going.

"Maybe if you stopped watching that shit, you'd shut the hell up at night! You fucking psycho!"

Something took over me when he said that. Before I knew it, I was out of my bed. Bent forward. Charged at him. Caught his sternum on my shoulder. Slammed his ass against the wall so hard it left a dent.

He yelped. Slumped. Gasped for air. I stood over him. Fists in knots. Teeth clenched. Breath sharp. And I knew if he tried me, I'd break bones and teeth. I felt it. Rage. I hadn't felt it before but I liked it. Screaming-me felt avenged.

He writhed and grunted, twisted around to his hands and knees. Started rocking back and forth like a dog fighting down a rotten meal. I might have even smiled watching his face turn red and veins bulge along his neck. But my rage soured when he stopped making sounds. I got nervous. Backed away. Tripped and stumbled toward the door. Bile rose in my throat. Head filled with static. My hand worked the wall. But my eyes were on him. I felt the metal edge of the alarm and slapped it right as he vacuumed in a breath.

"Cancel it," he coughed out.

I hesitated.

"Cancel it, asshole!" he croaked.

I did. But I stayed by the door. Watched him. Watched for loss of consciousness. Loss of blood. Loss of life.

He held his stomach and rolled himself back to sitting. Coughed and labored out some breaths. Let out more curses, too. He winced trying to stand.

"Are you okay?" I asked, more curious how alive he was than about his pain.

"Yeah."

"I can call med if you need it," I offered.

"No, no. No," he said, trying again to get up. It took a while but he hobbled to his bed and flopped onto his back. "I don't need this on my chart."

I hadn't considered that. It'd show up on my chart, too. Except not under Medical. This would be under Behavioral. Melancholy and antisocial were already stacked on top of depressive isolationism. I didn't need "violent outburst" added to the list, confirming my classmates' suspicions that I was, in fact, psychotic. But I started to feel bad. He didn't kill my parents. He didn't even know they were dead.

"I'd be the one in trouble," I said, hesitantly. "You'll get time in the infirmary."

"You don't get it."

What was there to get? I thought. "I'd love time in the infirmary, get to skip class and watch space docs all day."

That made him chuckle. He twisted his head around. Grinned with tears in his eyes, "You're so weird, man." He turned away and resumed staring at the ceiling, puffed out a few breaths and said, "I don't want to explain how a scrawny ass kid like you knocked the shit out of me."

I didn't understand at the time. But I'd eventually learn. Aristide meant *The Best* where he was from. His father didn't take anything less than that in any part of Beau's life. Beau was what his mother called him. Meant Beautiful, or Handsome. He told me to call him Beau a few days later. Aristide didn't seem to mean much after that.

***

That rage stayed with me, swimming below the surface. It kicked up less and less but it never went away. Scorching my hands in the bathroom sink helped burn it all back down. The screams, the memories. The anger and rage. I collected myself and steam-cleaned all that mess Ms. Laine broke free. But one thing didn't go away, a thought, a warning my father gave.

6

"Nothing good will come of this,** Tolulopé," my father grumbled from his office chair. He was a shadow dressed in a plain beige tunic with the sun pouring through the windows behind him. His lean, black body hooked forward over his work, head bowed, looking up only to show the whites of his eyes cupping their black centers. He waved me off and resumed working.

I thanked him for his time and counted the floor tiles back to my bedroom. Fifty-two to be exact.

I quietly closed my door and sank into my bed. I looked around my room at all the news clips about the upcoming mission. The posters of the Mars habitat structures stared back from all four walls. Smiling families waved from the mission headquarters. I wanted to be there more than anything.

I let out a defeated sigh and picked at the skin around my nails. My eyes stung and all I could think was how unfair he was. Everyone else in my class was going. Everyone except me and the Jehovah's Witness girl. She said it was against her religion and I figured my father felt the same. Any time I brought up the Martian mission, he'd say something about, "haste makes waste" and "all things in God's time." Whatever that meant was lost on me.

It wasn't just that everyone else was going, or that I would have given anything to go. It was the embarrassing fact that I wanted to *be* like everyone else. Besides the obvious physical differences, I was the youngest in my class by at least two years. By all measures I was a freak. Any deviation, including missing out on activities, was permission for my classmates to rub in my face how unlike them I was.

I heard my mother as I bit at the skin around my nails, tasting that first hint of blood. My father grunted back. Then she was in my doorway, face framed by a few coiled locs, the rest swaddled up in bright green cloth matching the loose kaftan she wore. She smiled.

"Your cousins will pick you up in the morning, Lopé. Kiss us *both* before you go."

***

Ten-year-old me would have wept walking into Command. All his dreams brought to life in neon blues and whites shining from floor-to-ceiling screens filled with data and video. His jaw would drop at the new monitor by the entrance, showcasing the immense crowd at the launch site. From the drone's view, the crowd looked like colorful static.

As much as I resisted all the fanfare, I had to admit it was beautiful. A million people gathered together looked like a well-earned celebration! Cartoon versions of the astronauts leapt around the sunshield and surprised the crowd where they landed; holograms flitted through the air, boasting the nations represented and the unifying Common Goal. The Global Children's Choir was on the stage, built around the shuttle's launch pad, heavenly singing the Global Anthem.

Ten-year-old me would have said, "See, Dad! Look how happy they are! It can't be all bad!"

He'd start asking how and what it would take to be part of the Galaxy Exploration Mission Command team. If someone told him, "Hard work," he'd grin and say, "No problem!" If another told him, "Sacrifice," he'd sign over his free time and sweets in humble offering. He would have given anything to be greeted with salutes from Dr. Jones, my team's lead, and the rest of the Command team. He would have gladly worn the uniform, slid an implant into his ear and got to work. Ten-year-old me hadn't experienced loss yet. He'd only known wonder.

It was wondrous when my cousins and I arrived at the ALN Martian launch that spring morning in 125. Ten-thousand people sang and danced to the music playing over the loudspeaker. It was the most joyous thing I'd ever seen. We apologized as we side-stepped through the crowd to a small section at the top of the bleachers. I was rapt when I saw the thirty rumbling ships half a kilometer away. The global anthem played. All ten thousand of us put our hands over our hearts and sang. We gave our allegiance to the Common Goal and prayed for a better future. I had never felt more committed to something in my short-lived life than in that moment.

I wanted to feel that excitement again as I watched our four astronauts cross the access arm leading to the shuttle. Part of me wanted to be wrapped up in the celebration like everybody else. The million or more-crowd gathered around our launch site, huddled under a massive sunshield was dwarfed by the three billion people tuning in from all over the world. Just for our four brave astronauts. What they represented. I wanted to feel proud.

The crew posed in the center of the footbridge and filmed a live video. It played on the sunshield, showing mostly the edge of their flipped-up face guards, their hairlines, their eyebrows, and the enormous crowd surrounding them. The sea of people surged in excitement when they saw themselves in the same frame as the global heroes. Heroes on the verge of sacrificing everything for us. For the Common Goal.

I don't know if I could have explained to wide-eyed me the choking difference between cheering on strangers and prepping for the possible loss of four friends. But I stopped breathing when the hatch closed.

"Transition to internal power," the launch director ordered.

As I watched the crew tether themselves down and run their checklists, I found myself thinking about their families. About Commander Beirdot's youngest. He was probably sobbing in his father's arms while her oldest tried to be brave; the pilot's fiancé, twirling his new ring, red-eyed from crying, wishing for one more goodbye; Chilikimari's wife watching from med as she managed her fifth pregnancy, their four other children in various states of nerves and naps; and Enros's family grieving his mother's death and praying for his safe return.

I couldn't conjure the excitement I felt decades ago. I hadn't for years, but this mission was different. Each phase of it held success in one hand and catastrophic failure in the other. I knew that if one of the thousand points of failure went wrong, I'd lose my mind. Because it was my engine taking them far, far away from their families.

"Thirty seconds. LD verify go for launch," Commander Bierdot said.

"LD verified. We are go for launch. Commence ignition sequence."

I looked to the launch arena again. The crowd looked delirious as vapors rose from the cavern-hold. *Lucky them,* I thought. I was knotted up in fear.

It was easier when I watched those thirty cruise ships take off for Mars. The way they roared to life and climbed up the sky, one after another. Like metal-clad thunder birds rising their way back to the heavens. The bleachers vibrated so much my teeth hurt. My bones rattled. My vision blurred. But I couldn't stop watching. They climbed higher and higher up invisible ropes that only presented themselves in the jet streams they left behind. I waved. Frantically. Enthusiastically. I laughed. I cried. I saluted them. All five-thousand volunteers on board those ships. All heroes. All journeying to fulfill the Common Goal! My heart nearly burst, spilling with joy, envy, and excitement as they disappeared into the blue. The perfect blue sky. And were gone.

7

All of **Command** focused on the split screen of the main display. One half showed the rocket boosters attached to the carrier shuttle below ground in the cavern hold. Vapors snaked through the air as the rockets readied and cooled. The other half of the screen was a top-down view of the shuttle's capsule, where the astronauts were buckled in and waiting.

The countdown at the top of the screen slammed to zero.

The boosters ignited. White light burst from their tail ends. Two million pounds of force erupted through the underground hold. The video blurred as the force grew.

The half second between ignition and lift felt like forever. I held my breath. So much could go wrong in an instant.

"Lift off, we have lift off!" the launch director announced.

The tension in the room eased a fraction.

We're doing it, I thought, *We're on our way!*

The launch director changed the video feed once the shuttle was well above the crowd. The split-screen became one. A blue sky, a red desert, and spiraling jetstream's of the rising carrier shuttle.

Once the shuttle rolled into position, thirty kilometers in the sky, angling just right to exit the atmosphere, I exhaled. That relief faltered when a relayer ducked in front of my station to approach Beau in the center of the room. He bent forward and whispered something. Beau's back was to me but I saw his body tighten.

Dr. Jones and I exchanged a glance.

Beau turned toward the left side of the room. "Shit," he whispered.

I looked. And froze.

Angry black clouds spewed from along the bottom left of the screen, just outside the sunshield. Not twenty meters from the crowd. Flames flashed within the black.

Beau shouted. "Groundkeep! Come in Groundkeep!"

The camera zoomed in.

Dr. Jones cried out, "Oh my God!"

I watched, speechless.

Spectators scattered into the desert. Some toward the medical tents. Fifty, maybe more. Some stopped. Ducked and hid under each other. Others scrambled. Doubled-back. Many trailed each other, until one of them stopped. Or something broke the line.

Then they were gone. The screen went black.

Command filled with worried murmurs. Beau stood at the podium at the front of the room and raised his hands. Quiet settled around us. He spoke firmly. "Our priority is the Umoja-19 crew."

The room went silent.

"Let Groundkeep do its job so we can do ours."

He promised to keep us informed if the situation escalated, if the mission needed to be scrubbed. Or if, for whatever reason, we needed to evacuate.

Something pulled in my gut.

Beau finished with, "We must remain focused on the mission!"

Most of us were prepared to proceed. Most of us. I felt my own resistance drag against me. My throat tightened the more I thought about what I saw. Black clouds. Red lettered flags. Running people. Flames. I shook the thought out. I knew Beau was headstrong, not heartless. If it was serious, he would call the mission off. I was sure of that.

Dr. Jones nudged my arm. "You okay, Dr. Morant?" she whispered. Her black skin reflected the blue light from our station. Her face showed open concern.

I thought about saying the mission should be scrubbed, but I didn't. Sentiment wasn't a reason enough. Instead I said, "Yeah, just a little rattled."

She nodded, whispered, "Me too."

We returned our focus to the main display and watched the shuttle pitch itself out of the atmosphere, into orbit. It hurled, over 40,000 kph, toward the space launch station. The launch director confirmed arrival time with the space station team, eight minutes to contact. The crew sounded off to assess communication. The medical team investigated each crew members' status.

No mention of the ground situation. Just business as usual.

The visual stream switched to inside the space station once the shuttle docked. There was a livability about the station. Decorations hung on the walls. Plants hung from the ceiling. They even had a station dog, named Luna, trotting through the corridors. It was far more pleasant than the functionality of the carrier shuttle or the Umoja craft. Something about it reminded me of the Mars cruise ships. And the Mars cruise ships were something!

They had terraces and playgrounds, food courts and movie theaters. I was jealous, like any space-case kid would be. The Mars kids were living my actual dreams. Every night of my young life, I dreamed I was an astronaut, or an interplanetary orbiter rocketing around planets and moons. Or a tourist turned explorer, jetpacking far away from Earth. The closest I ever got was the MarsPals app on the government platform. It let kids like me, reluctantly Earth-bound, jealous and fascinated, talk to kids on their way to Mars. It was actual magic.

My first question was, "What's it like in artificial gravity?"

I was in the middle of eating dinner when my rello buzzed an hour later. I leapt out of my chair. I asked to be excused when I was halfway down the hall. I tapped on my desk, opened my viztra screen, and there it was— a waving icon of a kid with bantu knots.

"A little loopy. I get dizzy a lot."

I rolled my eyes and thought, *what a weenie*!

Another kid with stick-out ears and locs split into pigtails, replied soon after. "I can do backflips when they slow the generators down!"

That was the kind of answer I was looking for. They sent a recording a day later of their low gravity backflip. It was more of a half twist-something but it was better than what I could do on Earth.

Those five weeks were the happiest of my childhood. I raced home after school every day, grabbed a snack and disappeared into the magic of MarsPals. I made more friends in that short time than the six years I was enrolled in school. I even talked to a few girls. The Mars Mission made all my dreams seem possible!

***

Luna, the station dog, and four techs greeted the Umoja crew. They escorted the astronauts to the medplex and helped them into their private pods, which earned the nickname "personal torture chambers."

They weren't kidding when they joked about it. Each pod was equipped with hardware to perform the genetic reiteration procedure. As awful as it was — and it was awful! — the science was fascinating.

Over the years we found that deuteron leaps, traveling faster than the speed of light, destroyed living organisms. So a medical procedure used to combat degenerative diseases was modified to make rapid space travel viable. Our astronauts were fed a biostimulant, aka Biostim. That was followed by a bioscan where they lay naked in a cocoon harness. Trillions of scanning nanofilaments generated a physiological snapshot. From there a genetic patch was made, and injected when the astronauts landed at their destination, healing any genetic fissures that inevitably occurred during the leap.

"Prepare biostim," the chief physician ordered.

That was the catch. Biostim. By any definition, biostim was as close to death as anyone could get voluntarily. Even Commander Bierdot, having birthed both sons naturally, agreed. She joked after her first biostim experience, "at least you get to hold a baby after delivery!" She's gone through the genetic reiteration procedure at least forty times since. She said nothing about it ever got easier. Enros, the crew navigator, described it as a screaming sixty seconds of infernal torture.

"Prepare bioscan," the physician ordered.

When I was young, I never thought about all the stress that accompanied space exploration and all the torture we put our travelers through to plant a flag, snap a picture, and leap our way to Neptune. I think about it now and question whoever thought it was a good idea to send children to Mars.

I remember asking my MarsPals, "Do you miss Earth?" It was probably two weeks after the ALN launch. The fleet of ships was a quarter way to Mars.

A little girl with big, dark eyes, replied, "Sometimes. I miss the wind."

That was the first time I ever thought about missing the wind. I stood outside the next day and tried to imagine what it'd be like without it. In the hot sun, I felt the wind cool my neck and forearms. I heard the palm fronds clattering a woody applause. Past the trees I saw birds strike poses in midair. I smelled my uncle's frying food. When the wind changed direction, I smelled my mother's flower garden.

I got a little sad and went back inside.

That didn't stop me from asking my questions. I wanted to know everything. What was the grossest space meal? How did they sleep when the generators slowed down? Did they have to study about Earth anymore? Were they excited about Mars?

The last question got mixed answers. Some kids were electric about Mars. They chattered through five recordings, each seven minutes long— the maximum time allotted— about which habitat bubble their family was assigned to, what their daily tasks were going to be, and how cool it'll be to see the first Mars-grown crops. They talked about that like they'd be growing more food than us in a year. One kid said, "We'll probably have to ship you some food!" I laughed at that. But it wasn't funny for long.

Other kids shrugged and said they'd probably prefer staying on the cruise ships. Less work, more play. That was understandable. I hated my chores, too.

A few kids cried and cut their recordings short. Those replies annoyed me. I felt like those kids didn't understand how lucky they were. I wanted to argue with them. Like didn't they know they were global heroes? That kids like me envied them? Didn't they know they were making history as the first Earth-born Martians? What was there to cry about?

Looking back, I wonder if their bodies knew that it would only be a few weeks before all there was to do was cry.

8

One evening, after I logged off MarsPals, I made my way to the kitchen for a snack. My father made peanut cakes— my favorite! He balanced the sweet and salty to perfection, and baked them to a crunchy crisp. The whole house smelled buttery, salty, sweet for hours! It took all my self-control to wait until bedtime to get my snack.

I turned the corner and paused. From the other side of the kitchen, behind my father's office door, I heard my parents speaking in low, tense tones that warned me to keep my distance. I hesitated. I thought maybe I should wait and come back later. But by the sound of it, they'd be in there for hours. So I snuck along the counter, quietly slid the glass jar closer to me. They stopped. I froze, held my breath. I waited until they started up again, quieter. I tried my best to move silently. I grabbed two plates, gingerly placed the cakes on one, but I bumped the other plate and it shattered on the floor.

Their voices stopped. The office door unlatched. I considered running, leaving my snack on the counter, and hiding around the corner.

"Lopé?" My mother stepped halfway out of the office. My father leaned over her. They looked tired and worried.

"I'm okay," I said quickly. "Just getting a snack."

"Did something break?" my father asked.

I dropped my gaze. "Yeah," I said. "I accidentally knocked a plate off the counter."

He stepped from behind my mother, and floated toward me in two smooth strides. I moved out of his way as he swept the pieces up and tossed them.

"More care next time, yeah?" He cupped my cheek and smiled. Then disappeared back into his office.

My mother stayed in the doorway a moment longer, nodded, then vanished and sealed the door behind her.

I carefully grabbed another plate and placed several crisps on it for them. I put their snack on a tray but halted when I got to the door.

"I do not want him talking to them anymore," my father said in a low rumble.

"Why? He's made so many friends."

"Yes, but what happens if they stop answering?"

I didn't hear my mother's response. I got caught up trying to work out why he would ask that. *Why would they stop answering? Surely not my MarsPals.* I sagged, dragged down by sudden doubt. What if they weren't my friends after all? What if they didn't even like me and were just answering my questions to be nice? But that didn't make sense. Everyone was so kind. Especially Amma. She sent me messages without me having to ask anything. That had to mean something, right?

I missed something my father said, only catching the tail end, ". . .out of the sun."

The sun? I thought.

"What are you saying?" My mother sounded skeptical and concerned.

I leaned closer, my ear hovered next to the door. My arms burned with the weight of the tray, but I ignored it. I wanted to know why my friends would stop talking to me. The idea hurt to think about.

I heard my father's chair creak as it did when he leaned back, hands clasped behind his head. He hummed out a low rumble. "An X53 flare would. . ."

I pulled away, confused. I knew plenty about solar flares. Every space kid knew about them. I knew they picked up this time of year. Satellites glitched most often during the late summer but there was no threat, as far as I knew, to Mars-bound crafts. No communication impairments had been documented about the cruise ships, according to all the updates I read. Even my friends on the ships confirmed it— they hadn't had any interruptions since they left despite a flare erupting right after the launch. He was making mountains out of mole hills again. Always worrying!

I leaned in, but missed some part of what was said.

". . . this is the third time I've sent documentation about the radars."

"And?" my mother asked.

"And nothing. They say nothing back."

There was a sadness in my father's voice that I didn't recognize. He sounded smaller somehow, more distant. It pinched something in my throat to hear him like that.

"If X53-alpha-alpha-theta erupts—"

My mother stopped him. I heard her move around the room as she hushed and hummed. I heard her softly say, "God's Will is His alone."

"But—" My father's voice was muffled, as if he were cradled against her.

She hummed, "But nothing. We pray."

***

The crew changed into compression suits equipped with their genetic patches, then boarded the Umoja craft. They floated to their stations and began their preliminary safety checks. When that was done, Bierdot requested a private moment with the crew. I knew she was checking in with each member. Everyone had to know that everyone else was committed and confident. That was her way. I always respected that.

But we never told them what happened at the launch site.

Once the crew cut the audiovisual feed and our main display went black, Beau returned to the podium and brought up the lights. Shadows cast down his face. He looked grave, mournful even. He cleared his throat to get our attention. Once the room quieted he informed us that he had been in contact with Groundkeep. "They've confirmed that the situation at the launch site has been contained."

I heard a few sighs of relief. Dr. Jones whispered, "Thank God," into her praying hands.

Beau went on, matter-of-factly. "There was a valve malfunction, resulting in damage to the hydro-reserve and a subsequent mechanical failure. All fires have been extinguished. Damage was contained within the exhaust evacuation system. There have been no reports of significant damage to the launch pad. According to Groundkeep, the incident occurred after the shuttle was thirty kilometers above ground. So, rest assured our astronauts are safe."

He paused and looked around the room like he was looking for something. A reaction of some kind. But most of us were waiting for directions. Proceed or scrub.

Beau cleared his throat again and dropped his eyes. "Unfortunately, there have been injuries."

I knew that was coming. We all did. We saw enough to know that there were more than just injuries.

Beau let the words fall out, flat. "There have been deaths."

I exhaled, not realizing I'd been holding my breath. Someone broke across the room. A cry spilled out. The launch team, stationed diagonally from mine, huddled around their newest recruits. I saw some of the same faces that spoke out against the protestors. Their boasting vanished. They crumbled into themselves and disappeared behind their superiors and cohorts.

Beau shifted his weight and gripped the podium. He raised his voice, quieting the rest of us. "GEM is attempting to contact the families of those involved and will take the necessary steps to ensure all parties are served in the best way possible. The crew is our priority and we need to support them more than ever. We must prevent any and all distractions to keep them safe and focused. Per GEM guidelines and procedures, what happened earlier did not endanger the Umoja-19 crew and therefore does not justify aborting the mission. We must let the crew make that decision for themselves."

The recruits, obviously distressed, excused themselves. The rest of the room resumed dutiful silence.

When the crew comms came back, I watched Bierdot on the main display. I looked for signs of what she might say. She looked straight into the camera, stoic and brave. That's how I knew her to be. Out of her cohort, she was the most courageous. She was often the only one to speak up when other recruits were too shy, or prideful, or too afraid to question. She listened and weighed the facts before she made a decision. She called off previous missions based solely on the trepidation of another crew member.

Beau stood with his back to everyone in the command center and asked, "What is your decision, Commander?"

"Umoja-19 is prepared to proceed."

I nodded in agreement. As did most of Command. There were some members who dropped their gaze, slowed their movements. I could understand their reservations. But there was a protocol to follow. And the crew were prepared to continue. Besides, there was nothing we could do about what happened.

Beau turned to us, face open and excited. He clapped his hands and boomed, "You heard her, people! Let's get it! This is the leap of a lifetime!"

Looking back, I should have spoken up, although I'm not sure how much that would have changed things. But like everyone else, I followed protocol. I donned my remote gear and prepared for the journey ahead.

My engine's hologram came to life, hovering above my station. My visual shield, gloves and audio implant buzzed when the engine fully loaded. I conducted the gravitom assessment. My team confirmed the astrydium fuel levels and navigation coordinates for the journey to Neptune. When I finished and confirmed with Chilikimari, the flight crew engineer, I looked around Command. I saw the strain in everyone's posture, more tension than other missions. I saw nervous flinches and quick apologies, glances and sad attempts at smiling. Pats on backs and a few brief hugs. And Beau, hands clasped at his chin, eyes wide as a hopeful child, at the center of it.

The crew tethered themselves, and confirmed their communications. Captain Enros keyed the moment coordinates for the leap to the Dragon's Gate, high over Neptune. Medical finished their final pre-leap assessment. I tapped my implant to engage the remote deuteron monitor. I could see, touch, and hear the engine as if it were in the room with me. For three hours, I'd be locked in, monitoring all its functions. I knew that engine and all its parts better than anyone. I could adjust fuel consumption or output during their leap. I could shut it down with a few quick taps. However, there was no need to.

The space station released Umoja-19. The craft eased to the launch zone, five hundred meters away. The crew-cams filled the display just left of the main screen as it connected with the quantum scopes positioned near Neptune. Commander Bierdot gave the countdown. Mansuri, the pilot, engaged the deuteron. The engine swelled with white light. Then they were gone. Vanished into the dark.

9

The **Dragon's Gate will forever** baffle me. It is terror and magnificence all at once. It hovers like a giant specter in Neptune's high orbit, past all her moons, away from the sun. It only opens two to three times an Earth year. I've never seen it with my own eyes. I mean I never sat in the deep dark out there and watched it morph to life. But it starts off as a blurry mist. When Neptune and its moons align just right, the mist rises to a deep blue. Blue grows into a crimson red that lingers for a while. Then shifts again. That's when something magical happens. That's when Dr. Dragonomassi, the astronomer who discovered the Gate, thought she was hallucinating and panicked in her small craft.

From her observation deck, she watched the red shear, revealing worlds on the other side. Worlds! And a billion stars beyond! According to her journals, she slapped herself to make sure she was of sound mind. No one had seen a Rosen-Einstein bridge before — the once theoretical wormholes that promised a way out of our solar system. From her memoir, she wrote, "to describe what I saw is to describe the face of God. Without weeping, impossible." She didn't know it at first, but she was looking through the bridge to the center of the Milky Way. To a promised escape.

When she returned to Earth, she spoke about her experience. How she had the unnerving urge to disappear, to "never come back — to leap and be one with the stars forever." I imagine to have seen all those worlds would have been proof enough to speak to God in poetry. She said it was a sight that brought her to her knees. She was either blessed or very lucky, because for most, it's the struggle that brings surrender.

From Command, I watched the main display in breathless silence. The Dragon's Gate, captured via the quantum scope, QS-N1, filled nearly three-quarters of the floor-to-ceiling screen. Black filled the rest. It wasn't Dr. Dragonomassi's view, but it was nevertheless entrancing.

Watching the blue rise and swirl toward red made me forget all the mess from before, even if for a moment.

That breathless wonderment dissipated when Umoja-19 landed in the satellite's view. Anxiety spidered up my back and down my arms as I watched. The six-by four-meter craft looked insignificant. Like a fly at a window, waiting for someone to draw back the curtains, open up the pane, and let it escape.

"Umoja-19 confirming arrival at moment d-naught." There was a sharpness to Commander Bierdot's voice, pitched up and nervous. Her vitals edged toward distress, but she looked focused. She looked ready.

"Affirmative. T-minus twenty-nine minutes until Dragon closes," Dr. Jones said, starting the countdown. Suddenly time picked up speed.

The crew did their pre-leap biostim and scan right there in their suits. Medical uploaded any alterations to their genetic patches. My team assessed astrydium reserves, ring dynamics and core connectivity. We ensured the engine was primed for the crew to leap through the Dragon, leap back, then leap home with fuel left in the tank. While I assessed the engine I tried not to think about what could go wrong. I tried not to think about Mars. All those children. All those families. All the shattered debris. But I couldn't stop the flashes of my mother crying and my father screaming.

I had just sent my last MarsPals question to the girl I liked, Amma Ore. She had shiny brown skin and thick, black, bushy hair which she decorated with the origami flowers she folded. She had a gappy smile with cheeks big enough to hide her eyes. She was sweet to me. I mean as sweet as a girl a million kilometers away can be to a boy stuck on Earth. She never once said anything about my looks. In fact, she said I made her laugh. Talk about an engine kick! Her laugh sent me to the moon. Each time I saw her icon pop up in my inbox, I forgot how to frown. I wanted nothing more than to make her feel that way about me.

I asked, "What's your favorite flower?" After I sent it, I pressed my palms together and prayed she would name a flower my mother grew in the back garden. I even thanked God for listening to my prayer.

Then I heard a scream. A ripping, bleeding scream. A man's scream. I raced out of my room. Bolted down the hall.

"Nne?! Papa!?" I yelled.

I found them, panicked, in the reading room. My father stood with hands on his head, back to the doorway. My mother was half sitting on the loveseat to the left with her hands cupped over her mouth. They didn't see or hear me. They stared at the viztra.

"Dear God! No!" my father bellowed.

My mother jumped up. She reached him just as he crumpled. Then she saw me.

"Oh, Lopé!"

My father screamed again. He dropped to his knees. My mother knelt and held him.

I looked up and saw what they were watching. It looked like an action movie. An old one. A bad one with hazy graphics. Space debris crashed and sprayed everywhere. There was no soundtrack. No filter. Then my brain slowly pieced it together. All the broken shards, scattering across the screen, my father crumpled on the floor, howling and screaming, my mother crying and praying. The news anchor, suddenly taking up half the screen, unblinking and red eyed, stuttered as they announced, "We have a heartbreaking update . . . Mars Mission has been declared— " they choked and swallowed as sparks flashed on the other side of the screen. "Declared a total disaster . . . Preliminary reports show . . . all five thousand are presumed dead."

Beau gripped my shoulder, jolted me back to Command.

"This is it, Doc!" he said. He looked excited and greedy. Like a dog eyeing fresh meat.

I nodded and nervously agreed, "This is it."

We both looked up just as the red sheared open.

Dr. Jones quietly prayed.

Command went silent.

A massive glow emerged. It looked like we were watching a fire burn through a forest. But we could only see the glow through the smoke.

"Twenty-two minutes, forty-seven seconds," Dr. Jones announced. Her time stamp flipped a switch inside all of us. It was nothing but call and response after that.

"Engineer, commence deuteron directional charge."

"Deuteron charging, Commander."

"Pilot standby to engage."

"Affirmative on standby."

"Navigation, confirm target."

"Target confirmed, Commander."

"Report deuteron charge."

"Deuteron at full capacity, Commander."

"Affirmative. Pilot, prepare to engage."

"On your count, Commander."

"Engage in three. Two. One."

I closed up. Stopped breathing. Fought back my growing memories. Pushed back my fears of them repeating.

"Umoja to Command?"

I opened my eyes, confused. Worried. Then I let out a breath.

There, in the center of the main display, buzzed the Umoja craft still tapping at the window. I had to hide my relief that all four faces were still on the screen, and still on this side of the Dragon.

"Go Umoja?" Beau said, hurriedly.

"We show a conflict with moment and transposition records. Please confirm," Commander Bierdot reported.

All of Command pivoted toward my team.

Dr. Jones confirmed the error, "Affirmative, Commander. We show conflict in records. Please hold for assessment." She looked up at me, confused like everyone else.

Before I could speak, Beau was in my ear, pressure in his voice, asking me what happened. I glanced at him. His face tightened in anger. I turned back to my station and tried to ignore his glare, but I felt him hot on the side of my face.

I opened the deuteron logs. What I saw didn't make sense. "Director, it appears they—" I started and checked again. "It appears they transposed to the same location."

I looked over to him. Even in the blue light of Command, Beau burned red.

"Umoja, did you copy that?" he spat, looking at me.

"Affirmative. Our findings are the same. Please advise."

Beau scrunched his lips, and jerked his head. Everything about him said, "fix it, now!"

I set in fast. Retrieved all the scenarios we'd coordinated. Not once had a static transposition been considered. I didn't know it was possible.

Dr. Jones stood next to me. Whispered as softly as she could, "Did we miss something?"

I didn't know. I didn't answer her. But I needed to do something fast, Beau was radiating nearby. I picked the scenario that considered the engine resetting itself. I figured that was the closest option. "Run scenario 15 with failover interface 5. Please confirm."

"Confirmed. What's our time?" Commander Bierdot asked.

Beau cut off Dr. Jones and blurted, "Plenty to get it right!"

We all stiffened at his tone. Even the crew.

"Thank you. Running scenario 15 with failover interface 5."

The engine activated. The throttle engaged. The charge beam pierced the Dragon. The room leaned forward. Bierdot gave the command. Mansuri hit the ignition.

Nothing.

How is this possible? Did I forget something? I thought.

Commander Bierdot cut through. "Dr. Morant, please advise." I could hear her worry building.

"Assessing gravitoms. Please hold," I said, urgently. My suit vented as my heart rate increased. My rello buzzed, warning me of high stress levels. No shit! But panic spreads quickly. Panic feeds fear. Fear breeds error.

I clenched my jaw and pressed onward. I palmed the hologram of the engine. Its shell opened. The core shifted. The rings froze.

Beau announced twelve minutes, seventeen seconds. He nearly shouted, "Let's get it right this time!"

I scanned through each ring as quickly as I could. The gravitoms were ready. The core was charged. But the fuel was low.

"Director, astrydium levels are—"

Beau cut me off. "This is our last shot! Figure it out!"

"Less than ten minutes, Umoja," Dr. Jones said.

I called out the scenario to offset the fuel loss. "Let's run scenario 7 with interlocked generator," I said.

Commander Bierdot looked into the camera. I saw her weigh the facts. If they successfully leapt, they'd battle the clock and the fuel levels to get back. If they didn't get back her two sons had their father and his new wife; Mansuri's fiancé knew the risks when he said yes; Chilikamari's family would be supported by GEM; and Enros already confirmed he'd prefer space to being buried on Earth. Bierdot took a breath and decided. "Confirmed. Run scenario 7, interlock generator."

The engine swelled. The fuel dropped. The transposition beam pierced the Gate.

10

The first to speak was Chilikamari, the flight crew engineer. He confirmed, cautiously, that Umoja-19 was nearly out of astrydium. The final attempt drained the reserves. They were stranded, billions of kilometers away.

I watched Beau's face contort into a snarl. He took a deep breath then announced, through gritted teeth, that a conveyance craft would be dispatched. He growled, "It'll take approximately twenty-four hours to reach you, Umoja."

Bierdot looked at the camera, exhausted. They all appeared spent. "Affirmative," she replied. "Setting comms to preserve mode." She and the other crew members saluted, hands over their hearts, "Forever onward."

We returned the salute, "Onward toward the goal," before their audiovisuals went dark. All we had was the quantum scope view on the main display. The Gate closed. The ship just sat there, flashing its hazards, drifting nowhere.

I itched with the need to solve this. There had to be a logical answer. There always was. This wasn't the first "failed" mission. Boosters leaked, systems glitched. Hell, Umoja-18 was postponed a Dragon cycle because the Aux on board kept powering down. Beau didn't bat a lash. But now he was on the verge of yelling at us. I'd never seen him so undone. So unprofessional.

As far as I was concerned, his anger was his own fault. Had he, and GEM, not made a spectacle of the day, no one would be embarrassed. No one would be injured. No one would be dead. Just science as usual.

Beau took to the podium. His face was all shadows when the lights turned on. He kept his focus on the floor, or the podium. Or the prepared script he had to read. "On behalf of GEM, I want to thank all of you for your sacrifice, time, and energy today." His words eased out like hot oil and he was trying not to catch fire. "Although it didn't go as we'd planned, or hoped, it will always be a day to celebrate."

Celebrate what? I thought.

Beau went on, "The world gathered together because of all the hard work and sacrifice of this team. So, thank you." He finally looked up. Anger written all over his face.

I joined in with the majority of Command and gave a half-felt clap for his half-meant words.

"We will debrief tomorrow at 0800 hours. I expect all team leaders to be in attendance," Beau said, stepping back from the podium and turning to leave.

The launch director, from the far side of the room, asked, "What about the launch incident?"

I looked back to Beau, glad someone asked before he left.

His response was curt and telling. "We will go over that in the morning as well. Dismissed." He left before any of us.

Pathetic, I thought.

I sent my team to their hub and made my way to my office. The framed schematic of my prize-winning engine lit up before the office lights. All at once it was too big, taking up nearly the whole wall. It looked ridiculous. I let out a sigh and sank into my chair with my back to it.

As I tapped in my security codes to power on the desk, something caught my eye. Something flat and opaque stuck out from beneath my wedding photo. I picked up the frame to see a small, folded piece of paper.

> *Sorry. Contact me. Anytime.*
> *199.23.3561*
>
> *T. Laine*

"Dr. Morant?"

Startled, I looked up. Dr. Jones stood at my door. She looked worried. I pocketed the note as I motioned for her to come in. She sat quietly for a moment. My head filled with questions, like why Tessa Laine left me her contact? Why on paper? Why hidden?

"Was there more we could have done?" Dr. Jones whispered.

Surprised by the sadness in her question, I assured her that we did everything in our capacity to succeed. "Failure is always a possibility, Dr. Jones," I said, "Be grateful it wasn't a complete disaster."

She looked up at me. Her face aged with worry. "I just feel like we missed something, you know?"

"If we did miss something, I'll find it." I claimed, trying to relieve her of the burden. As chief scientist, it was my responsibility to either solve the problem, or to sink with it.

She nodded, almost smiled, and left.

I saw myself in her sense of defeat. I knew the hours she and the seven other engineers spent in the labs, crafting this engine to perfection. I knew she spent nights in the lab more than anyone else, sacrificing time with her friends and partner. I understood that kind of sacrifice, that kind of dedication. I understood how much of herself she put into making this engine, and how much she, like the rest of us, hoped this mission would have ended in success. I also knew what ultimate failure could do to someone. What it could do to a family. To a whole nation. I knew it well.

***

When the news broke about the Mars disaster my world collapsed. My classmates, a few at a time, stopped showing up to school. Then the teachers stopped coming. In three weeks' time, all my courses were instructed over the viztra. Until the streamlines were cut, or "rationed" as we were told. I went mad after that. All I had left of Amma was in my MarsPals inbox, our back and forth that sent my heart galloping and tightened my stomach in a way that felt good and bad all at once. When the government started "rationing" streamlines, they rationed how often I could see her and watch back all the messages. Her smiles and laughs, all the origami flowers and animals she made, her hopes and fears about Mars. It was all gone. All that magic, rationed away.

My nnenne, my grandmother, came to live with us soon after the disaster. She cooked and cleaned and held me when I'd start sobbing.

My mother volunteered to assist with the increased mental health reports of Existential Hopelessness. For months, she snuck into my room before sunrise, kissed my cheek and left. I was already in bed by the time she got home. I pretended to be asleep when she snuck in and kissed me good night. I listened to her mournful vents to my nnenne while she warmed her late dinners or prepared for the following day. "I don't know what will mend them. I've never seen so much despair." I tightened my knees to my chest and let out what tears I had left.

My father was a storm when he was home. When he left for work, it felt like the ocean drew back from the shore, a sign of awful to come. His return was crashing anger.

A month or so after the disaster, I sat at the dinner table, looking down at my lap. My nnenne placed food in front of me and gently rubbed my back. She cooked another rice dish, spiced and seasoned with what she could find. But I couldn't and hadn't been eating for weeks. I couldn't stop thinking about the Mars crops. The ones pre-planted. The ones rotting. The kids and their parents who were supposed to have harvested them. Just floating out there. Frozen in crooked and shredded poses. Spiraling away, forever.

"Come, come, Lopé. You must let hunger in," she said. Her voice was always a song. A trait passed down to my mother.

I looked up at her. Saw my mother in her eyes, nose, and her smile. I picked up my spoon, scooped up the red rice, and brought it to my lips. But then I heard my father brewing in his office.

"If they'd listened to me, they wouldn't be dead!"

I shook, spilling rice on my lap and the floor.

"I told them about the radars!" he screamed. A crashing of things followed. He burst out of his office. His face stretched tight in fury.

I shrank. Prayed for him to pass.

"Nobody ever listened!" he thundered.

He slammed a fist against the wall, cracked open and wept.

11

Relief finally came when it was just me, in my office, alone with the data. In my element, doing what I loved: find the problem; solve the problem. Despite the absolute failure of Umoja-19, I was excited to find the cause. I started with searching the Oort sector conditions. I thought maybe Neptune whipped up a storm or maybe the Dragon had higher radiation emissions than usual. That was possible. It happened before. And when it did, some ships returned from the Dragon, whole but in shambles. Some came back in pieces. Even then, I took pleasure in searching for and understanding 'the why.' Plenty of missions ended in failure. This was just the first one that failed on the global stage. That pressure wasn't lost on me.

"Huh," I huffed, frowning at the perfect Oort conditions.

I asked GEMStone, the quantum OS, to display all the deuteron engine readings. My eyes ached as I scanned through the logs for twenty minutes, forty minutes. Ninety minutes. Nothing. Just the moment coordinate mismatch for each attempted leap. I should have found a cascade of errors already. I checked the sequencer, the ignition system. I ran through the generators. Nothing.

"Dammit!" I said, pounding my fist on the desk. It flashed yellow, warning me against that behavior. I rolled my eyes and pushed my chair back. Nearly two hours passed and I had nothing but the already-known evidence. I paced. I cursed under my breath. I rubbed at my temples so hard they ached. But I was missing something big. I clawed at my mind, trying to figure out what. And where to look.

I stopped and stared at the deuteron schematic.

"What the fuck is wrong with you?" I hissed.

I wanted to rip it off the wall, shatter it to pieces. That's what my father would have done, alone, in his office. It took everything in me not to destroy it.

To be clear, it wasn't just the mission failure that was getting to me. It was the publicity around it. The million people in the desert. The ones injured. The ones who died. I'm sure some part of me wanted to figure out the failure in hopes it would undo some of the suffering. But the child in me wanted to blame everything on Beau. He'd advertised Umoja-19 to be the "Greatest Leap in Human History." He had the nerve to call it the "Promises fulfilled" mission a few times. What an idiot.

Had he kept his mouth shut, and let science be science and not a spectacle, this failure would have stirred up the Doomsdayers as usual, maybe made a few headlines. But that'd be it. No injuries. No deaths. No damn desert city.

And yet, here I was, growling at a picture of the engine that I created. An engine that failed, breaking Beau's oversold promise, and I couldn't figure out why. Maybe I was the idiot.

Exasperated, I flopped back into my chair. "GEMStone, display external cams, reference deuteron log. Proceed from moment 7.39, 2.84, -0.093, -756, 82.9."

The office lights dimmed, and flight footage rendered in hologram above my desk. A ticker of data ran as the footage played. I glanced between the two, watching for anything.

The deuteron engaged. An error flashed: PROXIMITY SYSTEM ERROR. I ignored the warning. It was something I'd set up years ago but forgot to remove. Over time it became obsolete. Really, I hadn't seen it in years.

It flashed again. Immediately after the second time the deuteron engaged.

"What the hell?" I whispered. "There's nothing out there!"

It flashed on the third attempt.

"For fuck sake!" I said, "What are you complaining about?"

I tapped the error line. The footage halted, a data block appeared. The details read:

0.273 ml optical distortion detected.

"Oh come on!" I said, rolling my head back. "That's not even in the warning range."

I resumed the footage and saw nothing. So I started it over, squinting at the data ticking past.

PROXIMITY SYSTEM ERROR. Again and again. And again.

"Fine," I said, spitefully. I requested GEMStone to amplify the signal at the moment coordinate indicated. "Bet you won't find anything," I said as the hologram scattered then solidified at the anterior of the craft. Nothing. Just like I thought. But the error persisted. Begrudgingly, I requested GEMStone to play the footage, slowly, expecting more disappointing nothing.

But I was wrong. Something was there. Briefly. A wisp of something. A hint of a distortion. And then it was gone. Instantly. Even as the footage slow-crawled forward, the substance was only there for an instant. Appearing at the exact same time after each attempt.

I had to slow it to a painful pace to catch it, to isolate the frame. It felt like I caught lightning. A flash of something tremendous.

But what? The question felt electric.

I reviewed the Umoja Archives, going back through previous failed missions to see if something like this had been referenced. I looked through the Hakim reports for Umoja-17 and -18, our most successful missions to date. Nothing.

"What are you?" I whispered, studying it. My excitement rose. I countered it with mundane answers: a smudge on the camera lens, a smudge that appeared and disappeared three times? No. Perhaps it was a tumbling particulate. A tumbling particulate with a reflective quality. A tumbling particulate with a reflective quality on one side. That sounded plausible enough. Or maybe it was just frozen hydrogen. A minuscule amount of frozen hydrogen. How abundantly mundane.

I requested a neutrinic signature, sure my excitement was unwarranted. GEMStone finished quickly with a chime: NO NEUTRINIC SIGNATURE

I sat up straight and rubbed my eyes to make sure I read it clearly. At first I thought this was an error, so I requested GEMStone to run it again. Everything in our universe has a neutrinic signature. Everything!

Except this.

I shook as I made a note and saved it. Just something to reference later for the official report. I had to tell Beau.

12

I was thrilled to share what I found with Beau. I thought this could be about the best possible outcome: no harm to the crew and the failure could turn out to be a simple stellar factor that we hadn't encountered before. The thrill of discovery was an added bonus.

Beau's mood surprised me. He was on a call when I arrived at his office. He appeared upbeat, relieved, pleased even. Nothing like how he left Command. Here he was, appearing fully recovered. I was glad for it.

I knocked softly to get his attention. He looked up and flashed a smile, motioned for me to wait one moment.

"Mrs. Santigo, I have to go. Dr. Morant is here. Okay, yeah. I surely will. Thank you. Take care— uh, yeah, okay. Bye. Bye bye."

I smirked at his patronizing tone, the kind he used with his mother when she didn't want to release a pinch or a hug.

"I found something," I said.

His eyes got big. I motioned for him to follow me. He gripped my shoulder when he got to the door.

"I knew I could count on you, Doc," he said, smiling.

I dimmed the lights in my office. Beau stood in the center of the room, impatiently thumping his clasped fists against his chin. I pulled up the footage, played it in hologram mode at normal speed. I saw a flash of disappointment cross him. "What am I looking at, Tah?" he asked, hands now stuffed in his pockets, rocking back on his heels.

"Hold on," I said. I slowed the playback to a crawl, stepped through the frames and paused when the proximity sensor flashed its warning.

"What's this? I didn't see it live," Beau said, stepping closer to my desk.

"Exactly! I didn't either. But check this out!" I enlarged the image and requested the neutrinic assessment. The data repeated as it had before.

Beau looked surprised. Curious even. He leaned into the hologram. I felt myself leaning with him. He squinted at the foggy image. I bounced my attention between him and it, ready to share in my excitement.

"No neutrinic signature?" he asked, like he was still unsure.

I whispered, "Nope. Nothing."

He leaned back and requested the lights on. The hologram faded. "Nice work," he said, like a pat on the back for a job averagely done. I was startled by how uninterested he appeared. He must have noticed my confusion and tried to soften his dismissal. "It's a good start, Doc, but doesn't look like much."

"Beau, it's not about the amount. This is an unknown substance— we've never— no one has ever seen something like this."

"Did it cause the failure?" he asked, blunting my excitement. "Aren't you the one that warns us not to infer causality from coincidence?"

I raised my hands, conceding to that fact. "I'm not ready to pronounce that we located the cause of the failure, Beau. What I am saying is that we have a coincidence worthy of investigation."

He let out a long sigh. "We can check it out. Eventually. But I don't want to raise anyone's hopes. We have enough egg on our face."

I rolled my eyes. He wasn't a scientist. He didn't understand. "I'll raise it in the briefing tomorrow, see if anyone else noted it. We can figure out the investigation protocol and priority later," I said.

Beau's face hardened at my suggestion. "You want to say we found a minuscule amount of *something* that may or may not have caused the failure- which cost GEM *trillions* of hheqs, paid for by taxes— *and* you want to convince the Board that half a milliliter of said *something* needs to be studied?"

"Point two-seven—" I started to correct him.

He raised his voice, "I don't give a fuck how many milliliters it is, Tah, I can't take this to the board!"

The lights flashed, but we ignored them.

"You don't have to, Beau— that's *my* job! It's my job to report *all* findings. It's *our* job to investigate those findings."

The lights flashed again. We looked away from each other, cooled down. I was about to apologize when the office door opened. A guard appeared, bulked up with a vest and helmet. SECURITY stamped on his chest.

"Gentlemen, please make your way toward the underground transit level."

Beau nodded and stepped into the hallway.

"What's this about?" I asked, moving cautiously toward the door.

The guard didn't answer the question. "Sir, I ask that you follow directions for your safety."

I looked to Beau who appeared oddly calm about the guard and his warning. He jerked his head for me to follow. Further down the hall, I saw other department heads being escorted toward the elevators. I saw Dr. Jones and a few engineers from my team turn the corner, followed by two more guards.

"Sir, this is an emergency. We need to evacuate the building. Now!"

The escorting guards handed us over to the elevator guards. They told us to remain calm and follow directions. They warned that our safety depended on compliance.

Safety from what? I wondered, but they never told us.

The ride to the underground level was a nervous silence packed with too many people. I was grateful when the door opened. Fear has a particular odor. The elevator guards handed us off to the underground transit guards who directed us down a narrow, cement block corridor. The echoing footsteps gave good cover for our conversation.

"Look, Beau, I understand you're dealing with a lot, but I am obligated to report anything I find out of the ordinary."

Beau rolled his eyes. "I just don't think it's worth reporting, Doc. Less than a milliliter of something you can't name? That's hardly worth sharing."

We rounded the corner to a crowd of employees. I paused. The transit platform was busy with worry. Questions rang and echoed off the stone walls. Heads turned in every direction with wide eyes and bent brows. Team members huddled together in small groups, swapping what information they gathered. Beau and I followed the directions given to get in line with everyone else.

Another guard, standing on the edge of the transit platform, facing us, bellowed directions, slowly. His voice boomed over the *swoosh* of the transit pods and the growing crowd. He sounded bored, as if he'd been doing this for hours. "For your safety, only five people will be on each pod. Each pod will have a guard and an Aux. Please remain calm and follow all instructions given to you on board."

Beau and I took a step forward as a group of five boarded the next pod and disappeared down the tunnel.

"I disagree, Beau. It didn't appear in the last mission and it showed up this time. . . I think it's worth looking into. I'm bringing it up at the meeting tomorrow."

Beau glanced at his rello then back at me. His face tightened. "No, you won't!"

We stepped to the front of the line.

"Director, I am obligated by the Common Goal to report my findings," I said sternly.

The guard dropped his volume and quickly instructed Beau, me, and the three other people waiting. It was hard to hear him and I only caught the last part of what he said, "Please verbalize your consent and understanding."

We murmured, affirmatively. The guard nodded and resumed bellowing directions.

"I'm in charge of the incident report, Morant. Don't push me." Beau said, just loud enough for me to hear.

At that moment, a strong breeze pressed through the platform ahead of the next egg-shaped pod. It eased to a stop. The doors opened. I motioned for the three other employees to board and followed them. The doors closed. The lights dimmed. I turned to talk sense to Beau, but he was gone. The pod lurched forward as I watched the back of Beau's head work through the crowded platform.

13

The pod threw me off balance as it tore through the tunnel. I grabbed at a loop hanging by my head to keep from falling. I glanced a horror and froze. My skin prickled. My throat tightened. I wanted to look away but couldn't. Its malformed face scared me— the smashed flat nose, retracted lips, its teeth on full display. It was terrifying in the blacklight glow inside the pod. It stood, feet apart, hands holding its own weaponry, flat white eyes staring at nothing. Military Auxen were as horrid as I remembered.

"Sir, please take a seat for your safety."

I peeled my gaze from the Aux to the human guard on my left. His eyes and teeth flashed white against his black skin. His black gloved hands gripped his black rifle.

"Sir, for your safety, you need to sit down," he repeated.

"Okay," I whispered, and slowly lowered to the half circle bench behind me. It curved from where I sat, by the door, and ended at the Aux's knee. The other passengers didn't move right away. They eyed the Aux, threatening in its wide stance two meters from them. It swayed with the movement of the pod barreling through the near black tunnel.

I watched it and wondered why it was here. Military Auxen were only called in for serious disturbances. I tapped my rello to send a message to Itzel. *No Signal* flashed across its face.

Why is it here? I thought. *What aren't they telling us?*

I'd been around Auxen all my life. I admired the humanoids when I was a kid. They were able to exist without an atmosphere, without food or water. They charged via the sun and worked without rest. They were a marvel of science.

They propelled the ALN's bold vision of being the first to colonize Mars into a near reality. Five years prior to the Mars launch, Auxen were shipped to Mars in droves. They assembled infrastructure, piece by piece, allowing for subterranean living and farming in eco domes. They built the first and only city on Mars. Their purpose appeared to be great. But after the disaster, they were called back and reprogrammed for a different purpose.

The pod banked a curve, shifting everyone to the right. The person sitting closest to it braced and grunted as the others tumbled against him. I held myself straight and stared at the Aux.

The human guard swung his rifle around to his back and clapped his hands. "Alright, welcome to the UPS, the underground pod system!" He spoke to us like we were tourists. Like this was an excursion we all wanted and paid for. "Currently, you're traveling 200 kilometers per hour, cutting your commute in half! Pretty sweet, huh?" Outside the pod sparked hot orange-yellow. We all flinched— everyone except the guard and the Aux. "Perfect timing," he said, clapping again. "That was a flashpoint. There'll be five more along this route. Charges the pod. It's not dangerous and won't harm you."

I didn't care about the flashpoint. I don't think anyone else on board did either. It was the armed ghoul, unblinking, at the front of the pod that posed a danger.

The guard continued on, casual and lighthearted like that was enough to offset the fear fogging up the windows. "The Aux accompanying us on this ride is in standby mode. However, if aberrant behavior is detected, it will become activated."

My skin crawled beneath my suit when he said that. The fabric vented, lifting, like gills, at my neck, knees, armpits, wrists, and shins.

This can't be happening, I thought. I tapped my rello again. Still no signal. My leg bounced with worry. I just wanted to know what was happening and if my family was safe.

The woman next to me squeaked, "What do you mean, *activate*?"

The others looked from her to the guard to the Aux. I realized in that moment, I was the only one who knew what he meant. My heart rate spiked. I felt dizzy. My limbs felt heavy. My ears filled with static.

"Sir, are you okay?"

"Dr. Morant?"

The voices grew distant and murky. The purple glow faded to black. Suddenly I was in my childhood home. The sun burned through the dying leaves. I stood on the small balcony attached to my parents' bedroom. I peered around the trees at the mourners dragging along the other side of the security wall. It was blistering hot that morning, but they wore black. All of them— the parents, aunties, uncles, siblings, cousins, classmates, teachers, business partners, neighbors, lovers, and friends of the lost. A few wore small pins of red, or blue, or green, on their chests, matching those closest to them, but black was the aso ebi, the chosen color of their combined sadness.

Three months had passed since the Mars devastation. My classes were canceled. Streamlines were rationed, limiting the news regarding the victims and their families. Fewer and fewer updates were available the further time stretched on. Mourning parades started up and had been going for weeks. They sang their way to the West African ALN headquarters, half a kilometer north of our part of the campus.

I wanted to join them, sing my broken heart away with others who felt the same. My grandmother said they wouldn't let me join but never told me why. When I insisted on going, she warned, "If you only think of death, you will forget how to live."

That hot morning, I watched the black train of people pass. They got louder in the distance. Louder drums. Louder singing. Then shouting. Then loud cracks. Birds scattered into the sky. The air smelled like burning hair and something metallic. I heard screaming. More cracks. Louder screams. I ran inside, almost collided with my nnenne. She yanked me to the bathroom, and sealed us both inside. The gunfire cracked closer. Screams streaked past. I flinched with each sound. I cried for my mother. My nnenne folded me into her chest and rocked me. "They're okay, Tolulopé. They're okay."

Her humming mixed with muffled voices. Soon, the dark bathroom gave way to a sharp, purple light and two blurry faces.

"Sir, do you need medical attention?"

"Dr. Morant? Are you okay?"

An orange spark outside startled me out of the haze. I sat up, sweating. Everything swayed as the pod pressed on. Everyone stared at me. Except the Aux.

"Yeah, I'm okay," I said. My mouth was dry and my head spun slowly. "I'm okay."

"I'll have med meet us when we get to GEM City, Dr. Morant," the guard, squatting on my left, assured me. He radioed to someone on the other end. "This is pod alpha-five, we're going to need med at drop-off." Someone responded then asked for more information. The guard glanced at me, white eyes flashing up, then away. "One of the passengers passed out."

The pod finally emerged above ground in the industrial sector. Maintenance vehicles and storage buildings lined up impossibly close to each other, bordered the edge of the UV shield. When the door opened, I heard the shield warning, like a hornets' nest, to keep clear of its signal.

The other riders departed hastily. Soon it was just the Aux and me. It remained motionless, seemingly unaware of me. In the light of the dome, it looked more like a clothed statue– gray skinned and hairless. And even more hideous.

A med tech abruptly boarded, her bag knocked into my left shoulder. "Name and birthdate?"

"Tolulopé Morant, September 17, 115."

The tech scanned my fingerprints and retina.

I explained that I hadn't slept well and that was probably why I passed out. The tech wasn't convinced and recommended bloodwork, a metabolic scan, and a cognitive assessment. I declined the offer and said I just needed to sleep.

She scowled then shrugged. "Whatever you say, *Doctor.* Please sign to confirm you declined medical treatment." She handed me a small tablet, with space enough for my index finger to scribble a signature. "Forever onward," she said with annoyance and stomped away before I could respond.

It was me and the Aux again.

They were objects when I was growing up. Tools used for great feats, weapons used to suppress. In recent decades their initial purpose was reinstated. More human-like versions were created, designed to be hospitable, pleasant, less appalling to the eye. We used Auxen on our previous missions– better them than humans if we weren't sure about the outcome. Umoja-18 had an Aux handler to manage Jingles the Chimpanzee. And that mission was a jewel on GEM's crown of success! It proved that our methods would facilitate human exploration through and beyond the Dragon's Gate. I programmed that Aux to interface with the deuteron engine on the other side of the Dragon if my remote access failed.

I was very familiar with Auxen inner workings, but I never thought I'd be so close to a military Aux. Not since I was a child. I studied it as I waited for the guard to return. It had a broad square jaw, a heavy brow bone. Its shoulders were broad. Its hands were large. So were the boots it wore. Its ugly face had cheekbones. Even the gray skin had a brown undertone, like melanin had been there once, but drained out over time. I stepped closer, but stayed ready to run if it woke up.

"Ready, Dr. Morant?"

I jumped at the guard's question. "Yeah, I'm ready," I said, leaving the Aux on board, relieved to be outside. The air was stale. Cloudy white waxed over the constant blue of the city's UV dome.

The guard motioned me into a cherootza. I was the only passenger, a rare luxury. I confirmed my address and leaned back, relieved to have some time alone.

If it weren't for the security forces everywhere, GEM City looked dead from the inside. The day's decorations mocked me as the rootzi drove. Animated posters lit up with shimmering blue and golden lights, streamers and banners hung motionless above the tramlines and walkways. Shops and restaurants were closed. Parks were empty. Walkways were abandoned. The only people outside were the patrolling security guards.

My nerves kicked up, my insides tightened. "What is happening?" I whispered.

The rootzi replied, "Unauthorized inquiry."

14

When we first arrived in GEM City Itzel remarked how quiet it was. Besides the welcome committee and the floor coordinator, we didn't have any neighborly visitors. She said it was odd. It was cold and isolating. I told her it would get better. But I'm not sure it ever did. Not for her at least.

Our home in Chicago was on the second floor of a three-story walkup— a relic of a building. To Itzel, it had character. She described it as stately, unique, and a little lopsided. It was old brick and reinforced glass. I'd described it as archaic at best. We could hear the neighbors above and below us sing, laugh, argue, tip toe, stomp, and other activities. We could hear the trains race past a couple kilometers away. Neighborhood children playing outside was the springtime soundtrack when the temperatures weren't too high. She called it all the sounds of life. The disorder, the randomness, all a direct reflection of life and living.

She didn't complain about the differences between Chicago and GEM City. Instead, she pointed them out, as if she couldn't contain all of them. She'd just blurt out her surprised observations mid-conversation. We'd be walking down the street and she'd point out how the trees should be bigger for how long they've been planted. Or that there were no birds, no insects, just the rushing sounds of transit and people. And even the people were too quiet. Everything she pointed out were things I didn't really mind. Like the scented air. To me, it was pleasant. To her, it was strange.

"I'm just saying, it's a peculiar combination— those botanicals don't generally grow together," she commented during our first meet up with Beau and his wife, Sarathi.

I apologized, embarrassed that she insulted them somehow. But Beau and Sarathi laughed. They were tickled by her assessment.

We met them for lunch a few days after our arrival. It was the first time all four of us sat face to face, in person. Prior to our move, it was video calls over the viztra. Beau and Sarathi filled a whole window pane in our Chicago home with beaming smiles. They gushed over each other and how lovely GEM had been to them. They'd met before Beau joined GEM. In fact, Beau said, grinning one night, she was a big reason why he joined. "They don't pay nearly as much as I would have made with the family business, but, I mean! Look at her! Sure beats looking at my father!"

Itzel and I both agreed that Beau had done well for himself. Sarathi was lovely and they made a beautiful couple. As bright and shiny as Beau was, Sarathi was golden and warm. But seeing her in person was unsettling. Sarathi was gorgeous. In a way that startled Itzel and me. On the viz chats, we assumed it was the lighting or maybe she used a filter. But sitting across from her, in an averagely lit restaurant, she was unnaturally beautiful. And intelligent. And sedate. But oddly beautiful. Like she kept herself in her original packaging. Neither of us knew much about modifications at that time.

Sarathi blessed us with her smile after Itzel commented on the air. She explained to us, in her cool, languid tone, that "pollinating plants cause a lot of people discomfort. It's easier on the filtration system and people's well-being to scent the air, rather than grow flowers." It turned out she was part of the environmental engineering team for GEM. Itzel was quiet the rest of that conversation.

The automated condo was a constant source of startle for Itzel. She turned off the haum assistant most days. Said she'd rather talk to herself than the wall. Or the stove. Or the mirror. Or the washing machine. She didn't like the unsolicited advice it offered, either.

But she adapted over the years. In her own way. She petitioned for our condo, and anyone else's, to have a growing patio for a garden. The floor coordinator reluctantly agreed as long as there were no flowers. She'd have to aerate the soil, too. Insects were just too much of a nuisance.

Of the forty other households in our building, we were the only ones who grew our own vegetables. Everyone else peered over their balconies to see what dirt covered madness was sprawling around. It garnered attention that I could have done without. Neighbors asked me if it was permanent or if she knew how many or what bacteria was in the soil. I'd have to defer to Itzel to answer and to defend the decision.

The question that grated me the most was, "why doesn't she just work at GEM Farms?"

That was a sore spot I avoided poking as the years went on. Beau had set up a job for Itzel at GEM Farms. He negotiated a formidable salary for her. Even had a two-income home lined up for us– no condo. But Itzel declined. I was gutted. Beau was taken aback. Sarathi tightened her smile when she was around us. But Itzel made her decision, and I couldn't change her mind.

***

I raced out of the rootzi, into our building. The elevator couldn't have risen fast enough. I sprinted down the hall to our condo. I opened the door and listened for Itzel or Mai. It was silent.

I yelled, "Itzel?"

Nothing.

I rounded the corner to the kitchen. "Izzie?"

Mai's bedroom door opened and softly closed. I heard Itzel tiptoe down the hall, toward the kitchen. And then I saw her. I sighed with relief.

"Oh honey! Are you okay?" She looked anxious and tired. She wrapped her arms around my waist and I folded around her.

"Yeah, just a very long day," I said. "Are you okay? Where's Mai? Do you know what's happening?"

"Mai's in bed. I tried calling you, but the lines were jammed, I guess."

I glanced at my rello and saw the red circle on its screen indicating a poor signal. Better than none.

"Any instructions from GEM?" I asked.

"Just to stay inside and wait for more information."

I told her they made us evacuate the campus but no clarification as to why. She squeezed me tighter. "It's okay, Izzie, I'm sure security is handling whatever is happening," I said, trying my best to ease her nerves as well as mine. "We'll be fine."

We held each other until my stomach growled.

"You must be starving!" Itzel said. "I didn't know when you'd be home, so I put everything away. Do you want something?"

We'd planned a special dinner, a congratulatory feast. But as she pulled out the squash medley and roasted chicken, it looked more like leftovers from a repast.

I sank onto the stool and thanked her when she slid the plate in front of me. It wasn't the pre-packaged food GEM Farms produced, the food I used when it was my turn to cook. It was food Itzel grew on our patio: squashes, tomatoes, peppers, carrots. She combined the medley with rice and spiced it with homegrown chilis. It was good, but not as flavorful as GEM food. "That's because it's all natural," Itzel frequently reminded Mai and me. Itzel was an excellent cook. GEM Farms just tasted better.

Between mouthfuls, I told her about the interview which she was excited to hear. I didn't tell her it made me throw up. I told her that I found something that could be related to the failure, but Beau said it wasn't worth sharing.

"So . . ." she trailed off.

I looked up at her. Her thick black brows raised. Her forehead was lined with questions.

"So what?" I asked. I scooped more food in my mouth and chewed. I knew what she was getting at but she didn't understand.

"So you're just going to go along with him?" she asked.

I coughed out a laugh. "There's protocols, Izzie. I can't just go over his head." I stuffed another spoonful in my mouth.

"But you said you're obligated to."

"Hmm?" I mumbled, playing dumb.

She shook her head never mind. "The Dominion will appoint a commission to investigate. You know they'll call you to testify. Will you tell someone then?"

I shrugged, finished the plate, and thanked her again. She took the dishes, eyeing me for a response.

"There's a debrief tomorrow and we go from there," I said.

She nodded with her back to me. I felt her dissatisfaction like static. If I tapped too soon, I'd feel her spark. So I just waited for her to discharge on her own.

She turned to face me, leaning back against the dishwasher. "You'll bring it up then?"

I sighed and shook my head. "When the moment arises, I will. But I don't want to make a fuss."

"A fuss? Babe, you've found something really important."

I still felt bruised by Beau's dismissal. And there were bigger things GEM was going to focus on. I told her as much and got up to leave.

She wasn't ready to let go. She kept pulling me back with questions and suggestions. And all her concerns. "But honey, what if they send Bierdot and her team out there and something awful happens?"

"I don't know, Izzie—"

"You're obligated to tell someone your findings if Beau doesn't!"

"Please, Itzel. I don't want to talk about this anymore," I begged. My body ached with fatigue. I turned toward our bedroom.

"Maybe it's time you started talking more," she said, quietly.

Something tightened in me. Like a tripwire was crossed. But I didn't know who set the trap.

I turned around to face her. "What does that mean?" I asked.

"I mean it seems like Beau is ignoring important facts and protocol."

"Beau is just doing his job, Itzel."

"His job is to keep the board happy, Tah!"

"What are you talking about, Izzie?"

"I'm talking about you not getting lost in..."

"In what? The Common Goal? The thing that keeps me employed? That keeps us housed?"

"Don't do that, Tah."

"Do what? Provide for my family?"

"Please," she said, with her hands raised.

I should have stopped there. I should have seen the warning flag she waved.

"I work hard for this family, Itzel! I am literally working toward a better future for Mai—"

"Tah, don't bring her into this!"

"Don't bring her into this?" I said, louder than I meant to. But anger was talking. "She's the only reason I work this hard. Why I get up every day! Why anyone works at GEM! To make the future better for future generations! Maybe if you took the job Beau lined up for you, you'd understand!"

Her eyes widened. She nodded slowly, then said, "I have made my decisions so that both of us support her well-being." She paused, reached into her pocket and slid an infokey across the counter. "Your daughter was horrified by what she saw today, Tah. I'd think you, of all people, would understand."

I felt fire beneath my skin, like screaming-me was burning. I swallowed and fought the urge to yell, "*how dare you!?*" I squeezed my fists and stared at her.

She stared back with a look that let me know she saw me for all I was. I hated it. I hated feeling like I was the broken one. The one with secrets to hold, whose skin was searing. I wanted someone else to hurt.

"You don't think I know?" I asked.

She frowned at me. And for whatever reason, a reason I'm still not sure I understand, her questioning face pissed me off.

"You don't have to pretend anymore, Itzel!" I said, begging her to admit it.

"What are you talking about, Tah?"

I laughed, and slapped my hand on the counter. I told her that I wanted to hear her finally admit how she felt. I told her it wasn't lost on me. The reluctance she had for enrolling Mai in the advanced learning courses; the growing mess on our patio; the way she declined the job Beau and Sarathi had prepared for her— a job that would have set us up in a private home! Not a condo! I told her it was painfully obvious how she felt. And I needed to hear her admit it, out loud.

"I have no idea what you're talking about," she pleaded.

"Yes you do!" I yelled.

The kitchen lights flashed.

I dropped my voice, but I did not apologize. And I did not change my tone. "You don't believe in the Common Goal, do you?"

Everything froze. The air. Her face. My heart.

Then she left. She didn't deny it. She just left. She turned toward Mai's room. Not ours.

Whatever satisfaction I wanted was gone. Emptied out and sagging, I slumped into the stool and propped my elbows on the counter. I rested my head in my hands and cried. "What have I done?"

15

I didn't sleep. I tried. My body ached for it but my mind steeped in remorse. I yearned and hoped Itzel would slide into bed beside me so that I could apologize, atone, make amends. The bed felt too big without her. Twenty years of marriage and not once had an argument resulted in sleeping alone. We'd talk it out, cry it out, walk it out and find each other on the other side. But after what I did she was right to walk away.

Quietly, I walked to Mai's room, and held my breath. I didn't want to trigger the haum system and ruin their sleep. Everything looked so peaceful when I opened the door. A swirling nightlight of purples and blues moved along the walls and ceiling slowly. It played across the faces of her dolls and toy castles, her small art station. Propped up on her miniature easel was a work-in-progress of the Dragon's Gate. It glowed in neons as the light washed over it. Itzel curled around Mai in her small bed. Her back faced the door. I watched her breathe, her side rising and falling slowly. Mai twitched. Itzel tightened around her.

I closed the door and left.

In the kitchen, I quietly requested a choco-caliente to help me return to sleep. Itzel introduced it to me when we started dating. I hadn't expected the spice to be so spicy but I was surprised by the comfort it brought, especially on such a cold, winter night in her studio apartment. I knew the bevvy wouldn't make it the way she did, but I wanted as much of her as possible at that moment.

I sat in the same stool I sat in to eat the dinner Itzel made from food she'd grown. Food I was quick to eat and not comment on. I rested my head on my hand and replayed the argument in flashes. *How had I lost control like that? Idiot! Idiot! Idiot!*

The bevvy chimed. I stood to get the drink and saw the infokey Itzel placed on the counter. She said something about Mai being terrified by what she saw. I got hot and forgot the drink completely.

I grabbed the key and returned to the bedroom. I tapped the mirror over the dresser. The reflection of the empty bed was replaced by a black screen with a white-lettered menu. I tapped the option for private media and inserted the key into the tiny slot on the side of the mirror frame.

"Play," I requested and sat on the edge of the bed.

A smile broke across my face when I saw Mai waving, both hands, at the camera. Itzel's voice, from behind, told Mai, "Say hi to Daddy!" I melted, hearing Mai squeal, "Hi, Daddy! I love you!"

Itzel asked, "Are you proud of Daddy?"

Mai giggled, "Uh huh!"

"Can we tell him together?" Itzel asked, shifting the camera closer to Mai. Mai nodded, excitedly.

Then Itzel's beautiful face appeared right next to Mai's. My eyes ached as I blinked back tears.

"We're so proud of you, Daddy!" they said, singsongy and almost in sync.

I let out a breathy laugh and wiped a tear away.

Itzel shifted out of frame and I glimpsed the living room viztra behind Mai. Itzel pointed toward it, directing Mai to look and said, "Ten seconds! You want to count down?"

They did. Together. With the million-person crowd. Mai jumped and squeaked out each number, getting louder as it got closer to blast off. I was so caught up in her excitement that I forgot what was coming.

"ZERO!" the two of them shouted.

Then Itzel murmured, "Oh no!" The camera fell, facing the viztra. Mai cried out. Itzel stepped into frame, wrapped Mai in her arms.

"Everything is okay, Mai! It's okay!" Itzel said, nestling Mai against her, attention split between our daughter and what was happening at the launch site.

"Oh!" Itzel shouted, covering her mouth with one hand.

They saw it! I thought. *They saw the incident! Mai saw it!*

I heard Mai whimper something and Itzel agreed. She carried Mai out of frame. I heard distant sounds of Mai crying and Itzel trying to soothe her.

"Oh my sweet Mai," I whispered, holding the thought of her against my chest.

The camera continued to record. The living room viztra flashed black then flashed to the carrier shuttle disappearing into the sky. I was relieved to see that maybe they hadn't seen the worst of it. But the relief was short-lived when Itzel returned. She must have forgotten the camera. She stood close to the viztra, requested a satellite channel, one not presented by GEM. She stepped back, hands over her mouth. The camera bounced when Itzel sat next to it on the couch to watch what unfolded.

I leaned forward, horrified. All of it was new to me. All of it was horrible.

A reporter appeared, covered in a layer of soot and sand. He flinched and shielded himself with his arm as debris peppered him from above. "I'm on the ground at the GEM launch site and moments ago an explosion happened just over there." He pointed to his left. The camera swung shakily in that direction and panned up. Large black clouds spilled into the sky. Then the camera swung back to the reporter. "We're being told by officials the situation is under control—" He broke into a coughing fit as more debris rained down. He pointed behind them and coughed some more.

The camera jerked toward the medical tent in the distance. A red lettered banner flapped on the left side of the screen, reading TICK TOCK GOES THE DOOMSDAY CLOCK. More dirt-covered people ran toward the blue tent with GEM MED stamped all over it in yellow. Adults carried children in their arms and on their backs. Some carried other adults, who writhed in pain, or remained limp, limbs flopping as they rushed to find a place inside.

"We're unsure of the cause at this time, but it is apparent there have been significant injuries and possible deaths," the reporter announced, off camera, between coughs.

The camera jostled and bounced toward the medical tent. I looked away when I saw a mangled body, crushed under large metal debris. My stomach convulsed.

"Sir! Sir! Can you tell us what happened?"

I looked up. A wiry man with wild eyes, a fresh bandage around his head filled the screen. Blood stained his clothes. He stuttered trying to get his words out. "I- I- I-, I can't find her." The reporter asked who he was looking for. The man stuttered again, eyes darting everywhere. "I can't find Annie. I was holding her hand, but she tripped."

My stomach dropped. The man started crying but didn't seem to know. He kept searching the passing faces for his Annie.

"Do you know what happened?" the reporter asked.

"I, I, I heard something whistling. Then a bang. Then we ran. Everybody ran. Then I woke up in there." He pointed at the medical tent.

"Did you see anything? Where were you when you heard the whistling?"

The man pivoted his head around, searching the faces that passed.

"Sir, did you see anything?"

"Huh? See anything?" The man sounded angry. "I saw smoke. I saw fire."

"Anything else?"

I heard Itzel say, "I'm coming, baby." The camera jostled. I saw her face briefly before the recording shut off. The screen dimmed. The viztra inquired if I wanted to watch it again. I said no and requested the live newstreams. I needed to know more.

The first was a stern-faced reporter. "What should have been a day to celebrate, ends in failure." There was something about that reporter I never liked. I swiped to the next stream.

It was a round table of seven experts. They bickered back and forth so much it took a minute for me to catch up.

"It just appears to me that someone tampered with the hydro system," one expert said before the other voices piled on.

"That is a strong possibility, but there has been no evidence to back that up."

I sat up, curious about what they knew.

"No evidence? There is video evidence of an unmarked vehicle near the hydro reserve, Barry!"

"That hasn't been confirmed, Marvin!"

"All I'm saying is, there were a lot of people in attendance, thousands from around the world— who knows what their intentions were?"

I let out a sigh and changed the stream again. They'd be debating that for a while.

On the next stream was a replay of Prime Minister Cooper giving a press conference. I voted for him twice on account of his support for galactic exploration. Itzel wasn't impressed by his platform. She said he didn't give any funding to geo-terrestrial rehabilitation organizations, like the one she used to work with. But she was in the minority, especially in GEM City.

Cooper had aged over the five years he was in office. His olive skin was sallow. His graying hair turned white. He looked tired and distressed as he approached the podium. He gave a brief smile to the people in the room, then solemnly to the cameras, and began.

"It is with a heavy heart that I address my fellow Canadians and the world this evening. In times like this, we must reach out to each other in solidarity. The human race has survived innumerable devastations all throughout our history: famines, plagues, wars, and even the natural disasters that took so many from us in recent history. And yet, we persevered.

"What played out at the GEM launch site will go down in history as a tragedy we won't soon forget. We will grieve, together, the immense loss of our countryfolk and international brothers and sisters. There are no words I can give that will ease the ache shared by so many.

"I have spoken with leaders from around the world. Some of whom have lost citizens today. I send my gravest condolences to them, their communities and the families that lost loved ones. It is not enough and will never be enough to replace them in our lives. But you are not alone in your suffering. The world suffers with you." He paused, swallowed and adjusted his stance. "With regard to the destruction of Umoja Village, I ask that we, as a global community, consider what kind of society we want to become."

I hit pause. *Umoja Village? Destruction?*

I searched the streams for footage, horrified by what I saw. Smoke wrapped around the blue hotels. Fire burst out the windows. Billboards were shattered or torn down completely. Small explosions burst at random. Red and white emergency lights flashed. Security spotlights swept from above.

"I knew this was a problem as early as two-thirty! I could see it in the reaction, in the mood of the people around me," one witness said with his shirt wrapped around his bleeding hand.

Another bloodied witness jumped into the frame, "Some people came to start a fight!"

A security officer, lying on a gurney hovering past, mumbled to the camera, "I'm embarrassed for what happened and I'm sorry for what happened and I wish I'd done more to prevent it."

I was struck dumb by all of it. Numbed by the chaos. I muted the audio and just watched.

An Aux subdued two men. Two guards applied cuffs to their wrists and ankles. The Aux yanked them up. The two men struggled, but the Aux did not let go. It pulled, pushed, and dragged them to a windowless van with *T.P.C* on its side. One at a time, it threw them in. Followed by another Aux and another. Each one, tossing adults into the back of a van like bags of trash.

16

I arrived at the debrief just before the doors closed. The room was set up like an amphitheater. The entire sixty-six-person command team clumped close to the front. Beau sat in the first row, closest to the entry. I took a seat next to him. He greeted me with a nod and polite smile. I just nodded back. Nothing to smile about. Maybe he didn't watch the news. Or maybe the everything-is-under-control bit was second nature for a program director. Either way, he appeared less fazed than the rest of us.

Beau took to the front of the room, and called the meeting to order. "First, I want to give an update on the retrieval mission status. The Umoja-19 crew has been in communication with the conveyance craft. The retrieval team expects visual confirmation within the next four hours. They will keep everyone updated on the progress."

I was glad to hear they were okay and no further disaster had taken place. I don't know what I would have done had he reported otherwise.

Beau let out a deep breath and continued. "GEM has issued a formal statement regarding the riot and Umoja Village."

We all sat up, eager for information and possible good news. I wanted a solution.

GEM's official statement was that everyone at GEM sympathized with the frustration and anger demonstrated in Umoja Village. It emphasized what President Cooper urged, that the people must decide what kind of society we want to be. The statement ended with, "We, as a global community, need to make an effort to understand these emotions, and go beyond these difficult times." I felt sick.

I looked around and saw people wiping tears. I didn't understand why. Whatever Beau read didn't feel like enough. GEM didn't say how they'd remedy the hurt, just that they could understand. The ALN understood for a time. Then they unleashed the Auxen on the mourners.

Following that, it was my turn to report. I stood, eager, but nervous. I hadn't had time to prepare. Communications were limited underground. I couldn't review anything during my commute that morning.

As I took my place behind the podium, everyone adjusted in their chairs. I sensed their anticipation. Except Beau. He leaned back, legs crossed, and stared at me. I looked to the rest of the room and greeted them. Then I reported, "According to system logs, the engine showed no evidence of malfunction, however I did isolate what I believe might be a significant finding."

There was a shift in the room. Anticipation became curiosity.

"Milliseconds after the deuteron engaged, the anterior proximity sensor was triggered. This occurred during each attempt. But not at the initial leap from the space station."

I requested the room lights to dim and the system logs to project onto the wall behind me. I narrowed the log to the time I'd investigated. The vantage cam and the system log played side by side. I started it first at normal speed and watched everyone return their gaze to me, confused and unimpressed. I was ready for that.

"I'll slow it down," I said.

The vantage stepped along, frame by frame as the system log stamped out data point by data point. My heart raced as the moment approached. I was ready to pause the video at the millisecond when the wisp of a substance was sure to appear. But I missed it. The room looked at me again. I apologized. "Didn't sleep much," I said. A good number of them nodded and murmured some kind of understanding.

I requested GEMStone to step back to the appointed time frame and watched more carefully this time, absolutely sure I'd catch it.

But it wasn't there. No prox sensor warning, no wisp of something.

"Now hold on," I said, flustered. "Give me a moment."

Beau interrupted. "We've got other teams who need to report, Dr. Morant. And medical needs to check in with the crew."

I turned to him. He concealed a smirk then stood. "Look, we're all overwhelmed. Everyone is grasping at straws to explain what happened." I started to interject but he cut me off. "I think it's a shame how hard we worked for this mission's success only for some small mechanical failure to distract us. It's likely protocols got mixed up or something."

"Director Son—"

He cut me off again. This time, facing the room. "Some junior level error, probably a new recruit's fault, caused all this mayhem and destruction. It's a damn shame that all of you are being scrutinized so heavily!" Beau didn't look at me. He kept his gaze on everyone else.

I watched them nod and agree, loosening themselves from responsibility.

"Let's take five," he said. "We'll give Dr. Morant a few minutes to gather his findings."

I remained, speechless, at the front of the room. Row by row everyone filed out. When Beau made to leave, I grabbed his arm.

"Beau, what the hell? I showed you this yesterday."

He looked down at my hand around his forearm and back up at me. "Please release my arm, Dr. Morant."

I let go, unaware of how hard I gripped him. He turned to leave again.

"Director!" I said, loudly.

He paused. "Dr. Morant, I am advising you to keep your volume down."

"Beau, I showed you all of this yesterday. Why aren't you backing me up?" I asked the back of his head.

He turned half way and spoke to me like I was an indignant new recruit, "I am the director of the Umoja Program, Dr. Morant. I request you address me as such."

I could have choked on his attitude. "Sorry. *Director*. I showed you my findings yesterday. Did I not?"

He glanced at the doorway. Four people snatched themselves from view. "Dr. Morant, I recall you asking to show me something; however, upon reaching your office, we were escorted to the basement."

I felt twisted inside. He sounded so matter-of-fact about it, I started to question my memory.

Beau turned and strolled toward the door.

My anger climbed up and rolled forward like black clouds. "What the fuck is wrong with you, Beau?" I rumbled.

Beau stopped and turned abruptly. "Dr. Morant, I request that you adjust your demeanor and att—"

I couldn't take it anymore. "Director, I request you drop the bullshit! Why are you denying what we both saw?" I yelled.

The lights flashed.

"Dr. Morant, you need to calm down," Beau said, hands raised.

"Calm down? How can I be calm when I watched children die on the news? How can you be calm when a riot burned down your precious Umoja Village? You saw my findings, you threatened to write me up and now you're denying them? What the fuck is wrong with you?" In two strides I was in his face. He backed up, face so full of fear I could almost smell it. "Our crew is stuck in space and I'm trying to figure out why!" I spat. The lights flashed in double but I couldn't stop myself. I jammed my finger in his face and yelled, "All you care about is kissing the board's ass and hoping they like it! You bureaucratic whore!" I saw red. "Always ready to fuck someone for an extra hheq!"

Pain cracked the back of my knees. I folded to the floor. Cold hands yanked my arms behind my back. A knee pressed into my spine. A hand held my head in place. I tried to fight against it. Pain pressed into my cheek.

Black boots shuffled in front of my face. I saw the team leads stare from the other side of the door. Their eyes were big. Their mouths were covered. My heart pounded. My head felt ready to split. The guards yanked me up by my armpits. I looked to both sides and saw Auxen.

"No!" I yelled. "No! No! No! Beau, stop this! STOP THIS!"

He just stood there. Eyes wide. Watching.

I screamed at him, "HELP ME, BEAU!"

17

My memories of what happened next play like violent flashes: the guard shouted, Beau watched, horrified. The Auxen pushed me past shocked faces. They pushed me past all the offices and stairwells, past the elevators, past the security desk, down hallways I never knew existed. There were no windows or office doors. They yanked me around corners until the hallway ended and a large door blocked the way. The guard keyed in a code. A siren blared, growing louder as the door opened. The Auxen pushed me into the blinding sun. I closed my eyes reflexively and tripped. I slammed into the ground.

That's when time slowed down and I felt everything all at once. My knees and shins stung. The back of my knees throbbed where they hit me. My biceps pulsed where the Auxen gripped my arms. My hands felt like pin cushions, needled up and twitching. My face hurt. My head throbbed. And for the first time in years, my skin burned in the unfiltered sun.

The guard ordered the Auxen to stop after they dragged me a meter or two. "Sorry about that. Damn things don't have much sense," he grumbled as he helped me to stand. "All they know is to get you to the van." He took a step back once I was on my feet. "How tall are you?"

"Two-meters," I said, looking down at my dirty pants and shoes. It'd be my first infraction in seventeen years. A stupid thing to think about considering the circumstances, but I had a flawless record.

The guard whistled. "Gonna be hard to fit you anywhere!" Then he ordered the Auxen to resume getting me to the van.

Sweat leaked out my pores and stung my eyes. I kept squeezing them shut, catching glimpses of the van as they pushed me forward. Along the windowless side was stamped T.P.C in large block letters. The same vans on the news from the night before. It didn't make sense how I ended up in the same position. They fought security officers. They burned down a village! I just yelled at my program director. How did that warrant the same response?

The guard opened the back of the van. The inside of it was just two metal benches on either side. Heavy chains with large cuffs were bolted to the metal floor. Reddish-brown stains everywhere. I felt sick to my stomach.

The guard uncuffed one of my wrists and ordered, "Climb in. Watch your head."

I didn't move. I couldn't. I wasn't supposed to be looking at the inside of a van used to transport dissenters. I was a highly respected, integral member of GEM's Umoja program! *I built the goddamn engine that made half their missions a success! How did I end up here?*

"Do I need to repeat myself?" the guard asked.

"I didn't do anything," I said through clenched teeth.

"What was that?" he asked, leaning against the open door.

I turned to him and tried my best to stay calm. "This has to be a mistake, sir. I didn't do anything."

He was an older man with hard lines around his nose and mouth. White stubbled the lower half of his face. He looked annoyed to be in the sun. He sucked his teeth and nodded. "A Code-V got tripped and I found you screaming at a GEM Member. I'm just doing my job."

"It was a misunderstanding," I said, ready to apologize to him.

He shrugged. "I'm sure it was. But I gotta follow protocol. You can take it up with the processing agent when you get there. Now, watch your head."

He placed his hand on the back of my head and firmly pressed me forward and down, bending me in half. He followed me into the van and cuffed my wrists to the bench. I blinked back tears as he shackled my ankles to the floor.

"One of them is going to ride back here with you," he nodded toward the Auxen. "The other will be up front." He stared at me a moment. "Those tears won't get you far. I'd shut them off right now."

An Aux did as he said and climbed in after he got out. The other Aux closed the doors. I heard the lock latch. The front doors opened and closed. The engine revved. The van took off.

My mind raced. Maybe I should have gone for a psych assessment after my interview with Ms. Laine. Maybe I could have avoided most of this if I had. I was ashamed that I lost control and called Beau things that would have shamed my family. I should have listened to him when he told me to lower my volume and adjust my tone. I should have shut my mouth when the lights flashed. But I couldn't figure out the *why*. I never questioned the Common Goal. I didn't break anything. I didn't hit anyone. I just yelled at him. How does yelling garner the same punishment as destroying a hotel or water tower? Or even protesting the launch?

I was so caught up in thought, I didn't realize I said, "I don't belong here," out loud.

"I am unable to process your request. Could you please repeat it?"

I looked up. The Aux was looking at me. The fact that it mistook my statement for a request, and had a patented crescent grin on its face, pegged it as a XanTing model, probably 12th gen or so. They were designed to look more pleasant than the military Auxen.

I knew this was an opportunity I couldn't pass up. I could use this Aux, get some information. But I didn't want to say anything that could be used against me. Auxen recorded everything.

Since I had the right to know, "Why am I here?" The way it answered would tell me a little bit about its integration system.

There was a pause before it answered. "Your behavior triggered a Code Violet in the Social Threat System."

It was correct, but limited. Probably modified for simple answers only. I asked another simple question, "Where am I going?"

Another pause as it processed. "You are going to a GEM-designated Threat Processing Center."

GEM-designated? I'd never heard of that. I asked the Aux what it meant.

It replied, "I am unable to process your request. Could you please repeat it?"

I looked at my rello. It was only 9:30 a.m. No signal. *Perfect.* "What is your location?" I asked.

The Aux blinked then reported, "I am at an approximate location of 37° 19' 53" North and 104° 05' 55" West."

I took a deep breath before I asked where the processing center was located.

"The threat processing center is located at 36° 33' 18" North and 105° 06' 28" West."

My stomach dropped. Beau let me know after a few weeks of being at GEM, that anything beyond the border wall along the southern horizon— anything below the thirty-seventh parallel— was no man's land. GEM couldn't and wouldn't protect me.

"Who owns the threat processing center?" I asked.

"I am unable to process your request. Could you please repeat it."

I sighed and thought for a moment. "What nation has governing authority over the threat processing center?"

The Aux blinked and repeated itself, "I am unable to process your request. Could you please repeat it."

I leaned back and stared at the ceiling. "How much longer until we arrive at the processing center?" I asked.

"We will arrive in approximately one hour, forty-seven minutes."

I nodded and let out a breath. Itzel always reminded Mai to breathe when her emotions got too big. In through the nose. Hold. Out through the mouth. Hold. In, hold. Out, hold.

I figured I'd follow the guard's advice and explain myself. I'd tell the admissions officer to call Beau. Beau would explain the misunderstanding as a simple argument among friends. And I'd suggest the Social Threat System be updated! Volume and tone shouldn't be the only qualifiers to trigger the V-code. Subject matter should be considered as well.

I relaxed, convinced that this was just a malfunction in the system and everything would go back to normal. I'd be home by dinner. We'd even laugh about it one day.

Part II

18

The muffled thud of doors snapped me to attention. The back of the van unlocked. My stomach tightened. Hot air rushed in. I coughed and choked. The unfiltered sun blanched the inside of the van. Hot, white light flashed from every surface. The Aux across from me bent forward to disengage my ankle cuffs. As it moved to release my wrists, the guard climbed in. Through squinted eyes I saw the lower half of his face was covered by a breathing mask, the other half was shadowed by a helmet.

"Keep your eyes down or straight ahead," he said. "For your sake, I hope you're right about the misunderstanding, Dr. Morant, but still, keep your mind tight. Don't speak unless spoken to. Don't show any weakness. Keep your mind tight."

I expected to be re-shackled once I exited the van. But I wasn't. And it wasn't necessary. I was in hell. It was too bright, too dry, and too hot.

The Aux that rode in the back of the van slammed the door shut. The guard clapped a hand on my shoulder then climbed into the front seat. The engine revved and sand sprayed everywhere. I had to stop myself from yelling after them as they drove off. For a moment I thought I could follow the kicked-up grit all the way back to GEM. But the hazy bridge between ground and sky blurred the van and the cloud into one. And the sun was too brutal to run from.

I cupped both hands around my eyes and watched them disappear on the horizon. To the east and west were mountains. Panic clenched my throat when I turned to see behind the detention center were more mountains. The only way out was north following the van, into a sea of scorched earth. The only escape from the crippling heat was the crouched detention center ready to swallow me whole.

Bubbling out from the east-facing side of the building was a faltering UV shield. It offered a pitiful amount of shade to a growing number of gaunt-faced people dressed in yellow uniforms. There were no guards. No snipers. No barbed wire topping off an electrified fence. There was nothing to keep them from running away, just the buzzing UV shield to protect them from the sun.

"Ayyyy- fresh meat!" someone yelled.

"What meat? I only see bones walking!" another yelled back. That garnered some laughs.

"That's a mighty fancy suit? Where'd you get it?"

I ignored them as I tripped and staggered through the sand toward the building. My suit vented but that only drew in hot air. Despite my shoes, my feet burned with each step. I reminded myself it was all a mistake. I wasn't supposed to be there. A foreigner left in the wrong land. I'd file my complaint by dinner.

I could hardly breathe when I got to the large, steel door. My flesh stung from the sun above and felt like it was being seared off by the heat radiating from the building. I looked around for anything to press or wave at. There was no button or sensor to trigger the door open. Seconds felt like forever as I stood there, waiting for something to happen.

The prisoners kept up with their insults. I glanced over my shoulder at them. Most just stared. A few chuckled and sneered, joking about my shiny shoes and gold buttoned suit. No one offered any advice or instruction.

When I felt ready to collapse, an alarm sounded followed by a buzzer. Bolts released with startling clangs. The door dragged open. Cold air rushed from the darkened entry, like it was making some great escape.

Right as I crossed the threshold, I heard an inmate from outside shout, "Welcome home, Bones!"

I walked into a melee of screams and yelling, ringing bursts of metal on metal. It took a moment for my eyes to adjust. I expected to see a room full of people, but I stood in an empty lobby. Steel benches lined the walls. Lights buzzed and flickered from overhead. Cold air blasted from large, overhead vents. But even they couldn't drown out the mayhem coming from behind a barred door on the other side of the lobby.

The alarm sounded again as the door slowly, loudly dragged itself closed. The bolts locked with echoing clangs.

All of it had to be a mistake. I did not belong there.

A glass enclosure across from the entry housed an Aux sitting behind a desk. It waved me over. I had to nearly press my ear against the glass to hear it. ". . . Center 5. Your identification is important to us. Please stand on the footprints in front of the camera and remain stationary until confirmed."

I stepped back. A light flashed. I jerked away.

The Aux said, "Please stand on the footprints in front of the camera and remain stationary until confirmed."

The light flashed again. I did my best to not move or blink.

The Aux looked down for a moment then back at me. "Thank you, Toolooloop Ahiodoggy Morant. Please have a seat. A processing agent will be with you shortly."

An old model, I thought. Newer Auxen could decipher non-Anglosaxon names.

I sat on the bench closest to the barred door to get a better idea of what was happening, what I may walk into.

A man shouted, "This is fucked up! We don't belong here!" Other voices rallied, repeating the sentiment.

A voice boomed, "SHUT THE FUCK UP!"

For a moment it was silent. Then I heard shuffling and low murmurs. Then the same man started up again, yelling about his rights and freedoms and threatening to sue. "I was practicing my right to protest!" he shouted. "This is a violation of my rights as a Canadian Citizen! You're violating my rights, you bald fuck!"

Another voice shouted back, crudely, "I got your rights right here!"

"That's sexual harassment! That's fucking sexual harassment!"

"I SAID *SHUT THE FUCK UP!*"

Everyone went silent.

"Now, I want to welcome you to Jarret Detention Center 5 of the Greater Texas Federation's Department of Corrections!"

"What the fuck?!" the freedoms guy and several others shouted. "We got fucking trafficked into another country!"

Others joined, shouting their objections.

"ENOUGH!" a man bellowed. He continued with a chilling sense of humor in his voice, "You want to be free? Be my fucking guest! A-5 and A-8, please escort uh— Mr. Dobryivech– Dobyrivich– Dobrivick– however the fuck you say it. Escort him off the premises. We would hate to violate his rights any further."

I heard beeps. Then metal scraping. Shuffling and grunting. Then the man, adamant about his rights and freedoms started shouting again, more desperate this time, "GET OFF ME! DON'T FUCKING TOUCH ME!" No other voices joined. The barred door to the lobby opened, its hinges whining. Two Auxen carried a man by his arms. His clothes were torn and stained. He kicked and screamed. His bulging eyes found me. Clung to me as he cried for help. He begged me for help. His voice ripped and echoed. Spit flung as he screamed at me to stop them. He apologized when the bolted steel door dragged open. Hot air rushed in. I looked away.

It took eight seconds for that door to grind itself closed. Eight seconds of hearing his screams grating like the sand on the door's well-worn track. The bolts clanged into place. The freezing air rattled out from the vents overhead. And that was it for a moment. I was relieved by the silence. I don't feel good saying that, but what was I supposed to do?

From the other side of the barred door, the booming man, the man I'd learn was in charge, said, "Now, anyone else worried about their rights?"

No one answered.

When the barred door opened again, I looked down. I didn't want to witness anyone else being dragged out. That man's bulging eyes, his face stretched in horror, fouled my stomach.

"Toolooloop Ahiodoggy Morant, please follow me."

I looked up to see another Aux, dressed in fraying navy blue, in front of me, set to servile and pleasant. They all were. Like they were attendants at a hotel or day-spa. Their cheeks plumped just so, corners of their mouths curved up slightly, blank behind the eyes. These models didn't have sympathetic expressions. Just constant politeness.

I rose and followed it, heart thudding in my chest. What choice did I have? If the processing agent was behind that steel-barred door, and that's who I had to explain my situation to, then that's where I had to go.

Everything was worse on the other side. The cold air warmed and thickened with the smell of urine, feces, rotting onions and spoiled potatoes. Moisture dripped down walls and gathered on the floor. The lights cast everything in a dull white but I couldn't tell if everything was gray, or brown, or just covered in dirt. I did my best to keep my focus straight ahead, like the transit guard told me. I wasn't staying long and I didn't want to make eye contact with anyone who was. I didn't need their stares clinging to me.

I blinked hard with relief when the Aux opened a door labeled ADMINISTRATION. I straightened my suit and stood taller with each step. Each step was getting me closer to home. I was almost smiling by the time the Aux stopped and motioned me to enter a room labeled Admin Bay 4. It seemed too small of a room to fit more than one person in. I thought maybe it was another waiting room. More palatable for someone like me. Closed off for the ones who belonged there. But I was wrong. A hardened knot of a bald man, in a tan uniform, sat bunched up behind a desk, staring at a screen embedded in the wall to his left. The top of his head was shiny and pale. The rest of his skin looked like oiled leather left in the sun to bake. He motioned for me to sit in the only other chair in the room without looking.

"GEM always sends their fuck ups over here, but do they ever send resources? HA!" His bark of a laugh jolted me. But he didn't notice. He rumbled about shortages and rations as if I were his contemporary. As if I understood the politics. "This place isn't even full and I can barely keep everyone fed! And then they dump load after load on my doorstep like I'm the fucking shitter!" He tapped the screen with meaty fingers. "At least they warned me you were coming, Too- uh, how the hell do you say that?" He turned to me. Surprise spilled over to excitement as he eyed all my buttons and service ribbons. The GEM crosshair pinned over my heart. "Interesting. . ." His hard, lined face creased into a smirk. "How do you say your name?"

"Tah Morant is fine," I said, resisting the urge to squirm. He looked like he had plans for me. Like I really was fresh meat.

He took his time turning back to the screen. "Hmmmm. . . Pleased to meet you, Tah Morant. I'm Warden Nattle. Now, what'd you do?" He huffed and scrolled for an answer. His eyes bounced around the screen. Then he stopped. "A scientist? That's a first!" He cut a glance at me as he continued looking for my offence.

"Set off a V-code, huh? What the fuck happened, Mr. Scientist Morant?" he asked, entertaining himself as he surmised about my violent behavior. "Wait one damn minute." He jabbed a finger at me. "You're *the* chief scientist, Dr. Morant! Holy shit!" he exclaimed like he won a prize. Like he'd get to hang my head on the wall.

Before I could say anything, he held up a finger. "Hold on." He turned toward the Aux standing behind me. "A-4, I need you to bring me a cup of water from the Level 2 common room."

The Aux stepped forward. "Your request would leave you alone with detainee Toolooloop Ahiodoggy Morant. Are you sure you want to do that, Warden Nattle?" the Aux asked.

"I am sure I want you to get me a cup of water from the Level 2 common room, A-4," Warden Nattle said, rolling his eyes at me.

"You are aware that detainee Toolooloop Ahiodoggy Morant has a history of violent outbursts and may pose a threat to you."

"Yes, yes, yes! I confirm my understanding and consent to being alone with the detainee, A-4!" Warden Nattle barked.

The Aux processed the request. Then left.

Warden Nattle leaned forward and dropped his volume. "What'd you do, Doc? Fuck around with the controls?"

"No. I–"

"Oh, come on," he coaxed, "you can tell me. I'd understand. All that Common Goal shit don't do fuck for us. But you? You're a big fish! You must of really fucked up to be sent all the way out here!"

"No," I said. I looked him right in the eyes and explained what happened. "It was a misunderstanding. I got into an argument with the program director. That's all. Just words, nothing violent. You can call him. Aristide Soncal."

Nattle leaned back, crossed his leather-bound arms over his chest. "Is that all?" he huffed, disappointed. Possibly skeptical. It was hard to tell with all the lines on his face. He shook his head and grumbled, "That doesn't make sense. You must've pissed somebody off!" Then he shrugged and rocked himself forward. "But they do enjoy eating their own over there. Guess it doesn't matter how high you sit."

I didn't have time to ask what he meant. A-4 returned, holding a brown cup. It placed it on the desk and returned to its position behind me.

Warden Nattle held up a finger at me and addressed the Aux. "A-4. I think you made a mistake."

"I apologize, Warden Nattle. How did I incorrectly execute your request? I would be happy to execute a correction."

The way it used the word happy bothered something in me. Like a faint but foul smell. I never liked the servile setting. Auxen were tools. Tools didn't need to be polite.

Warden Nattle chuckled, "It was supposed to be a red cup, A-4. I can't drink water from a brown cup. It has to be red. Please take this back and bring me water in a red cup."

The Aux processed the odd request, took the cup and left. I looked between the warden and where it had stood, confused.

Warden Nattle explained, "That's a little game we like to play—Moron Mission. It's the only way to get any privacy around here. And it's free entertainment for us!"

I didn't get it. But the warden liked to talk, so I sat and listened.

"They're programmed to tolerate that shit! I got one of them to go all the way to the basement and back to tell me the temperature of each inmate in the lower level. Celsius. Then Fahrenheit! Took damn near all day!" He barked out a laugh. "Shit is never not funny!"

I forced myself to laugh with him. He seemed like the type of man who required that. He was also the man who held the keys to my freedom, so what he found funny, was funny, even if it was the stupidest thing I'd heard.

"They're an older model than what you're used to, I'm sure. GEM saves all their new gadgets for you scientists. We get scraps if anything. But they prove useful. Incredible strength. No need to waste food and water on them."

"These models perform their tasks well," I said, agreeing with his every word. Whatever got me out the door.

Warden Nattle considered what I said with a nod. "But that's like complimenting the sun for shining." He shrugged. "They do what they're supposed to do. I don't qualify it. What pisses me off is their confirmation questions, though."

I surprised myself, finding more things to agree on. "We have similar frustrations with the ones we have at GEM. Especially when the safe guard is so astringent." I stopped myself before I let slip that I'd programmed half a dozen over the years. That was something I knew he shouldn't know. He seemed like the kind of man who would reprogram them for the wrong reasons.

Warden Nattle leaned back in his chair again and locked his hands behind his head. "I just wish they could shut off! It's like having a supervisor follow you around all damn day, making sure we don't *violate prisoners' rights*," he said, rolling his eyes. "Sending them on moron missions gives us a little breathing room!"

I made a noise that sounded like a grunt of approval. But it was disgust.

A-4 returned with a red cup of water and my shoulders relaxed a little. The warden chugged the water and tossed the cup at the Aux. The humanoid snatched it out of the air and resumed its guard behind me.

"Well," Nattle said with a sigh, "better get you to a cell. Detention Center procedure and all." He tipped his head toward the Aux and rolled his eyes again. He took my rello, told me it was for my own safety. "Don't want to tempt these animals with something shiny," Nattle said. He pointed at my buttons and offered to take those, too. I think he was half joking. There was greed in his smile. "You'll be with the degenerates, but my guess is your people'll fetch you this afternoon and everyone will kiss and make up."

I let out a soft chuckle and nodded. That was another thing we agreed on.

He tapped through some screens, then turned to me. "Just don't give us any shit, all right."

"Yes, sir," I said.

"Good!" He stood, gingerly placed a wide brim hat on his head and led the way to the cells.

The smell was putrid. The floor was slimy with dirt and God knows what else. My "cage" as he called it, had two bunk beds and four dirt covered men, and one angular outgrowth from the wall, disguised as a sink and toilet. I looked around the cramped space quickly, avoiding staring too long at the men inside.

Warden Nattle barked at a young man lying on the top bunk furthest from the toilet-sink combo. "Get up!"

The young man, hair tangled with what looked like dried blood, objected. "What the hell, I just laid down!"

"Get the fuck up, dummy! This is *his* bed! He's actually supposed to be here! You dumb fucks were dumped on me!"

I started to say I'd be okay with sitting on the floor, but Warden Nattle turned to me. His face was cracked mad. "I gave you both an order! Get in that bed, Morant. Show these idiots what respect looks like and don't you dare talk back to me!"

No one had ever spoken to me like that. I felt stripped of all my medals. My service to the Common Goal made meaningless.

The young man climbed down and I climbed up, half reluctant and fully repulsed. A choking odor was left in his place.

"Now, talk nice. I got ears on all of you," Nattle said before he left.

The cage door slammed shut. The lock clanged into place.

With each nauseating breath I reminded myself that this was all a mistake and I'd be home by dinner. Just had to keep my mind tight. *Keep my mind tight.*

19

A fight broke out. I was face up in the top bunk, calculating my approximate arrival at home when I heard a "fuck you!" I turned to see two men nose to nose. One shirtless; the other in blue. Both of them were filthy.

The man in blue pushed the shirtless man saying something about the launch site. Like lightning, the shirtless man cocked an arm back and punched. Two hits, *crack crack*. The man in blue stumbled backwards. The others moved out of the way. He raised his fists but the shirtless man was too fast. He connected with the man's cheek CRACK. I turned away as he stumbled and fell. I didn't have to see it to know what was happening. He slammed his fists into that man's face so many times, it started sounding like he was hitting mud.

I don't think he would have stopped had the Auxen not pulled him off. One caught his arm mid-swing with one hand and used the other to subdue him with a baton, thwack thwack thwack thwack across his back and shoulders.

Seconds later, two guards entered the cell. One of them closed a collar around the shirtless man's neck. He did it so deftly. Like he was casting a fishing line. Then he pressed something on the back of the collar. The man released a scream I didn't know a human could make. Then he fell limp. The Auxen cuffed his ankles and wrists and dragged him out.

My heart slammed recklessly in my chest. I was too horrified to breathe. *Where the hell am I?* I thought. *I don't belong here. I'm not like them. I don't belong here.*

The guards ordered everyone to shut up or be shut up. "We've got a surplus of yokes! All charged and ready to go! Keep messing around and you can join your little friend in the basement!"

"That's not my friend," someone shouted from down the hall. Some laughs followed.

"Shut the fuck up! I don't care if you're friends or fuck buddies! Not another word!"

It got quiet after that. I heard the guards gripe about paperwork and how this was going to mess up their lunch time. Their boot stomps dragged at a lazy pace.

The man in blue lay where he was left, bleeding on the floor. His nose was a mess of red flesh. His lips were busted open. His left eye was swollen shut. His right eye wound around the cell then landed on me. He spit blood and some teeth out. I heard them tick-tack to the floor.

"What are you looking at?" he growled.

I didn't answer because I didn't know. Nothing made sense. I shook my head and looked away. I sank back into the bunk and swore I was going to make Beau pay for this.

I heard Beau's laugh flow down the corridor an hour or so after the blood dried. A few minutes after I heard him, an Aux beckoned me through the opened cage door. I heard Beau buttering up Warden Nattle, complimenting the man on his wide brim hat. The warden harharred at the flattery and bragged how it was passed down to him from his father, the warden Nattle Senior.

I was a mix of anger and relief before I got to the visitor door. But a familiar face does wonders to smooth out bitter wrinkles between friends.

"Here's your boy!" Nattle said, tipping his hat to me. "Signal to the Aux when you're ready, Morant. C-8 will be right outside the door."

"Warden Nattle, it was a pleasure meeting you!" Beau said, beaming a little too brightly for the circumstances. The two shook hands while the Aux cuffed me to the table. Then Nattle left, chuckling to himself.

"Fuck, Tah. . ." Beau trailed off once we were alone.

Forgetting about him owing me anything, I asked, "How's the crew?"

He raised his hands to calm my angst. "Everyone is fine. The crew is healthy. Contact has been made with the retrieval craft. They should be docking in an hour and heading back."

"ETA?" I asked.

"Tomorrow, about this time," he said. He looked me over. "What about you?"

I let out a big breath. "I'm okay," but something caught in my throat. I swallowed and tried again. "This place is. . ." The memory of the fight flashed. *Crack crack*, two swift hits.

"Tah, are you okay?" he asked more seriously.

I blinked the thought away and told him that I was fine but I had my complaints. I listed the awful air quality and general lack of sanitation. I mentioned how everyone had short tempers. But I didn't tell him about the fight. "The Auxen are programmed to be pleasant, so there's that," I said with a laugh but didn't mention how pleasantly they likely carried a man to his death in the desert. Or how they kept a calm demeanor as they beat the man in my cell. I wanted to keep my mind tight, like the transit guard told me. "Good place to visit, but I wouldn't want to live here." I forced out another laugh.

Beau tipped his gaze at my cuffs and said, "This all could have been avoided. You know that, right?"

I scoffed. "What I said was way out of line but no way should it have tripped a behavior code. It's not like I was throwing things or had my hands around your neck. The sensor needs some tuning, don't you think?"

He didn't agree with me, not immediately. "I know you didn't mean it, but suggesting that the GEM administration is corrupt. . ." He looked like a disappointed father sitting across from me. "That's what set off the V-code, Tah. You can't make accusations like that. The security of the mission— of the Common Goal— requires discipline and dutifulness. Challenging the higher ups puts everyone at risk."

"That wasn't my intention, Beau."

"Well, what did you mean? And what's going on with you? I hadn't seen you so worked up in a long time, Tah."

"I don't know," I said, playing back the past thirty-some hours. "I didn't sleep well the night before the launch. And then Itzel and I got into a fight when I got home. Then I didn't sleep last night." I shook my head. "I know that's not an excuse. I know everyone was affected, but I. . ." I looked up to see Beau watching me intently. He gave me a sad smile. "I'm sorry, Beau. My temper got the best of me." He bobbed his head in agreement. "And you know I don't like things being swept under the rug. I just felt like I'd found something important and you needed to listen. I needed your support."

Beau reached across the table and grabbed my hand. It felt like a promise to help me. "Hey, I'm here with you, Doc! It freaked me out when they tackled you. That was awful. And you're absolutely right, the response was uncalled for! Bringing you all the way to Texas is crazy! Absolutely crazy! I thought they'd take you to a different conference room and let you cool off. But out here! This is nuts!"

I nodded and took deep breaths to keep from welling up. Hearing someone else say what I was thinking assured me that it was a mistake, and I'd be going home soon.

But then he let go of my hand and said, "Dr. Jones is covering for you while we finish the mission report and get everything worked out."

"What do you mean, covering for me?" I asked, curling my fingers away.

Beau adjusted in his chair and cleared his throat. Suddenly there was space between us. More than the table. "Since your outburst was logged during a debrief it may take a few days to get it—"

I cut him off. "A few days?"

"Yes, Tah, a few days."

I felt sick. A few days. A few hours had already been some twisted type of hell. A few days in that place was going to end me.

He went on, ignoring my obvious distress. "Everything said and done during a mission becomes part of the record, Tah. You know that."

I saw an opening and took it. If I wasn't getting out that day, I asked about the findings being included.

He stumbled through his words for a moment, then said, "No. No, no. You weren't able to show anything so it's irrelevant, Tah."

I wanted to yell bullshit, but didn't. "Beau, you and I both know that's not right. A finding like this needs to be mentioned in the official report." He looked away. I softened my tone, "Just a mention, that's all." He drew in a big breath and let it out. I got desperate and begged, clasping my hands together. "I went through Dr. Hakim's logs to see if she had mentioned it. I didn't find anything! I just want it mentioned for historical purposes, Beau, that's it!"

Beau frowned. "You went through Hakim's files?"

"Yeah, and I didn't find anything. Please, Beau," I pleaded, "just a mention."

He swiped a hand through his hair. "Tah, if we even mention those *findings* in the report, sandbaggers will pore all over it and want to study it to death. That'll set us back a decade, maybe two!"

"Oh please, Beau! No they won't!"

He dropped his volume and rested his arms on the table. "This is just between us, but the board is nervous about the upcoming election. If we don't get Umoja-20 going, they're worried we'll lose all credibility! Funding goes to the next in line! Great Brazil and South Africa are chomping at the bit!"

I rolled my eyes. There was no way one anomalous observation could stop a whole mission or dry up all the funding.

He leaned in closer, stretching his neck half way across the table. He whispered at me, "Don't you want to be on the team that finds the Novi Dom, Tah? We're so close."

I scoffed.

"Well, I do!" he said. "Sure, I wanna save the human race and all that! But really, I want to find that planet! I want to send my dad the newstream and rub it in his face!" He grinned at me, summoning that younger, dumber version of himself. Fifty acting like a fifteen-year-old. All cocked up on out-doing his father. I just stared at him. And I kept staring as he tried to convince me to dismiss the anomaly. He tried flattery, telling me the whole Umoja team wanted me back, I just needed to sign off on the report sans the anomaly. He said he'd even make sure I'd get to do my own investigation once Umoja-20 was in the works. God forbid we stall a timeline during an election cycle. He even pulled our friendship between us, waxing about how long we'd known each other and that we shouldn't let something like a little wisp of nothing come between us.

I leaned further back in my chair unconvinced. And just when I started to question if he knew me at all, he swung hard.

"If you don't agree, they'll start an investigation into your whole life, Tah. You want to drag Itzel and Mai into your mess?"

My ears got hot and I stopped hearing things. I barely heard the cuffs rattle as I grabbed at him. But I saw him flinch. That little school boy was still there. I warned through clenched teeth, "Leave them out of this, Beau!"

The fear dried off of him as he realized I couldn't actually hit him. "You said some pretty damning things, but if you cooperate, I can see about GEM dropping the charges."

I slowed my breath. "See about it. And I'll see about signing."

He rubbed his forehead. "Fine. A liaison will contact you later," he said, exhausted.

I didn't have anything else to say to Beau. Itzel was right. He wasn't there to help me at all. He was doing his job flawlessly, keeping the Board happy and his ass covered.

I called for the Aux and enjoyed the worry in Beau's face once my hands were free. He was lucky the Aux was there. If it wasn't, I would have made mud of his face.

20

I don't know exactly when the other men were taken out of the cell. I didn't pay them any attention. Why should I have? I wasn't going where they were going. I only had two strikes against me: My *verbal* assault and Itzel's views of the Common Goal but that was a moot point— she hadn't actually done anything wrong. If anyone deserved to be in a detention center, it was Beau! *He* suppressed a significant finding. *He* violated GEM's reporting policy! And more importantly, GEM needed me for Umoja-20. They needed *me*.

I was confident I'd be home for dinner. I was even more confident that this game of chicken between Beau and me would end in my favor. But then dinner came. An Aux delivered it through a slot in the cage door. I pushed aside my doubt, choked that food down and swore I'd never forget to compliment Itzel's cooking. As soon as I got home, I'd beg for forgiveness and devour each meal in honest-to-God gratitude. As soon as I got home!

Then the Aux returned. I stood ready to receive news of my departure, wide eyed like a kid ready for dessert. But it was only there for the tray. As I handed it over, I thought about choking that Aux. Reaching through the bars and choking its circuits.

Tighten up! I thought. I couldn't give Warden Nattle a single reason to keep me longer than necessary.

I started pacing. The click of my uniform shoes bounced off the concrete walls with each gritty step. When I started to worry about nightfall, my thoughts ran to Mai. Her sweet, brown face and corkscrew coils. Her squeals and giggles. Her brilliant mind. She'd be asking about me, not having seen me in over 24 hours. We had bedtime stories to read. It was my turn to tuck her in. God, I hurt to hold her!

Then Itzel and I's argument crept in and gripped my insides. My eyes stung thinking about her silent pleas for me to stop talking. The face she made when I questioned her integrity, out loud for the haum system to record.

Dear God! What have I done?

Beau was right. If I didn't acquiesce, Itzel would be investigated. How could I protect her from this remote prison? And what would happen to Mai? My sweet, sweet Mai.

How could Beau do this to me?

We'd been friends, basically brothers since secondary school. I backed him up through all his adolescent missteps— cheating on tests, pulling pranks on admin. Defacing the school mascot with a giant penis costume. I defended him against his father's raging disapproval. I stood by his side through all of it. Sure, we were kids but that was the foundation of us. All we had was each other in those four years. He was all I had. I never imagined he'd betray me.

By the time an Aux returned and told me I had a call from the GEM legal department, I'd argued my case to the empty bunks and walls for a good fifty minutes. As far as I felt, I was ready. I was going home that night! And GEM was going to know about that anomaly and Beau's transgressions!

The Aux entered the cage and set up a projector call. An oval faced woman appeared on the wall over the sink-toilet. "Good evening, Dr. Morant. My name is Lilly McLeod, I am your liaison with GEM Legal. I regret these unfortunate circumstances but it is my pleasure to meet you."

"Nice to meet you, too, Ms. McLeod." *Not too much*, I thought. *Don't want to show any weakness.*

She was straight to business. "Due to the shortening window of time, I encourage you to consider this preliminary agreement. Your immediate consent will guarantee a dropping of all charges, clearing of your record, and reinstatement of all security clearance. You would have to—"

I interrupted her, "What window of time?"

She smiled and explained, "There is a twelve-hour window that allows for quick resolution to system-generated alerts like this. After those twelve hours, you will be automatically required to attend a disciplinary martial regarding your, um, behavior." Her face sagged slightly as she said it.

Why didn't Beau mention this? I reflexively glanced at my wrist. No rello. "When did the clock start? How much time do I have?"

She made an odd noise before she told me I had twenty-three minutes to make my decision.

The walls pressed in. My chest tightened, my ears buzzed.

"Dr. Morant?"

"Yes?"

"I am going to share the preliminary agreement now. It is brief due to the time constraints. I encourage you to read quickly and confirm your decision." Her face faded, replaced by a bulleted list of items.

I sagged as I read it. Beau stuck to his guns. It said everything he said with no hand holds. I needed to be quiet about what I found and agree with the general consensus that the mission failed due to a procedural mistake. I needed to focus on making Umoja-20 a success. And once I agreed, witnesses would sign nondisclosures. All of it would be swept under the rug. Right next to my findings.

The liaison reappeared and asked, "Do you consent to the agreement?"

It must have seemed reasonable to her. GEM wasn't asking for too much, just a simple list of Do's and Don'ts– Do play ball, Don't be an idiot, Do your little experiments on your own time and let GEM know if that foggy mist actually means something. Don't talk about it to anyone unless it actually means something. Do ignore that gnawing feeling in your stomach. Don't bring it up.

"Dr. Morant?"

I hardly heard her. I couldn't quiet the voice screaming that the anomaly had to be investigated. I knew in my bones it was related to the failure. I just needed to figure out how. And what if it posed danger? Itzel had asked the same thing. I had pushed back and dismissed her worry when she said it. But what if she was right?

"Dr. Morant, I need an answer."

"I just need a few more minutes to think," I said.

She raised her brows at me, but said nothing.

I returned to my pacing as I worked through the facts. What was there to think about? What was stopping me? GEM agreed to let me explore it on my own, but in seventeen years, I never had time outside of the lab to take on another project. No one did. And outside of work, family was my top priority. I knew Itzel would be supportive but–

"Dr. Morant, you have less than 10 minutes." Her soft tone hardened toward impatience.

For fuck sake, just agree and go home!

"Can I speak to my wife?" I asked.

She looked puzzled. "Uh, no. No, you can't, Dr. Morant. Texas does not allow consultative phone calls. Director Soncal's visit was a courtesy to you. Not everyone gets that kind of treatment, sir."

I nodded at her but something was wrong. Why was Beau so hell bent on excluding this single observation? He mentioned the election and funding but that couldn't be it. Funding for research was guaranteed under the Interplanetary Safety Act of 142. There had to be something else.

I spun around. "I want a lawyer," I blurted.

"This isn't an interrogation, Dr. Morant."

"I know that Ms. McLeod. I am formally asserting my rights to guidance and counsel before I make my decision."

She repeated her warning. "Dr. Morant, you have less than five minutes before an automatic disciplinary martial is set."

"I'm entitled to counsel as a team lead at GEM. I am formally requesting—"

She cut me off. "GEM Labs is not obligated to assist you in providing counsel due to your behavior."

My vision blurred when she said that. My chest felt heavy but I tried to explain, "There is something going on that needs to be uncovered—"

She cut me off again, "You understand that the earliest martial will be in three months, Dr. Morant?"

A wave of nausea crashed into me. Three months without Itzel or Mai. Three months. No giggles. No soft kisses. No velvet warmth. No *I love yous*. I swallowed the bile in my throat.

Ms. McLeod gave me one more opportunity to take the deal.

I shook my head, "No." I hoped Itzel would understand.

"To be clear, you are declining to consent to this agreement?" she asked, face full of worry.

"Tell my wife I love her."

21

"**Y**ou're so opposite of each other," Itzel had said, one day, carrying a small basket of half ripe tomatoes from the porch. We were considering a family vacation with the Soncal's, but Itzel had reservations.

I was folding Mai's clothes. She was an infant, burbling on her belly next to where I sat and her clothes were hardly big enough to fold.

"Well, you know, he kind of grows on you," I said, matching two tiny socks.

"So does mold," Itzel mumbled from the kitchen, assessing each red-green fruit.

I frowned, "What's that mean?"

She shrugged. "Just that *growing on someone* isn't always a good thing. Not a good sign."

"Like there's something wrong with me?" I asked, picking up another two small socks. They didn't match, but Itzel said that didn't matter, so I folded them into each other and tossed them into the basket.

"No, I don't think there is something wrong with *you*. I just think. . ."

I watched her. She stared at the kitchen counter like it was telling her something. Her brow tightened. Her lips pursed.

"Itzel?"

She shook free whatever the thought was and smiled. "It's nothing, honey. I didn't mean anything by it."

At that time I couldn't see what she saw. I didn't see the gradual changes that took place over the seventeen years we lived a short tram ride to the Soncal's. But there were signs, like his face. The thought of it made me clench my fists as I stared at the ceiling in the prison cell.

His face never changed. Even on the morning of the launch, he looked young. Living under the GEM sun shield slowed the aging process in general, but his seemed to stop. His and his wife's, Sarathi. Both of them looked brand new to adulthood, far younger than their actual age.

Itzel had pointed out modification adverts when we watched a program or the news. I downplayed them, thinking Itzel was interested in what they had to offer. That's what I assumed when she showed me how much certain procedures cost.

"Five-thousand hheqs for plasma infusions, Tah! That's so expensive!"

"Mm hmm," was all I said. But I realized, thinking back on those conversations, that she had caught onto something I had missed. Beau and I had similar salaries, so there would be no way he could afford a plasma infusion or a contouring, or whatever youth-enizing procedure he had. At the time, I had thought maybe with their combined salaries they could afford the procedures. It guaranteed them a stand-alone home. I thought a dual-income came with other perks. Like their property upgrades.

Since I was the only GEM employed member of our household, GEM provided us a condo. Our neighbors were mostly single individuals. We were a rarity if not an odd couple. There were few children for Mai to play with after school. So naturally, Beau and Sarathi invited her to play with their daughter, Abby. Mai loved going over to their place.

One afternoon, she came back excited to tell me that she got to swim in Abby's pool. I chuckled as I lifted her and sat her on my hip. "That's not Abby's pool, honey bee, that's GEM's pool where everyone swims."

She defiantly shook her head, drops of water sprinkled onto my face. "Uh uh, Daddy, it's Abby's pool!"

I looked past her as Itzel walked by. She gave me a look to tell me Mai was right! The Soncals had a pool.

"Well that is wonderful, Mai! That must have been so much fun!" I said as I kissed her cheeks. I tasted salt on my lip. I mouthed to Itzel, "When did that happen?"

She shrugged back and headed toward Mai's bedroom. "Come on, my little mermaid, we gotta get you washed up."

I messaged Beau to congratulate him. He buzzed me back with a thank you and a casual invite to a small get-together at their place the following week. "Bring the family!" his last message read. I told Itzel and we went.

Mai tore out of the tram, through the house and cannon balled into the water before we could reach the door. Itzel and I were gobsmacked at the updates since the last time we visited. It had been a few months but it was like walking into a new home.

"Beau, I didn't realize GEM gave out bonuses!" I said, as he pulled me in for a hug.

He laughed, slapped my back and said, "Oh, they don't!"

Most two-income homes under the GEM dome were single story. Some even had planted trees. Beau became the proud owner of one of the two-story homes inside of GEM. He was prouder still to be one of the few homeowners with a yard, two trees, and an in-ground pool.

When we returned home, Itzel remarked about all she saw. "The light fixture in the foyer costs 450 hheqs, babe! Would you let me buy a 450 hheq light fixture?" she asked from our bathroom doorway while I brushed my teeth.

"How do you know how much it costs?" I mumbled, cradling the paste beneath my tongue.

"Sarathi told me! She told me about the new flooring, the new automated appliances, the garment service included. Their bedroom could fit half of our entire condo. She's done an amazing job with the furnishing but my goodness!"

I wanted to joke about how she could still apply to work at the Farm so we could start the Morant Estates, but decided against it. I spat and rinsed. "But I'm your garment service, babe," I said, swooping in for a kiss.

She was too distracted. "That's not what I mean, Tah." She looked up at me with big, serious eyes. "They live better than anyone on their block. That's not weird to you?"

I let her go, a little bruised by her lack of affection. "Not really. Beau has been here awhile, Sarathi even longer. Maybe they saved up," I suggested. "Besides, Beau comes from money. His parents might have pushed for better accommodations. His dad is pretty convincing."

I told her about the time his father barked down our dorm coordinator's throat in high school. He was furious that Beau didn't get the corner room our senior year. It took less than a day for the school to shuffle the rest of the students around to accommodate his request. "My room was between the kitchenette and the bathrooms. I thought myself lucky to be close to the necessities and told Mr. Soncal Senior just that. The old man warned me to never settle between the shitter and the sink."

I sunk into a bottom bunk, oblivious to the smells. I was blind to everything around me. Been blind to who Beau really was. He'd used the system against me. Got all he needed from me and shuffled me off to prison. And there I sat, right next to a toilet and sink. But I wasn't settling. I had three months to prove my innocence. And Beau's guilt.

22

I didn't hear them coming down the hall. I hardly noticed when they entered the cell. My head and heart were battling over the decision I made. Whether it was righteous or a mistake. Whether I made it out of stubbornness or plain stupidity. A man ordered me to look up and "show some respect." I followed orders and saw a guard accompanied by two Auxen.

"Detainee Too- toolop—whatever—Detainee Morant, you have been charged with violation of Dominion statute 97.07.53, Seditious Obstruction to the Common Goal."

My body tightened at the word seditious. Who had I incited? Were they blaming me for the failure *and* the riots?

The guard proceeded reading off his tablet. "You will hereby be held in detention until your disciplinary martial at which time you will be transported to a predetermined location. Upon determination of your status, you may or may not be required to return."

I started to object over the charge, but the Auxen were on me. They yanked me by the arms out of the bunk. Then out of the cell. Down the hall. Through windowless doors. Left down another hall. Away from the main entrance.

"Where are you taking me?" I demanded. I stumbled, trying to keep up as the Auxen pivoted a corner.

The guard, following behind, rattled on with practiced boredom. "At this time, you will be inspected for contraband and given your uniform."

"Inspected for contraband? I don't have anything!" I pleaded.

"Do not interrupt me!" he snapped. "Dammit! I lost my place," he mumbled, before returning to his instructions. "You will receive two sets of prison uniforms, shoes, and toiletries following the inspection."

The Auxen stopped in front of an elevator. Authorized Access Only was stamped above it. The guard stepped around us and swiped his badge. A buzzer sounded. The door slid open. The Auxen pulled me forward. The guard followed and used his badge to activate the lift.

"Your current attire will be kept until the conclusion of your disciplinary martial and will be returned to you *if* you have been deemed *innocent and acceptable* to return to society."

The lift dropped. My stomach leapt up my throat. If *I was innocent?*

"You will be provided a solo unit at this time," the guard said. Then he whispered how lucky I was but that I shouldn't get my hopes up. "A martial ain't a promise, but a cellmate is a guarantee."

I turned slightly, trying to catch a glimpse of him. I swear he said that with a smile on his face.

"Face forward, Morant!" he shouted. "It's been a long fucking day and I do not have the patience for this." He sighed then spoke softer, "just follow directions."

There was something in his voice—pity. Maybe it was concern. Whatever it was, it was enough to make me nervous. I wanted to ask what was going to happen next but the door in front of me opened. Light from the elevator spilled into a darkened hall. A large pipe ran along the ceiling, like a hardened vein. The smell of sour water and bleach choked me. The Auxen yanked me forward as I coughed and struggled to breathe. I glanced back to ask the guard where they were taking me. But he stayed in the elevator, waving goodbye.

The door slid shut. The light went with the elevator. Fear filled me as the Auxen marched me further into the dark. Their boot stomps pounded off the walls. The pipe rattled and whined overhead. Deeper into the dark, I saw a faint light flicker on. As I got closer, I could make out a sign, pointing toward Decontaminator Bay 1. My knees buckled but the Auxen kept stride. My feet stuttered to keep up, but everything in me wanted to turn and run.

I dug my feet against the Decontaminator threshold when I saw what was inside. Four steel bars hung horizontally from the ceiling. Beneath each one was a pair of metal posts protruding from the concrete floor. Between the posts were grates. But it was cuffs that really scared me. They dangled from the bars, swaying like they'd been used recently. The floor was still wet. The bleach was freshly poured.

I struggled against the Auxen until they reached for their batons. I knew I had to obey.

One ordered me to remove my clothes. I complied, slowly. I felt like an animal as I stood between them. Embarrassed, naked. And terrified.

The one on my right stepped behind me and said, "A cavity search is required for contraband. This is for your safety. Please bend forward."

I protested and swore I didn't have anything. That didn't matter. One held me still. The other inspected.

After what felt like too long, the Aux announced that my cavity was clear. Its programmed polite setting made the Aux sound impressed, almost pleased by my suffering.

I prayed it would end but then they cuffed my ankles and wrists in place, making an X of me. Then they stepped out. I was terror and fury. Like an animal, caught in a trap. Ready to break my bones or gnaw through them to get out. I shouted for help. My pleas echoed back.

And then I heard rattling. Overhead, pipes were rattling.

Water. Unstopping water beat against me with skin tearing pressure. I gasped for air. I choked. My face, my arms, my back, my buttock, my genitals, my thighs, my finger nails. All on fire. All at once. I screamed for it to stop, and choked on more and more water. I was drowning and on fire at the same time.

Then it stopped.

I hung there, sagging against cuffs. I coughed and threw up water. When I opened my eyes, I saw reddish orange streaks swirling down the drain between my legs. I don't know where it came from. I closed my eyes again. Afraid of what would be next.

The Auxen returned. One released my cuffs. The other handed me a towel. Then it handed me yellow, folded clothes and blue shoes, a wash rag, a lump of soap, and a toothbrush.

After I dressed, they escorted me to my cell. It had a cot with a thin mattress pad, thin pillow and blanket, a toilet and sink combo. It was a quarter the width of the holding cell. I couldn't spread my arms if I wanted to.

The Auxen informed me that my day would start at 6 am. Further instructions would be provided for the rest of my intake process. They welcomed me, with polite, unblinking stares to Level 1, closed the windowless door and it locked.

That sound, a bolt dead-ending into place, stopped my heart.

23

I had a dream that night. I sat at a table. In the center was a bowl. Golden light shone from it. It lit up the faces of everyone there: Itzel sitting to my right, Mai on my left. My father at one end of the table, his piercing stare softened to a striking smile. My mother sat opposite of him, beaming at my family. Across from me sat Beau and Sarathi. Their children, too.

"Mrhbaan! Mrhbaan!" My mother and father called, singing in a chorus. "Everyone. Please eat. Eat. There is so much. You can have all you like."

I reached forward but found my wrists were bound to the table. I panicked, but Mai assured me it was okay. "I'll feed you, Daddy," she said, raising a long spoon to my mouth.

I went to sip the golden light, but something drew my gaze toward Beau. He was rotting. Maggots crawled in and through large wounds on his face. His wife, Sarathi, paid no attention to the swaying corpse beside her. She looked beautiful as always, and fed her children, who fed her in return. I tried to speak, to tell her that Beau was dying. Or dead. Or very sick. But I couldn't. I had no words.

Beau's jaw opened, unhinged on one side. Black oozed out and spilled down his chest. His eyes shone, entranced by something behind me. I tried to lean forward, away from whatever it was. I tried to lean toward the light. But it pulled me back. It was a woman. She stroked my cheek and whispered, "I have something I need to ask you." I liked her voice. It sounded like liquid gold. I relaxed into her. Beau's rotting face smiled at me as blood poured from my ear.

Sarathi tried to feed Beau, "Aristide, darling, you'll starve." But Beau was mesmerized by the woman drinking my blood. I did nothing to stop her. I let her drink freely. Then there was blood everywhere. Covering the table, drowning the bowl of light. Beau gurgled out a laugh. Sarathi fed her children. My parents disappeared. Itzel stood. "Come Mai, we must go. Your father's heart is drained."

I watched them leave. Panic filled my chest. I tried to scream. I strained against the cuffs. *Don't leave me! Please don't leave me!*

Finally, I shouted, "Don't go! I can fill my heart back up."

I awoke into complete darkness. I had to think fast to remember where I was. What all had happened the day before. The night before. Nightmares on top of nightmares. I didn't know which was worse.

The light cracked on, blanched the small cell and blinded me. Then my door swung open. I jumped to standing, ready to defend myself. But no one came. Instead I heard movement outside, a constant shuffling with occasional coughs and curses. I steeled myself and stepped into the doorway. Prisoners, in yellow uniform, passed without looking. Except one. He walked differently than the rest, off-balance and shakily. He eyed me up and down and swerved in my direction in a jerky gait.

"Face forward, Sam! Don't start with me today!" a voice boomed from down the hall. "Morant!" the voice erupted, "Fall in line! Face forward!"

My body obeyed. I stepped behind the last prisoner. I did as they did. Mimicked their shuffled gait, their hunched postures. I'd disguise myself as a prisoner if I had to. For three months, I'd play pretend. I'd do whatever I needed to to get back to my family.

Breakfast was a flavorless gruel lumped out of one spigot. Dirty brown liquid sprayed out of another. There was a hint of coffee that served as a disappointing mask for the sulfur. I sat alone that first morning. I watched the rest of the prisoners notice me. No one greeted me. *Just as well*, I thought. I wasn't one of them, and they knew it.

After breakfast came "dawn time." The Auxen lining the walls of the mess hall directed everyone outside. The UV shield flickered on as the sun rose higher. Even that early, the air dried up my nose and throat. I shielded my eyes against the sun and followed the craggy slope of the mountain to the north. Something closer caught my eye. A vulture. It hopped around a lump in the sand then tugged at it. Then stuck its head inside. My breakfast threatened to return. I swallowed it back down and turned away.

The memory of fetching water rose. It was months after the Mars disaster. My grandmother had taken charge of the house duties and suddenly I had chores, too. The kind that made my body hurt. The worst was fetching water. Two kilometers out of the ALN compound, two kilometers back with 75 liters of water. Once or twice a week.

My grandmother and I would join others. We always had to go in groups. Always. We walked in the middle of the streets. My grandmother warned me every time, "keep your eyes straight ahead so your feet don't wander." That rule was hard to follow. There was so much to see. So much I didn't want to see but couldn't help to look. There were bodies along the gutters. The newer ones buzzed with flies. The older ones crawled with maggots. Some were too charred even for the insects. Those were for the vultures. They sat in the trees and watched us pass. I'd look over my shoulder and watch their black wings stretch wide before they'd swoop down. I learned to look away before they started to pull the flesh out.

"Another one come crawling back!" someone said from my left.

A withered man stood next to me. I asked, "Crawling back? How'd he get out there?"

He puffed out his cheeks. "Auxen, probably."

I felt light headed as I recalled the man from the day before. His contorted face, a horrific scream, begging me for help.

"He was so close," I said. "Why didn't they let him back in?"

"My guess, he wasn't officially here."

"What?" I asked, eyeing the frail man. "He was here. I saw him."

"Oh, well, if you saw him, then that's all that matters. Better tell his family he's dead!" He coughed out a laugh and walked away.

I turned back to the body. Three vultures worked around him. They hopped and bobbed their heads. Raised their wings in apparent excitement. He died where I had been dropped off. A few meters from the edge of the UV-shield. How far had the Auxen carried him? Did he fight the whole way? Did he have enough sense to relax and save his energy for the trek back to prison? Did he know he could have tripped the Auxen's command and made them his own? I looked around at the Auxen. Their placid faces turned up and open to the sun and I wondered which ones I could make mine.

24

The intake officer rolled her eyes at my name. She confirmed my official status as a registered prisoner of the Jarrett Detention Center in the great Nation of Texas. *At least they'd let Itzel know if I died*, I told myself whether or not it was a lie. I had to find solace where I could.

"You are entitled to seek legal counsel and advice. However, under Texas law, we are not required to assist you in securing said counsel. Do you understand?"

Behind her was a newsstream playing. The sound was turned down but I didn't need it to know what was happening. Umoja Village, established just a few weeks prior, was smoke and rubble. Over 1,000 people were arrested. *Was that all?* I thought. One million people attended the launch, 0.001% destroyed the temporary city. One-thousand was not that many. And where were they? I couldn't imagine Warden Nattle letting that many people enter his castle. He seemed like the type to raise the bridge when he saw someone coming, just for the joy of it.

The agent tapped the monitor again. With a tired sigh she instructed my escort, Aux D-5, to take me to medical. I stared at her, unwilling to move. My body still ached from the night before. I couldn't go through something like that again. She cocked her head to the side and glared at me. I understood that to mean, "Fuck you waiting for? An asskicking?"

The medical facility, tucked further to the west side of the prison, behind five secure doors linked together by five long hallways, didn't offer any welcome. The air smelled like the wrong combination of bleach, urine, feces, and iron. The lobby was mostly empty except for a few prisoners and their Auxen escorts. Something I noticed about the lighting in that place– it made more shadows than anything. A couple of the prisoners raised their stares in my direction. All I saw were sunken eyes and cheekbones looking at me.

After I took a seat, I glanced around at the Auxen, making an effort to not look too long. A few of the prisoners looked agitated enough without my eyes on them. The last thing I wanted was to set any one of them off. Based on my experience from the day before, I figured the chance of violence was pretty high.

My random glances informed me of one thing: all eight Auxen were different, like they had been acquired at different times from different military surplus stores. A few were the same model but different generations. I could tell by their ear shapes and whether they had the outer part or not. The three with flat, round ears were the ones I was most interested in. I perked up thinking what modifications I could do. With the right patching and the right amount of time, I could send a message to Itzel through their internal network. I just wanted to tell her I was okay and that I loved her. And how sorry I was. I looked up at my escort, D-5. It had pointed ears which meant it communicated with local frequencies only. It'd be of little use to me.

Not fifteen minutes after my arrival, I heard my name called. Standing at the admittance door was a nurse, covered head-to-foot in protective wear. As I made my way toward him, I heard someone snarl and spit. "I been here two hours! No food! Why you not calling my name? Why you pulling him back? He ain't been here more than a second!" It was a man bent unnaturally at his upper spine.

"Don't mind him, he's always here for something," the nurse said. "I'll bump him down on the schedule for that."

I frowned. The last thing I wanted was an enemy this early in the morning, this soon in my 90 days.

Nurse Tidwell was young, maybe in his early thirties, and eager. He exclaimed how they never got to treat celebrities, let alone a *Global Contributor*. That didn't exactly comfort me, but I smiled at the sentiment. The other medical providers watched me as I followed him. Some saluted, hands over their hearts. I reflexively did the same. Others turned back to their work and shook their heads. I wasn't sure of the offense I made, but I didn't really care. I wasn't going to be there long.

"So you'll have to forgive my excitement!" he said, closing the treatment room door behind us— us including D-5.

The treatment room, at first, reminded me of the ones on the space station, adequate but limited in supplies. With a little more time to look around, it was far less sanitary and most of the equipment was, by GEM standards, outdated.

Nurse Tidwell didn't stop talking throughout the examination. He shone a light in my eyes and said, "You guys use that bio stuff, huh? Biostim? Heard that shit is crazy!"

"Yeah, it is crazy," I said with a soft chuckle, blinking away the residual blue circles. I recalled Bierdot's joke about it and childbirth, "at least you get to hold a baby after delivery!" *What's my prize for this?* I wondered.

He pressed a metal funnel in my ear. A thin ringing sound played under his voice. "We don't have that kind of stuff here, but my crew is pretty good." He switched sides and tested my hearing again. "Haven't had any serious infections in a few years. Which is kind of a big deal!" He took some notes. "Especially that lower level!" he said with a whistle.

"Lower level?" I asked, rubbing my ears. I could still hear the ringing in the right one.

He motioned for me to lift my uniform shirt and placed a large c-clamp around my chest. It was so cold, I flinched as he closed it. He tapped something into his monitor and the clamp beeped on. "Yeah, we call them Dungeon Crabs. I hate getting one of them on the schedule. It's always something heinous: cracked skull, punctured lung, missing finger or limb–"

"Missing limb?" I asked, interrupting him.

"A lack of sun will drive you crazy," he said, frowning at his screen.

I imagined hunched bodies with joints like barnacles, gnarled and callused, creeping through the dark. "What gets someone sent down there?" I asked.

He cut his eyes over to the Aux and said, "Hard to say."

I understood that to mean he probably said too much about what I wasn't supposed to know. I knew starting a fight got a collar. I could avoid that. I just had to keep my temper in check. But how was I supposed to survive if I didn't know where all the mines were buried? I got nervous thinking that was the point. And maybe that's how Warden Nattle managed the population. Maybe that was where some of the thousand rioters were.

Tidwell told me to take some deep breaths, then made me sit and stand several times. He did some strength tests, took a pin drop of blood and said I was the healthiest prisoner there. I forced a smile that time and told him GEM kept us up on all our vitamins.

But I didn't like being called a prisoner.

"You're good to go," Tidwell said, with a smile in his voice.

"Hey, at GEM we have monthly check-ups. You all do that here?" I asked. *He'd make a good ally,* I thought. *He could get a message to Itzel.*

I saw his cheerfulness shrink behind his mask. "Uh, no. Annual check -ups, or necessity only."

"Oh," I said.

"Limited budget and all," he explained, apologetically.

I thanked him and half jokingly said, "In that case, I hope I never have to see you again."

He let out a short laugh and wished me all the best. He sounded nervous for me.

I followed D-5 out. The bent man was still waiting in the waiting room. He hawked spit and flung a hand gesture at me. I looked away as his escorting Aux backhanded him in the mouth. I took that to mean a few things: The Auxen might be my closest allies, that I better keep my eyes down or forward. And above all, keep my mind tight.

25

And then I met Sam.

It was after the medical assessment and the Aux led me to the laundry room where I was put to work at my first "activity." I made the mistake of thinking it wouldn't be so bad. But the door opened and I was smacked silent by its atmosphere. The air was so thick and awful it was hard to breathe in there. When I did take a sip, bile rose into the back of my throat. The sound was constant, grating and somehow nauseating. The machines, which were as tall as I am, lined the walls and shook loud and angry as they spun and tumbled. In the middle of the room was a long table and four long-faced men surrounding it, sorting the soiled linens. I joined them with a nod and did as they did.

Silly me thought laundry was laundry. But prison laundry was a new type of torture. We had to sort by color and state. Some sheets were dirty, but dry. Others weren't. It only took one time for me to learn to look before I grabbed anything. A cold squish in my palm sent rivers of disgust through my whole body. But I tried to keep my reaction to myself. I didn't want to show any kind of weakness. I did look around for gloves, but no one else had them on. I spotted a sink in the back corner. When I looked harder, I saw dusted cobwebs making a canopy over the basin. I wiped my hand on the cleanest part of a bed sheet and tried not to think too much about it.

We had to move loads of laundry. I mean two-men-required sized loads of laundry. And even then we had to take a rocking start to heave the sacks high enough to toss into the machine door. The worst was the transfer from wash to dry. I know I pulled a muscle on the second one.

I was well focused when the room door opened. I looked over and saw the man from the breakfast march that morning, the one who teetered in my direction as he passed my cell. He was limping behind a large laundry cart now, grinning.

"I knew I'd meet you soon enough" he said as he slowed the cart. He smiled up at me like we were old friends. "Name's Sam. Sam Truce." He moved around the cart, keeping one hand against it as he teetered toward me.

Sam was small, the same way an over-blown balloon is small when all the air is let out. His walnut-colored skin was wrinkled and very dry. I saw puckered scars on his arm when he extended his hand for me to shake. I didn't take it immediately. Something about him made me nervous. Maybe it was his eyes. They constantly jerked to the left, like he had an accomplice behind me and I was going to be the victim of something only they'd find funny. I shot a glance at the men standing across from me. They kept their focus on the sheets and uniforms, but I knew they were listening. One shook his head, subtly. I took that to mean I should stay focused on the sheets and uniforms, too. But Sam was persistent.

"And you are?" he asked. I was surprised by how his voice carried over the tumbling washers and dryers and the screaming whine of a loosened pipe.

I looked again at the other men for a hint of advice but they'd turned away and were dumping a sack of soiled uniforms in an open washer. The other men to my side looked determined to mind their business.

I gave in and shook Sam's hand. I opened my mouth to introduce myself but he beat me to it.

"Dr. Tah Morant!" He announced my name loud enough to startle the others. Which was pretty loud considering the jumbled rhythm of the room. "I know who you are!"

My stomach tightened. But just then an Aux entered. It made a direct line toward Sam. He rolled his eyes and lost his balance. I caught him and helped steady his stance. He swatted me away and beat the Aux to its warning of "no touching." I think I heard Sam laugh as he braced against the sorting table. He mumbled something, but I assumed it wasn't for me.

About twenty seconds passed before he stood upright. The Aux produced a cane from its belt. I braced myself, ready to witness a beating, or to receive one. But the Aux handed it to Sam.

"We all know who you are!" Sam said with a smirk.

The first breath I took once we left that room felt medicinal. The dryness reached down my throat and cleared out all the pneumonia I was positive I developed. I coughed up some phlegm and got worried. At GEM, this was a sign of infection, a reason to quarantine. But the Aux escorting us to the mess hall didn't pause. The other four men cleared their throats and moved along. I wondered how long it'd take to acclimate. I had ninety days. Hopefully it was less than that.

Lunch was different by substance but just as bland as breakfast. Thin bread, a thin slice of meat, and a short glass of foggy water.

"It's mineralized!" Sam said.

I jumped at his voice. I hadn't noticed him slide into the seat next to me.

"So," he said, "how did such an illustrious scientist— no, *theee* chief scientist! — nay, the *award-winning*, Chief Scientist Dr. Tah Morant, end up here with us rejects?" He said that last part loudly, with pride. As if being rejected and relegated to Nowhere, Texas was an honor. I hunched forward and tried to disappear. His eyes skipped to the left but he was focused solely on me.

"It was a mistake," I said finally. He raised his eyebrows and waited. "I got into a disagreement with my program director and triggered a behavioral code" I said, avoiding the violent part of the title. It felt like I was lying on myself if I did say it out loud.

Sam nodded with his whole body. "Hmmmm. The system. . ." then bellowed, "the system always reacts! It's a reactionary system!"

I wanted him gone. He was drawing too much attention to me. I noticed that most of the men kept a solid meter between them and us. And I was still convinced that I was all I had and that was all I needed.

He dropped his volume to just above a whisper. I felt my heart rate slow. "Everyone in here triggered the system somehow."

I turned to him and waited for him to say more. I immediately regretted that.

"But Chief Scientist Dr. Tah Morant, you're different! You're part of that system! You are a glorified fingernail on the hand of the arm of the system that serves you!"

I hunched further over my food tray and barricaded myself between my elbows. This man was insane and my father warned me about men like him. Better to ignore crazy so nobody mistook me for crazy, too.

"Do you know where you are, Dr. Tolulopé Ayodege Hudu-Morant?" he asked, quiet and low.

I pulled away from him, startled that he knew my whole name. "How do you know my name?"

Sam dismissed my question with a groan, "Ugh, don't flatter yourself! We all know who you are. Now answer the question: Do you know where you are?"

I straightened up and growled out, "Texas. Now answer mine!"

He was unfazed. "Do you know why you're in Texas?" he asked, squinting at me. His eyes jerked a little less.

"How do you know my name?" I demanded.

"Shhhh, shhhh, you're making a scene, doctor!" Sam whispered. "I know things. I'll teach you what I know, but you have to relax."

I looked around the cafeteria and saw most of the prisoners were occupied with their lunches. I frowned at Sam but nodded for him to continue.

"Now, do you know why you're in Texas?"

Still frustrated, I started to answer, "I already told you, it was a mista-"

"No, no, no, not why you're here sitting next to me, dumdum! I mean, *why Texas*?"

"No, I don't," I said, tethering my anger down. "Why Texas, Sam?"

He leaned back again and said in a whisper, "All those brains and not a single bit of knowledge."

I let out a sharp breath. "I know about things worth my time."

"All you've got is time here, my friend!" he chuckled.

"I'll be out of here in ninety-days," I said, grabbing my tray to leave. "Now, excuse me. I have my defense to prepare."

He cackled. "A defense! Oh, that's rich." He banged on the table three times. Two guards shouted for him to knock it off. He ignored them and continued. "Your defense is simple, Dr. Tah Morant."

I stopped mid-stride and turned.

He leaned in my direction, and smiled wickedly. "Go back to GEM. Bend over. And take it up the backside."

26

I was on wall duty on my second day. I was with seven prisoners, supervised by two Auxen. Six buckets between us, three with bleach, three for rinsing the bleach off. We got grime covered rags to wash grime covered walls. No gloves. No masks. I tucked my nose in my yellow shirt. My sour odor gave some relief to the pungent cleanser. But lifting my shirt that high and reaching overhead (I was the only one who could clean the ceiling line when standing on my toes) exposed my low back. That drew attention from a few of the prisoners. I didn't notice the sudden silence behind me. I didn't have time to react. One, two, three stinging snaps and cold water ran down my backside, dribbled down my pants. I turned and pressed myself against the bleaching wall. The rest of the crew muffled their laughs and turned away. The Auxen stepped forward, scanned for aberrant behavior, then stepped back to their positions.

I eyed them all, bleach-water dripping down my buttock and thighs. Three men working on the opposite wall kept glancing at me and snickering. I wanted to get my revenge but I also wanted to hide. Forty-eight years old and pride stinging like a child's.

"Don't let them get to you, man. It's just a little hazing," the prisoner next to me said. For a moment I felt comforted. But only for a moment. He followed up with, "I wouldn't hit back, though. We all know where you sleep."

I shrank after that. I stopped reaching so high. I stopped covering my face. I kept pulling my top down and my pants up. I did it all trying my best to not let it get to me. I still had eighty-nine days to go. *Tighten up.*

My pants were dry by the time Sam limped his way down the hall, pushing a mail cart, his private Aux in tow. He bumped the cart into me. My guess, on purpose.

"Tye-dye is so vintage!" he said. "Way to bring it back!"

I didn't know what he was talking about. The seven wall washing prisoners let out some versions of disapproving laughter. I was starting to get the sense that Sam was someone I should avoid but as his Aux passed, I noticed it had flat round ears. I had to make a decision. Sidle up to Sam so I could reach Itzel, or take the hint from everyone around me and keep to myself.

Turns out, I didn't have to decide. Sam did it for me.

He hobbled over to me at lunch and plopped his tray down with a clang. He braced against the table as he slowly maneuvered his legs over the bench. "Have you figured it out yet?" he asked, out of breath and swaying once he sat down.

"I don't know what you're talking about," I said, frowning at the thin, grey slice of meat between thin, grey slices of bread.

"You forgot already? Better get that head checked!" He bit into his sandwich greedily. "Ham! What a treat!"

It wasn't ham. And just because I didn't recall what he was referring to didn't mean I was losing my mind. He was messing with me. He liked to mess with me. But that was an easy price to pay to get a word to Itzel.

I told him I must have forgotten and asked him to remind me.

"Why Texas?" he said, impatient with his mouth half full.

I hid my eyeroll with a blink. "No, Sam, I haven't figured out why I'm in Texas." I hadn't thought about it since he asked the day before. Honestly, I held onto that last part he had said– the part about bending over and offering GEM my backside. I was motivated to keep my dignity and prove my innocence. Texas could wait.

"Ah! Well, since it didn't strike you as something worth questioning, I think we should start with some history!" He took another bite and grinned at me.

***

Sam wasn't a succinct teacher. Maybe he was when he was younger, before his rehabilitation fried his nerves. But by the time our paths crossed, his thoughts wandered. If I didn't press him to stay on target, I would have learned a lot about nothing.

"Do you know how Texas became the *great nation* it is today?" he asked.

I disguised a sigh and shook my head.

"It's kind of like your neutron stars," he said, chomping another bite.

I scoffed. "What do you know about neutron stars?"

He stared me down best he could. His eyes still jumped to the left. He asked, one brow cocked, "What do you know about Texas?"

I groaned and nodded for him to continue.

"Like a neutron star," he said, smacking his lips, "it formed once a supergiant collapsed. . ."

A high school memory from a history class dusted off. A doodled rocket overlapped a subtitle of the chapter section. The words were hazy. The particulars were distant. I remember thinking what was in the past ought to stay there. Thirteen-year-old me wanting nothing more than to escape it.

"They called themselves the most powerful nation— how up your own ass can you get?" Sam wanted to know.

I let out a short laugh. Time was running out, and I had more walls to wash.

"Well, eighty-three years before the reset, Alaska— you must recall that was their most northern state— started getting cozy with Canada and Russia. Who kissed whom first isn't important. What is important is Alaska was holding hands with those two before the folks in Washington, D.C.— the old capitol— could do anything. But honestly, I don't know how they didn't see it coming! I mean you have an entire nation between you and one of yours, of course they're going to start fraternizing with their neighbors!"

I rolled my eyes. "Get to the point, Sam," I said.

"What's the rush?" Sam asked, looking around. "We're not going anywhere."

"I have—"

"Your defense? Please!"

I moved to leave, but he gently grabbed my arm.

"Alright, we've got a few minutes before the bell. Let me just get this part out of the way." I gave a curt nod and off he went.

"Washington D.C. responded, sending thousands of troops north. But Canada wasn't going to let them just pass through or set up shop along the Canadian-Alaskan border. In fact, the Canadians saw more benefit defending Alaska's sovereignty than letting America keep it. So the big boys fought it out. No one expected Canada to win. But at the time, the United States had spread itself thin, fighting in the Middle East, fighting North Korea, fighting all of Latin America over the Panama Canal. Rumor has it, Russia sparked off another international crisis just to pull more troops away from Alaska. After all, Russia did "give" Alaska to the United States. That's beside the point. The U.S citizens were pissed at the government for wasting more lives on another war. See, thousands of troops went north. A few hundred came back. Frost-bitten. Blind. Delirious. In less than a year, the United States conceded. Fifty states became forty-nine. But that was just the start."

The bell rang. We all rose. Except for Sam. I asked him if he needed help getting up. He waved me off. And just then, his Aux appeared. The same one from earlier. It reached under his arms, and pulled him up by his armpits, like a child.

"My consolation prize for surviving rehab," Sam joked. The Aux handed him a cane.

I studied the humanoid. It would do nicely for what I needed.

"Careful D-7, I think you have an admirer!" Sam nudged the Aux. It swiftly gripped his elbow. Sam and I both winced. "D-7 is sensitive," Sam joked. "If you want one, they'll make it happen!" he said as the Aux pushed him past me.

For a second I thought he was serious.

"Just need to cook your goose first!" He stuck his tongue out and shook his head like he was being electrocuted.

As I found my work crew for the afternoon I started wondering about Sam. I started wondering about everyone: the seven prisoners sharing sloshing bleach buckets with me, the three-hundred or so other prisoners sharing meals every day. Sam was a history teacher. I was an award-winning Global Contributor and as far as I knew, still the chief scientist of the Umoja program. What was everyone else if not violent? And what were *they* doing in Texas?

27

I woke up squeezing the flat pillow in my arms. The Itzel that I'd dreamed of evaporated in the heat of the cell. I strained to hold onto the last part.

We were younger in my dream, before Mai was conjured up. We were in bed. Itzel was lying on top of me, her ear pressed against my chest. I ran my fingers through her hair, then let them wander down her back. The room was quiet. I felt her heart slowly thrumming to my beat. She smelled like roses and morning affections, sweaty and sweet.

She had asked, "Do we want to have a child?"

The question wrapped around us, pulled us tighter against each other.

I asked her why she asked it that way, a little sad around the edges. I told her of course I wanted to have a child with her. I stroked her arm, the one that stretched behind my head. Her fingers pressed against my scalp.

She said with a wavering voice, "There's so much suffering already." The room darkened with her tone. "We work so hard to grow food, harvest it, send it to market, prepare it and then throw thirty percent away while a million people starve to death at the same time. Can you imagine the feeling of watching your own child starve to death?" Her voice drifted away. "Those things haunt me."

My chest tightened. The lights cracked on. The cell door opened. I got in line and marched to breakfast.

I missed Itzel so much I wanted to cry.

***

I was ready for Sam when he sat down that morning. "What happened after Alaska left?"

He brightened immediately. "A curious mind is so refreshing!" He shoved a spoonful of gruel in his mouth and resumed his lesson.

"Hawai'i was next to leave. They saw Alaska do it with the help of Canada, and Russia— rumor has it-"

"You told me yesterday," I said, trying not to be rude.

"Oh." He looked around for a moment, gathering his thoughts. "Well, anyway, Hawai'i joined the Pacific Island Pact, backed by Japan and *BAM*— forty-nine became forty-eight. It started out as a peaceful transfer of power, but the military personnel who'd been stationed in Hawai'i for most of their lives thought they should be in charge and—"

"Sam, breakfast is almost over," I warned.

He let out a sigh. "Anyway, forty-nine became forty-eight. And for a while, everyone thought that would hold. The continental forty-eight. It's all connected. It would make sense to maintain forty-eight states, right?"

I agreed with a nod.

"Right, except!"

My patience was running thin. "Except, what, Sam?"

He held up a finger and just then the guards announced Dawn Time. I wanted to scream. He was dragging this out and for what?

The air outside was hot and getting hotter. The sun crawled up the mountains and scorched what it touched. The UV shield glitched then stopped working all together. The early slivers of sun felt like needles in my skin. Hot needles. I pulled my arms inside my shirt. Pulled my shirt up to cover my nose and found a wall to stand with my back to. But my forehead. My scalp. The sun was branding us, searing without distinction.

"Hot one!" Sam said, as he teetered out, cane in hand. His Aux followed right behind him. Like the others, it faced the sun fully, eyes open to charge.

My heart kicked up. This was my chance. I whispered to Sam, "Why do you get an Aux?"

He chuckled. "Why does anyone get an Aux?"

I only had ten minutes to get what I wanted from Sam, but he was going to make a maze of this back and forth. I snatched the sweat from my brow. "Assistance," I said. "Is it the same one every time?"

"Who can tell!" he said. He turned to the Aux and asked, "What's your name?"

It slowly pivoted its head to Sam and responded, "D-7."

I decided to go bold. I asked, "D-7, what is the–"

Sam cut me off. "Ah, ah, ah! D-7 is *mine!* Get your own!"

It got hotter as the sun showed half its face. My forehead felt like it was stretching, cracking, peeling and bleeding. Breathing hot, muffled air inside my shirt was suffocating. But that realization damn near killed me. His Aux was programmed specifically for him.

"They'll give you one, too," Sam said, enthusiastically. "Just gotta cook your goose first!"

Frustrated by the heat and his response, I asked, "What does that mean, exactly?"

"Start mouthing off and they'll fry you up, too!" He pointed at his jumping eyes. "If enough people know you're here, they'll keep you above ground and give you a personal assistant! Ain't life grand!"

Dawn time ended. I felt sick. Maybe it was the mandatory sun exposure. Or maybe it was the feeling of defeat mixed with a hopeless longing for my wife. *Eighty-eight days, Morant. Tighten the hell up!*

***

The next time I saw Sam, or the next time he found me was at dinner. I had looked for him at lunch but he wasn't there. I almost asked a couple of the men I'd mopped floors with that day if they saw him. But I decided against it.

He looked worse than usual. Paler than he had been that morning. A fresh bandage appeared around his left elbow. Even his eyes twitched a little slower. He didn't seem fazed by any of it. He plopped his tray with a clang as usual, struggled to fold his legs, one at a time over the bench and promptly asked, "Where did we stop this morning?"

I found myself admiring him. Even a little energized by his determination. "Forty-nine became forty-eight. Except. . ." I said.

"Right, so Texas once called itself 'The Lone Star State' but that was *after* it joined the Union. This is centuries-old history, but it was once called the Lone Star Republic— had declared itself a sovereign nation once those settlers fought off the natives and made it theirs. But there weren't enough people to hold it, so they agreed to join the Union, stretch that border a few hundred kilometers south and became the 28th state.

"And it stayed that way for a long time, about a decade short of a quarter millennia. But the itch was always there. Once Alaska and Hawai'i broke free, Texans got to scratching!" Sam mimed, with exaggeration, scratching his crotch and buttock.

I let out a nervous laugh. The men sitting across from us hid their laughs, too.

Then Sam abruptly stopped. "They were just about to close their borders off to the rest of the forty-eight, but one of their richest— I'm talking old money! Ancient money! Owned the oil reserves when they were still *oozing* out black gold money! One of them ran for president."

I looked around and noticed more heads tipped in our direction. Sam was gathering an audience. And I was seated, front row.

"He saw the risk in leaving the Union— a man who knows his history makes different decisions!" He wagged his finger in the air. He sounded like my father for a moment. A deranged version of him, but he used to say something similar. Sam continued, "He decided instead of ceding from the Union, Texas should engulf the rest of them." He took a huge bite of meat. Then he started choking. I went to pat him on the back, but he stopped me with a wagging finger. A guard shouted, "No touching!" Sam rolled his eyes, as if to say *how moronic* but that made him lose his balance. I couldn't help but hold him up.

A guard shouted, closer this time, "I said, *no touching!*"

Sam flung himself forward against the table. The chewed lump shot out.

I raised my hands. I heard the guard's weighted belt, his heavy boots. I tensed my back and shoulders. Tipped my head forward slightly, closed my eyes. Clenched my jaw, prepared for a beating. "I'm sorry. I didn't mean to!" I pleaded.

"Oh, leave him alone boys!" Sam said, coughing, "He's just human!"

I heard it before I felt it. The snap-crack of electricity. A whining buzz ripped through me. I bent away as it bit my side. My scream reduced to a groan. All my pain was trapped in my mouth. The buzzing stopped. The grip released. I sagged forward.

"No touching!" a guard shouted. His spit mixed quickly with my sweat. "Do you understand?"

I nodded. I understood that a fight gets a collar. A collar makes a corpse. Too much talk earns a frying. A touch gets a torch.

I washed up at the sink, put on the cleaner uniform, and stiffly bent into bed. The lights blinked off. I curled myself around the flat pillow and dreamt of Itzel.

28

It went on like that for several more days. The lights cracked on. I'd crookedly rise out of bed with the mirage of Itzel against my chest. The door opened. I'd march to breakfast behind the rest. I'd find a seat close to the same one I sat in the day before. I learned to do that by someone else's mistake. Or maybe it wasn't a mistake. Maybe he sat in another man's seat because he felt like starting a fight. A fight earned a collar. A collar made a breathing corpse. Maybe it was his way to escape. The alternative was the desert, but the collar is quicker.

At a random meal, Sam would teeter over to me and tell me more about how Texas came to be. Others would listen and pretend not to. But Sam cracked jokes that caused them to crack smiles. Quivers in weakened muscles. Flashes of rotted or missing teeth. I think that's what I admired the most about him. After all he went through, he still liked to make people laugh.

It took another five days to get the whole story out of him. This is what I remember:

The Texan gentleman ran on the platform of rehabilitating the soulless state of the Union. "Going back to Glory" was his campaign slogan. Sam said, "Most people didn't know what the hell he was talking about, but enough people liked the word *Glory*." Some people attributed it to God, others figured he was talking about the flag and patriotism. Some associated it with all their family and friends who died in war and were *gone to Glory*. He inspired reverence and solemnity which helped calm the people. Wars, famines, hurricanes up and down the eastern seaboard, sand storms devouring the west, earthquakes sloughing off another chunk of California— all of it was decimating the national psyche.

"Hundreds of thousands were homeless and hopeless. Crime was on a steady climb. The haves were terrified of the have-nothings. And the have-nothings were starved for anything! Then came this stoic Texan, a symbol of yesteryear, to ease their nerves." I remember this is where Sam paused. His eyes bounced to the left but his gaze was up like he was looking at God. I was leaning toward him, holding my breath. He looked like he'd been saved. Like he was one of the starving many, gazing upon Glory. Then he clapped his hands and startled me and about five others. "That was until he won the election!" Sam said. The bell rang and we had our duties, but I was eager for more.

At another meal, Sam said that's when "all hell broke loose!" He said, "the Texan president might not have been a dummy but he sure was a bigot!" He didn't like how Latinos were the majority race. He didn't like how many women held office. He didn't like sixty percent of the American population. And after the first month of his first term, sixty percent of the population didn't like him. Sam wagged a finger and said, "that's a bad time to have the majority of your constituents turn on you." Sam made me guess why, but I couldn't. So Sam answered himself, "tax season came around and sixty percent of tax paying Americans abstained from their national duty!" The president sent out tax collectors. Sam said the government underestimated the people severely and how strongly they clung to their second amendment right, which I never heard of. Sam briefly entertained my startled questioning about the logic of such a right. He said emotions tend to outweigh logic when under immediate threat. I asked if there was always a threat since it was added to their Constitution so early? He said, "If someone is always telling you there's a threat, then you start believing them, right?" I remember shaking my head thinking, no one can be that passive or that dumb. But Sam went on and listed all the peoples' armaments, things I couldn't imagine in my childhood home: automatic handguns, machine guns, bazookas, and anti-aircraft weaponry. Anyone who couldn't purchase a gun made them. Printed them in their garages and sheds. Sam said they probably did it in their living rooms, watching a sitcom and eating dinner. "Kids, too! Everyone had firearms!"

At another meal, Sam told me the worst of it. He said, "When those tax collectors came around the people straight up killed them.

Slaughtered them on their doorsteps." He went on and said in response, the government deployed armed forces. They snatched up anyone who breathed in opposition. But the people weren't having it. They lit up the soldiers so bad, most of them retreated. A lot of them turned-coat.

Then the people gathered the dead bodies in the middle of their villages, towns and cities and set them on fire. They sent selfies to their mayors, governors, senators and the president as proud evidence. "They weren't taking any shit from anyone! Thousands! Millions! Smiling in front of burning corpses."

I made Sam stop during that meal. Whatever the protein was for dinner that night was well done. Charred. And the memory of burnt bodies in the streets wafted by on a hot breeze. We'd let them lay where they fell, my nnenne and I and our neighbors. We averted our eyes. We let the vultures and insects have their way. We never showed the carnage to anyone.

"That president was a coward!" Sam said in a firm whisper over another dinner. "He ran back to Texas, kicked the governor out of the mansion and crowned himself King of the Lone Star Republic. He even made a new flag! A white star in a field of red. Texas was a star all on its own! He left the American people to tear each other apart. Many starved. Plenty fled. To Canada and Mexico. Some went to Alaska. But he wouldn't let anyone into Texas. Walled it off from the rest of the world. And boy was the world knocking! By that time, the United States of America was nearly one-quintillion dollars in debt."

A man sitting across from us quietly asked, "How much is that? In hheqs?"

Sam looked at me. I couldn't imagine it. Sam answered, "We'd all be wealthy. Everyone on Earth." The man was satisfied with that answer. I'd never thought about it like that.

Sam continued. "What was left of the American government, military and all, couldn't pay those debts. So came the Continental Divide of 85 NC. Mexico took back the southwest, excluding Texas of course— they could have, but it wasn't worth the stress. The Dominion of Canada absorbed the rest."

"So why Texas?" I asked.

Sam smirked. "Texas isolated itself. Then lost most of its population due to starvation. It was on the brink of death, when that cowardly cowboy had an idea— *Give me your thieves, your murderers, your rapists!*"

I looked around nervously, but Sam swatted my arm.

"That was nearly a quarter of a millennium ago! They don't have as many of those and if they do, they get sent to another prison."

"Another prison in Texas?" I asked.

Sam mumbled a yes with a mouth full of green mush. He swallowed. "That's all Texas is. A nation of prisons!"

"Sam," I asked, slowly, "how did you end up here?"

For the first time in the ten days I'd known Sam with his shaky walk and twitching eyes, I saw him perfectly still. Eyes locked on a memory.

He had a full life. He taught history to high school kids and started teaching evening classes for adults. He had a family, a wife and two kids. He hadn't seen or heard from them in nearly two decades.

He said his life ended because one student in his night class had a problem with his curriculum. Sam said this one student brought the whole lesson to a halt all because of one line in the text: The Common Goal is a reactionary solution to a greater problem. He asked the student why he objected. The student said it was irreverent to speak that way. His parents served the Dominion and firmly believed that the Common Goal brought peace among the nations. It brought focus and camaraderie that the world had never seen. To call it reactionary made the efforts seem irrational, not purposeful.

I didn't say it out loud, but I agreed with the student.

Sam said it was only two weeks before he was arrested. He said his wife had pleaded for him to stay home that evening. She even begged him to quit his job and suggested they move out of the city, away from people, where it was safer. Where he could start over and start a new career. Sam said he couldn't do that. He felt called to tell the truth.

Auxen barged into his night class and took him. He said he fought back and they tased him. He woke up with a collar around his neck, strapped to a table staring up at bright light.

"Then all the lights went out. I couldn't see anything. . . but I felt pressure at my temples. Then. . ." he trailed off.

"Then what, Sam?" I asked.

"They called it rehabilitation. It– it felt like all my thoughts, lined in razor wire, got shuffled in my head. I heard screaming. I think it was me, but I couldn't feel myself scream. Just the inside of my head." He rubbed his temple closest to me. "They were trying to mix up my memories and words— but they fucked up and now I'm like this." His voice cracked. "Years ago, but they did this to me. Because I wanted to tell the truth."

I didn't sleep that night. Each time I closed my eyes I felt them jerking to the left, like Sam's. I didn't want to be like Sam. I didn't want to be stuck in prison like Sam, without my family like Sam, maimed and limping like Sam. I wanted to get out, not by collar or desert. I wanted to get out with my life intact. With my mind intact.

29

Warden Nattle sat across from me, and cocked back in his chair. His bald head shone as the sun worked through the window to his left. He pressed his finger tips together as he studied me. His leathered skin matched his brown uniform and brown desk, and the brown leather chair he sat in. The only contrast in his office was the large Texan flag, hanging on the wall behind him. The star in the middle of all that red made me wonder if it represented its single purpose— prison, the nation's single point of pride according to Sam.

I hadn't expected this meeting with the warden. Eleven days passed since my arrival and I only heard his bark on occasion. He tipped his head to the side and asked, "How you doing, Morant? Everybody treating you okay?"

His question took me by surprise and I wasn't sure how to answer it. I hated being there, but I'd gotten used to the schedule which gave some semblance of purpose to my days.

"I'm getting by, Warden. Thank you," I said.

He smirked and leaned forward, clasped his hands and bounced them on his desk "That's good to hear. I let all my guards know to keep an eye on you, make sure you're keeping your nose clean and out of trouble."

"I appreciate that, Warden. Everyone has been treating me. . .well enough," I said.

He nodded. "Good, good. And the other prisoners? Anyone giving you a hard time? You know I'd take care of them if you ask."

I told him I had no complaints.

He nodded some more. "You know, there are some nut jobs here. Got a lot to say about nothing."

I let myself smile but only for a moment. His stare didn't let me relax.

"There's one in particular we've always had a problem with. He can't seem to keep his mouth shut. You know who I'm talking about? Walks funny? Looks funnier?"

I didn't answer. There was a threat on the other side of those questions.

"Yeah, you know him. I know you know who I'm talking about."

His words hung between us. I kept my breath even and my eyes on him.

"A-1, go fetch me some water from Level-2," he ordered, keeping his sight trained on me.

The Aux asked its usual confirmation questions, making sure the warden knew I had a history of violent outbursts.

"I am fully aware, dammit!" he barked and slammed a hand on the desk.

I flinched.

The Aux left. And I got nervous.

"One day, Imma pop each of their heads off," he growled, looking down at his desk for a moment. I could see him doing it. Wrapping his thick hands around their necks and squeezing. He'd laugh, too, like a kid on his birthday, tearing open present after present, taking more joy in the destruction than the gift inside. He regained his composure and returned his attention to me. "I got word some media types have been looking for you."

It took a moment to register what he said. *Media types*, I thought. I recalled Ms. Tessa Laine leaving her contact information, that folded piece of paper tucked under my wedding photo. My heart rate quickened. *Had Iztel found the paper? Alerted Ms. Laine when I didn't come home?* I didn't want Itzel or Mai drawn into my mess. I had to take responsibility for being there. I had to be the one to get me out. But more than anything, I needed them to be safe.

I felt him watching me so I released a breath slowly and said nothing.

"It would be a damn shame if, oh I don't know, some footage of you consorting with a convicted dissenter got out there and hit the newstreams. Wouldn't it? It would be a damn shame! Sure would be hard to shake all those rumors about you." He smirked and watched me.

I fought to keep my breath steady. Control was key. I had to stay in control of my anger. But this felt dangerous.

He smiled. Wrinkles etched through his weather worn cheeks, but the smile never made it to his eyes. They sharpened, the way a hawk sees its prey. "I really like you, Morant. I would hate for anything to happen to you because you got caught up with that whack job. You're smarter than that. You're a goddamn Global Contributor, son! You don't belong here— we both know that! Don't let these fuck ups pull you down."

A-1 returned, holding a white cup. Before it could place it on the desk, Warden Nattle chastised it. "Come on A-1, you know I can't drink water from a white cup! It has to be blue!" He winked at me then scowled at the Aux.

A-1 computed the request and left again.

"Now look here," Warden Nattle dropped his volume to a growl. "I don't want anyone coming around here making trouble for me. You being here is bringing the type of attention I'm not interested in. So listen to me when I say this." He held up a finger and hissed, "If you make one wrong move, I can and will make your lil stint here a thousand times worse! Do you hear me?"

I jolted when the door opened. A-1 returned with a blue cup in hand.

Nattle abruptly turned to A-1. I watched his face loosen and curve into a smile. His voice sweetened, too. "Thank you so very much, A-1. I do appreciate you doing that for me. Now please, could you escort Detainee Morant back to where you found him?"

I rose and started toward the door.

Nattle took a swig and said, "I'll be watching, Morant!"

***

I did my best to avoid Sam after that. But I couldn't keep it up until my disciplinary martial. I couldn't even avoid him for a whole week. He caught me after breakfast, three days after my meeting with the warden.

He tugged on my shirt. "I'm on hallway cleanup today," he said. "You?" He smiled excitedly at me.

I knew he was on hallway duty. I saw the schedule the day before. It was going to be the two of us and ten other prisoners, dividing up the sweeping and mopping and wiping down the walls. I'd asked the guard manning the "Activity" station if I could do something else, preferably a solo job.

"I don't give a fuck," the guard grumbled, looking down at a tablet he was holding.

I looked behind him and studied the chart. I saw a shipment was coming. So I asked, "Can I do deliveries?"

The guard looked up from the tablet, annoyed that I was still there. He paused whatever had his attention and said, "Whatever, man. I don't really care." He tapped the station monitor and I watched my name disappear and reappear away from Sam's. I thanked the side of the guard's face and left, sure that I made the right decision.

"I'm on deliveries," I said.

I saw disappointment dampen Sam's mood. I felt bad. Sam wasn't the issue. But like the warden said, I needed to keep out of trouble. According to him, Sam was trouble.

Because delivering office supplies was a solo job, security bracelets were placed on my wrists. They tracked my movements and would shock me if I stole, tried to run away, or attacked someone. They weighed a kilo each, adding some difficulty to the task of lifting and lowering the toiletry and office supplies but I wasn't in any rush. No one was behind me, nagging me to move faster. No one was around at all. The silence gave me time to focus on my disciplinary martial. I needed to convince the GEM board that I wasn't the dissenter. I needed to show that Beau was working against the interest of the Common Goal and the safety of the mission. I kept getting stuck on how I was going to prove that when I couldn't find the data. I knew my notes weren't enough.

I wheeled the cart into the administrative wing and dropped off light filaments, screen cleaners and protectors in the admissions office. The officer behind the desk didn't even notice when I entered the room. She was occupied with a news report. I saw the stream broadcast and quickly turned to leave. It was the same channel that linked the explosion with the failure and called it international sabotage.

I moved down the hall to the break room. I grabbed their boxes and backed into the room. Four guards were in there, watching the same broadcast with great focus. I kept my gaze down and placed the boxes on the counter. Right as I turned to leave I heard my last name. I turned, expecting one of the guards to be requesting something, but they were silent, staring at the news. I looked up and saw my face — my prison mugshot taking up half the screen.

"Now he's being investigated as having possible ties to the horribly failed mission – "one commenter said.

"It is astonishing to think how much damage he could have caused!" the other commentator interrupted.

"Absolutely! Absolutely! So many people were injured and died. So incredibly tragic! Now, some interesting findings have been shared with us. This is exclusive. The source is unknown at this time, but we do have exclusive footage–"

The screen divided into three panels, the commentators on either side of a hazy video. I felt my heart thudding in my chest. Slowly the hazy image cleared. I recognized the solar-capped roofs and all white buildings. The balconies. My whole body started to shake.

"Now, this is drone footage of the disgraced scientist's neighborhood. In just a moment it'll zoom in and we want our audience to look closely and there– can you freeze it, Jim, and zoom in a little more. Thank you."

The commentators vanished and the drone footage filled the screen. My knees buckled.

"Right in the center of your screen, you can see– what would you say that is, Sherry?"

"I'd call it a damn biohazard, Raquelle!"

I wanted to scream. It was our balcony. Filled with plants.

"Now, Jim, can you skip forward just a second or two."

The video jolted then stopped. There was Mai. Tiny and brown, dressed in pink and orange. Pointing up.

"I think it is absolutely disgusting to have your child living amongst all that filth!" one of the commentators said.

"Absolutely! And not to mention the risk to their neighbors! My goodness, all that bacteria and fungus in that soil, they could kill someone!"

"Here's what I'm thinking: If they're willing to jeopardize their neighbors, or really the whole GEM family, because they all live under that dome, then it's no stretch of the imagination that he'd be willing to sabotage the whole mission!"

Something broke inside me. "LIARS!" I shouted. I charged the screen. "THEY'RE LYING! LEAVE MY FAMILY ALONE! THEY'RE LYING!"

An arm wrapped around my neck.

"GET OFF OF ME!"

I punched, slamming my fist into a guard. The security bracelets fired. My hands and wrists contorted. I screamed in pain.

Suddenly, my face was on the floor. Left cheek against the tile. "THAT'S MY FAMILY!" I shouted. Again and again, "THAT'S MY FAMILY!" I strained against them as they forced my arms behind me. I didn't feel my shoulder dislocate. I only saw my baby, my sweet little Mai, pointing up at the drone. For the world to see. The footage paused again. Itzel.

"And here's his wife, allegedly a dissenter herself."

"NO! NO! THEY'RE LYING! THEY'RE LYING!" I screamed.

I watched Itzel step onto the balcony. She looked up. Then she grabbed Mai and disappeared into our condo. "NO!" I shouted. "ITZEL!"

A hand yanked my head back. I choked. Something pressed against my throat. I heard a metallic click. Then a beep behind my head. Someone screamed. Then everything went black.

30

There was no light in the dungeon. And without light, there was no time. And without time, I can't relay all of this coherently.

I woke up in a black pit.

Pain crawled up and down my spine, through my head and tore open my shoulder. That is what told me I was still alive. I was on a metal slab. It pressed into the back of my calves. I tried to bend my knees, but pain coursed through each leg and bent my feet in spasms. I couldn't cry out. My mouth wouldn't open. My tongue wouldn't move. My lungs sagged in my chest. I heard groans and cries. I heard water trickling. I smelled rot.

Slowly, I drifted away from the sounds.

My father, lying in the hallway.

How long has he been here? Why isn't he moving? 'Papa? Papa!'

I awoke, screaming. Soaked and shivering. My fists clenched. I tried them first. I released my fingers, careful to not wake the pain. I felt grooves in the metal, erratic like scratches. Were they mine? Probably not. Probably the leftovers from someone else's madness.

I could move my ankles and knees. I could relieve the pressure in my back and hips. I tried to sit up. Something pressed into my throat. The wide, curved shape wrapped around my neck and connected to the bed. A collar. *The newstream. My wife and child. The guards pinned me to the floor. There was a scream. Was it mine? Probably.*

I tried to reach overhead, feel what could be felt, see without seeing. My left shoulder spat daggers of pain. I cried out. Cursed. Pain tumbled into agony, agony grew into anger. I cursed Warden Nattle. I cursed Beau.

"It won't help," said a voice to my right. It was rough, and sounded close. Close enough to reach me.

Scared, I shouted, "Who's there?"

"It doesn't matter."

"Who are you?" I tried to keep my voice firm, but even I heard fear.

"It doesn't matter."

It took all of me to reach toward the voice. The tip of my middle finger felt the edge of another metal slab. I pulled back, relieved. They were strapped to a table like I was. Powerless.

"How many. . . how many people are here?" I stammered.

There was a long silence before they spoke again, "Depends."

"On what?" I asked.

"Time."

I stiffened at their answer. When I asked what that meant there was silence.

"Fuck you," I whispered. Then anger surged and heaved out of me. I cursed until my head hurt.

When I stopped, the voice returned, "That won't help either."

Dungeon crabs. Punctured lungs. Missing limbs. Missing limbs? A lack of sun will drive you crazy.

***

I saw things. Small things at first, like lines and dots moving in the black. Gradually those shapes morphed into each other and grew in size. They resembled stars, swelling and bursting open. Some were violent explosions. Others were slow and beautiful. At one point I saw the Dragon's Gate easing from blue to red, to all the worlds at the center of the Milky Way. I saw it like Dr. Dragonomassi saw it. Captivated by it. I saw the Umoja craft land in front of the Dragon, pathetic in comparison. Pathetic in its attempt to cross the Gate. Dr. Dragonomassi compared her discovery to the face of God. Who were we to broach that? Who was I to think I was capable?

I lingered there. Asked myself who was I to broach the face of God?

A man who can't hold his tongue. A man who unleashed his temper like a dog on his wife.

Who was I to broach the face of God?

Dragonomassi never touched it. She never tried to leap in its direction. She fell to her knees. And wept.

Who was I to broach the face of God?

A man who hadn't talked to God in decades. Would God listen if I asked Him? What would I ask Him? If I was right? Would I argue if I was wrong? Would I listen? Would Itzel forgive me? Was I worth forgiving?

I whispered a prayer, "God, help me. Please."

***

I see my mother's feet. One with a slipper, the other without. Both right behind the loveseat in the reading room. I stop breathing and stare. I wait for her to move. Then I'm there. Seeing her. Her knees bent at crooked angles. Bullet wounds in the palms of her hands. She's wearing the gold bracelet I picked out for her. In the moonlight creeping through the windows and skylights, I see the dark smattering. I look away. Gasp for air. And see it. All of it. The upturned chairs. The broken glass. The stamped footprints across the room. I look down. See my blood-stained feet. And scream.

I screamed into the black. I strained against the collar. I felt stubble on my cheeks.

"Something's eating you," The low, graveled voice startled me.

"What do you mean?"

"Whatever you've got inside you, is eating you."

I didn't respond. How much of my nightmare spilled out of me?

"We've all got something eating us. Chewing up the walls and floorboards. You gotta get rid of them before they eat you up completely."

"It's nothing," I said.

"Doesn't sound like nothing. I miss my family, too, but I don't cry out for them. Not like you do."

***

There was a door. I opened it and stepped onto a balcony. I felt the breeze and smelled the mix of flowers wafting by. I looked up and saw my mother. She appeared like the sun, face full and round, with so much life in her eyes. I melted like honey when she said, "Lopé, my sweet string bean." I smelled her perfume and inhaled deeply, hoping to keep her closer to my heart forever. Then she vanished. The sky darkened. Fear wrapped around me. I sank and curled into a ball. My grandmother kissed my cheeks and forehead. She said she loved me. Her face was a map of wrinkled sadness, rivered in tears. She said, "I love you, Lopé," like my mother.

"All things in God's time," resounded in the lonesome dark. It compelled me to look up. When I did, I saw my father. His cherry black skin shone like the moon. He never turned away from me, but drifted behind shadows. I cried out for him until he showed himself fully. He didn't speak. He only showed me our home at night, tucked back from the security wall, hidden behind trees, with my uncles' homes on either side.

There were lights on in our home, where the reading room was. I saw movement behind the curtains. I saw flashes. One. Two, three.

Four.

Inside, I found my father in the hallway.

I fought against it. I tried not to see my mother.

But the moon was bright and glinted off her bracelet and shattered across the floor. I looked down. Saw my blood-stained feet.

Suddenly, there were lights. Bright, painful lights. Dizzying in the dark. They surrounded me. Hands grabbed me. I struggled against them. I cried out for my mother. I reached for my father. I searched for the moon.

I screamed, "God, help me!"

31

There was so much light, it was painful. I squeezed my eyes shut. But I swore I saw sky.

"Dr. Morant, we have to move you now," someone said. It wasn't rough like the voice in the dungeon. It was a man with concern.

I gave a small nod thinking it must be nurse Tidwell. The guards must have brought me back to the surface. But something was different. I didn't hear the sirens of doors opening and closing. I didn't smell the foul of other prisoners. I heard shuffling feet on gravel. I heard soft tones and a hiss. Muffled echoes and a hushed breeze. The smell of minerals and something sweet. I was lowered onto a firm, grooved surface, long enough to fit my whole body.

When I opened my eyes again, black figures stretched high above me. I stopped breathing, willed my mind to clear. I tried to turn away as one of them lowered to my height. But my neck was too stiff, rusted into a partial turn.

"Dr. Morant, you're very sick," the man said. "We're going to give you myogen and something to help you sleep, okay? You need to rest now."

I felt a pinch in my shoulder. Then I was surrounded by black.

Black like what the mourners wore.
Black like their charred bodies.
Black like the center of my father's eyes.
He hummed, *All things in God's time.*
God.
Help me.

***

The darkness ebbed like an ocean, gradually drawing back its hold. It lapped against me, offering its nothingness in rhythmic waves. But voices dragged me back awake.

A woman said, "Yeah, I let Kin know."

"Did you tell her how bad he looks?" a man asked.

"I said, I let her know," the woman hissed.

"Kin hates surprises and whew!" The man whistled.

"She's pissed, not surprised," the woman said.

"Yeah, I'd be pissed, too. She said she'd pick him up today?"

"I told her she has to get him out of here before we open," the woman said.

"We can't say there's a repair or something?" he asked.

"You don't think that'd look suspicious, Sol?"

"You're thinking too hard, Mar."

I searched for them. Rolled my eyes around and saw a stone table directly next to me and a stone bench on the other side. Four or five meters away, a hazy figure sat behind a counter. Then it saw me and stood. I swear it tripled in size. A stack of boulders with legs and arms strode toward me.

"How are you feeling, Dr. Morant?" the man asked.

I answered with a blink.

He came closer and smiled. "Good. That's good. I'll be right back," he said, then silently walked away.

I waited until he stepped around a corner then scanned the surroundings for a clue. Everything was blurry shadows– rough walls, a high, jagged ceiling with low hanging lamps. Nothing was familiar. Nothing made sense.

I heard a spigot open, liquid splash then shut off. Then the giant returned, blocking the light. I strained to move my hand. My legs. Anything to get away. But then he was beside me. Bending in my direction.

"I'm going to help you sit up, okay? It might hurt a bit."

Powerless, I blinked again.

He put a glass on the table, and with one hand, shifted the table out of his way. He lowered to my height and wrapped his arm around my shoulders.

I closed my eyes. Inside I screamed, *No touching! No touching! A touch will—*

He raised me, gently, like he was moving a sleeping child.

There was pain. It sparked in my spine, but settled to an ache in my lower back. I swayed, lightheaded. I couldn't remember how long it'd been since I sat up. How much longer since I'd been treated with care?

He steadied me with one arm and pulled the table toward us with the other. He brought the glass to my lips. The first drop of water awakened an animal in me. I needed it. I needed all of it. He warned me to take sips. "Too much will make you sick." I didn't care. I tipped my body to finish the glass. I licked my lips and huffed at him, like a dog panting for more. Glanced a wordless please and thank you.

"That's enough for right now," he said.

I finally looked at him, ready to growl. A deep brown, oval face smiled at me, with a patch over one eye. "Hey there, Dr. Morant. I'm Sol."

Sol remained by my side out of caution. I was weak. Pathetic, like a newborn deer, unsteady in my body.

The myogen injection took its time to mend and repair. Not like biostim and its sixty second broil. This felt like a slow simmer to normal. Thirty minutes passed before I could sit up without Sol. Forty-five minutes before I could hold a cup on my own. Ninety minutes before I felt strong enough to stand.

Maryene, Sol's sister, had little patience for me being there. She checked her rello frequently and seldom looked me in the eye. She left at one point and returned with a backpack, a change of clothes and boots. "You need to bathe and get dressed. We'll eat after you wash."

The mention of food made me nauseous, the way starvation does.

Sol helped me to the bathroom, said he'd be by the door if I needed anything. I thanked him again and limped in alone. Lighting, pulled down by mirrors from the outside, made the whole bathroom glow. A pleasant surprise, really. But then I saw the mirror above the sink and a dead man stared back at me.

Jaundiced eyes, cracked lips. I reached toward my face and watched bone and tendon roll and stretch under thinned, dried skin. I saw my heart behind my ribs when I removed my shirt. I saw wounds where the collar had gripped, weeping sores along my spine and pelvis.

I winced where I touched. I cleaned what I could. I asked Sol to bandage my back. He did. Carefully, he applied pseudo-skin patches to every open wound, and said, "That should hold for a few days."

Maryene brought stew. With onions, carrots, tomatoes, celery, garlic, herbs, spices. Flavors that reminded me of home. Of Itzel. My throat tightened at the thought of her, her garden, our daughter. I stared, unblinking, at the stew, thinking of the last time I saw them. Itzel curled around Mai. Them, breathing together. Without me.

Maryene interrupted my thoughts, warned their bar was opening soon, and I'd better take another dose of myogen. Sol explained that this was just a pit stop. I had another leg to journey and that a friend— someone named Kin— was coming to get me.

I told them that I didn't know anyone named Kin.

Maryene said that was beside the point. She placed a rack of glasses on the bar, and glared at me. "You aren't staying here."

I told her I understood that much. "There's something I need to make sure of," I said.

She rolled her eyes and walked away, the rack of glasses rattling with each step. Sol stepped in her place. "What's that?" he asked.

"Do you have stream access?"

Sol frowned and affirmed that they did.

I considered if I should try to contact Itzel, or if that would put her in danger. More danger. If I could reach her, I'd at least know she and Mai were okay. But that's assuming she was still in GEM City, where everything is recorded. I decided against it. "I need to make sure— I need to get into my GEM account."

Glass shattered. Maryene shouted, "Are you joking?"

I looked at Sol. "I have information I need to access," I said.

He grimaced and stepped back as Maryene stepped between us. Her eyes tightened. "We busted ass to get you out of Texas. That's what Kin asked. That's what we did. We did *that* for *Kin*. Whatever else you want, you ask her!"

"I don't know Kin and I didn't ask to be broken out!" I shot back.

Sol's eye widened. Maryene's face turned furious.

I started to explain myself, that all I needed was access to data that would prove my innocence. That the system over-reacted.

She cut me off. "Do you want to go back?"

The question silenced me. I dropped my gaze to the empty bowl. "No," I said.

"Then shut up, eat up, and be ready to go when she gets here."

Maryene stormed off as Sol ladled more stew for the both of us.

"She's got a good heart," he said, apologizing for her.

He shouldn't have. She was right.

32

We finished our stew. The chairs were tucked in place. The tables and bar top were wiped down. But they kept disappearing around corners to whisper at each other. Maryene whispered in worry, Sol whispered to calm. But then Sol started to sound worried and I started to worry, too.

"Why don't you sit back in that corner," Sol suggested, pointing at a dark table with only one chair. Away from the door and the bar.

I took the meaning. I wasn't supposed to be there. Kin was late. The bar was open.

Customers eased in. A few at first. The regulars greeted the siblings and found their seats at the bar. Others picked tables, or slid into booths. I watched Maryene work the bar, deftly taking and making orders without pause. I took comfort in the fact that she had little patience for everyone, even the regulars. Sol hustled between tables, minding each customer like old friends before disappearing back toward the bathroom and returning with large barrels over his shoulders. Their bar was a finely tuned operation. One where I knew I didn't belong and did my best to stay out of their way. As many questions as I had– like who was Kin? Why did she ask *them* to break me out? How'd they do it? Where was Kin going to take me? – I knew this wasn't the time. I'd have to wait for Kin.

An hour passed and the cave was nearly full. I overheard someone say it was half past one in the afternoon. Sol looked to Maryene. She checked her rello, frowned and shook her head. I pressed myself further against the wall and chewed on my cracked lip.

Then someone shouted. "You!"

I looked up. A big-eyed man pointed at me.

My heart rattled in my chest, *They found me!*

Maryene yelled for Sol. A muffled shout came from down the hall, past the bathroom.

The man charged across the room. Pushed tables and chairs and patrons out of his way. He came at me, pointing and shouting, "You! You did this!" He pulled his shirt up, eyes burning through me. "You did this!" he screamed, pointing at the angry purple scars lashed against his body.

"I don't know what you're talking about," I said, hands raised.

"Bullshit!" the man screamed.

Maryene yelled again for Sol. He yelled back, closer this time.

The man spat, "You and your space ships!"

I moved to put another table and chair between us.

He shoved the chair out of his way, screamed louder, "You told us we were safe! You told us this mission would save us!" He mocked, shrieking, "The leap into the future!" He shoved the table into me, knocking me off balance. "You and all of them like you!" His eyes bulged as he screamed, "*YOU KILLED US!*"

I scrambled away. But where I went, he was there, raving.

"I hope they find you! I hope they lock you up for the rest of your life! I hope they—"

"ENOUGH!" Sol boomed. He grabbed the man by his shirt.

The man screeched as he fought against Sol's grip, "I hope they fucking find you! Fucking murderer! MURDERER!"

Sol struggled as he carried the kicking, screaming man out. The door hissed closed. The cave was silent. Patrons stared. *Murderer* thudded against me. Soon, the quiet grew to whispers. The whispers grew louder, and suspicion grew to recognition. I felt the room shift against me.

Sol returned. Moved quickly across the room. He grabbed my arm and my backpack. Pulled me past the bathroom. Through a door and down stony stairs. Past stacked barrels, down steeper stairs. Deeper and deeper through a maze of narrowing corridors. Then suddenly into black.

I froze, fearing the worst: The black of the prison's pit.

"Change of plans, amico," Sol whispered. His voice echoed around us, like the darkness shared his secrets. "Too many eyes and wagging tongues up there. I'll take you myself."

I was too knotted up in fear to ask where he was taking me. My ears filled with static, my heart pounded. I heard Sol fumble with something in the bag. I flinched at a click. Winced when light fanned out.

"Where are we?" I asked, shivering. It was damp and cold. I heard water trickling in the distance.

Sol handed a headlamp to me while he continued to rummage through the bag. I searched the tunnel for a clue.

"The net," he said. He placed a headlamp on himself.

I asked what the net meant.

"The network. The tunnel network. It's how people got out," he said. He produced a compass and handed the bag back to me.

"Out of where?" I asked.

"America. Texas." He powered on the compass and thumbed in a location.

"Is this how you got me out?" I asked.

He nodded, "Not this tunnel, but yeah."

I thought back to Sam's lesson. I wondered how many had used the network, how often they still used it.

A green light beamed out of the compass and a grid lined map unfolded between us. A large green dot flashed where we were, Phoenixia, and from it a dotted line bent and curved beneath mountains, followed an underground river, climbed up to the surface and climbed up some more. It stopped where an upside-down triangle pointed to *S-245*.

"That's where we're going," he said.

"How far is that?" I asked.

"Oh, sixty kilometers or so," he said, as if it were a short jaunt. He tapped the compass and the map folded away. He handed it to me, and proceeded off to the right, deeper into the dark.

33

I hated the tunnel. I hated the low ceiling, sometimes so low, we had to crawl. I hated the constant and increasing narrowness. At several points I wondered how Sol could flatten himself between the all-too-frequent jagged walls and rounded boulders, while I felt the need to collapse my chest to slide through those passages. I hated the stale, wet and limited air. Our headlamps played tricks on me, casting shadows in every direction, moving as we moved. I hated the sudden pools of water that were "cold as a witch's tit in February," as Mr. Soncal Sr. would say. I hated how the pools never revealed their depths. I'd watch Sol and be glad when the water was only ankle deep. The one time he stepped down and half of his body disappeared into rushing, freezing, silt filled water, I considered turning back. But we had just crawled on our stomachs for ten meters and before that, scooted on our sides for another eighteen. There was no going back.

We took breaks. We had to. Despite the myogen, my body was not prepared for this journey.

The first resting spot was surprisingly open. I could stand up completely straight, spread my arms out and above my head with my palms pressed against an angled boulder, a stoic threat of death.

"Who's Kin?" I asked as I collapsed to catch my breath.

"She knows you. Used to work with you. Short. Wild eyes."

I perked up. "Locs, blue and black eyes? Shakina?"

Sol arched backwards, expanding his chest. "Yeah, that's her. Guess she goes by Kin now." He grabbed the bag from me and dug through it.

I looked around, stunned. Shakina Hakim, former lead astrometer for the Umoja mission. It had been years since she left. "I can't believe she got me out," I said, laughing and bewildered.

"Kin's a good one."

"Yeah. She is a good one," I said thinking back to when I introduced Shakina to Itzel.

***

I was nervous at first. Shakina was like me in some ways. Reserved. Stand-offish. I worried Itzel would be too warm, too sunny. But that wasn't the case at all. I was surprised by Shakina's knowledge of ancient civilizations which coupled well with Itzel's love for agriculture. The two sat for hours, talking, laughing. After Itzel got the building manager to sign off on her patio garden, Shakina sent her ginger root to plant.

When Itzel was pregnant with Mai, Shakina left gifts on my desk. Swaddle wraps, calming teas, body butters. Each one wrapped in plain brown paper, signed SH. No heartfelt message. Just her initials.

A month after Mai was born, Shakina brought food over. I was surprised when she asked to hold Mai. I placed my tiny daughter in Shakina's arms and the two stared at each other for a good long while. I left them in the living room to grab the food, and heard Shakina softly humming.

I never thought I'd see her again.

***

"How do you know Shakina – or Kin?" I asked.

He pulled a well wrapped paper bag out of the backpack, sniffed it, then slowly unwrapped it. "Phoenixia is at a crossroads. Some people stay. Some pass through. Kin stayed for a little while. But found her peace at the Spot."

"*S-245*?" I asked.

"Yeah. We'll see it tomorrow. Eat."

"Will my family be there?" I asked, eagerly.

He reached in the backpack and handed me a sticky ball and a strip of dried meat. "Fruit snack to get your blood up. Meat to balance it."

"Please. Sol," I begged. "Will my family be there?"

He eyed me a moment. "Can't say. We'll see tomorrow. Eat."

My mind raced as I chewed. *He didn't say yes, but he didn't say no.*

We rewrapped our snacks and resumed our trek. But I had more questions.

"That man in your bar. What happened to him?"

Sol grunted, maneuvering around a small boulder. "Lost his fiancée."

My stomach soured. "At the launch?" I slid around the rock to find Sol quiet on the other side. He continued without a word. My shoulders ached, my thighs burned. I was grateful for the pseudo-skin bandages. I could only imagine the infections I'd collect.

"Did anyone you know– or love– die that day?"

He sighed. "We all lost someone that day. Or the days after. . . or years before."

"What do you mean?" I asked.

He said he'd tell me at the next rest stop. "Best to focus on these next kilometers. Floor's slick.

I nodded and followed. Focusing on my feet, ignoring the ever-present worry about shifting boulders. But my mind filled with questions: *Where's my family? Are they safe? What if I never see them? What if something happened to them?* I couldn't think of anything else. I just needed to find them. I needed to know they were okay.

We took another break in another open pocket. I collapsed to the ground, unfazed by the pain it caused. I was just happy to be still, to let my arms and legs rest. I closed my eyes and heard the muffled sound of water and my breathing. I felt my heart thudding. I almost slipped into sleep, but flinched when Sol started talking. His voice didn't fill the space.

"Mar and I were babies when GEM moved to the desert. We didn't know any difference, but our father used to tell us about the desert before GEM. There used to be a deep-water pool out there. Near your rocket campus."

I frowned and said I wasn't aware.

"Yeah, our dad and his buddies used to ride out and go black water diving. That's where he met our mother. Black water diving in the desert. . . He said he never met a woman as fearless as our mother."

"Does Maryene take after her?"

Sol let out his booming laugh, relieving some tension I felt. "Yes! Pops said Mar was her spirit double!"

"Spirit double?"

"Personailty-wise, Mar takes after her. But mom was built like me."

I choked and started coughing.

He let out a cascade of laughter that resonated in every direction for seconds after he stopped. "Our mother came from a long line of strong women." His laughing tone slowed. "She died when Mar and I were young."

"I'm so sorry to hear that, Sol. My parents died when I was young."

"How?"

"Murdered."

He held silent for a moment. "Did they catch the ones who did it?"

"I– I can't remember." I drifted, trying to recall it. I saw the emergency lights and tape. A man talking at my nnenne. Sol cleared his throat, pulling me back. "I left soon after. But I remember they said something about a robbery. . . Sorry. I just know the hole that leaves."

He eyed me like he'd found something he'd been searching for. "You lost your roots. You're tumbling."

I shook my head, confused.

"Better get going. Don't want to miss the sunset!"

"What?" I asked. For the first time, I realized he didn't have a rello on his wrist. "How do you know what time it is?"

"Comes with living in the desert. Nothing else but the sun."

I struggled to get to my feet and stumbled to keep up. Steadied myself between two mounds as I stepped onto a narrow third. After some time, I asked, "How did your mother die?"

Sol grunted, raising himself onto an incline. Before he crawled down the other side, he answered.

"Rocket debris."

34

The sun was setting when we emerged. That first breath of fresh air. I wanted to drink it. I closed my eyes, drew in as much hot air as I could while the melting light waxed over me. I'd never been so free. In the desert, unrestrained. No trams. No UV shields. No uniform. No prison. Just openness in every direction. It was liberty manifested. Silhouetted mountains to the west, and a rising dark to east, early stars and no moon. It was hot as hell, but it was beautiful.

I looked down at the black crevice quickly disappearing into a shadow and thanked God for holding it true.

I took off my soaked garments, laid them flat on the still hot rocks, then laid myself down and let my body liquify. Sol told me to eat and hydrate as he pulled two firesticks out of the backpack. He shoved them between rocks. "A fire for later, when the heat goes."

"How long have you lived in the desert?" I asked, chewing on a strip of meat.

Sol huffed out a laugh. "Since before my grandfather was born."

I smiled at that. "So, your family has been here since before the calendar reset?"

"And proud of it!" he said.

I tried to imagine an ancestor of his, with the same size and temperament killing off tax collectors. Maryene fit that role a little easier. I had imagined everyone left the southwest, fled to Mexico or Canada. That's how Sam told it. "Why didn't your family leave?" I asked.

Sol chugged some water and laid back. "You ever been in love, Dr. Morant?"

"Yeah," I said, "have been for twenty-eight years."

"You're married, then?"

"Yes." I raised my hand to show the ring. The reflex brought back our wedding day. The placing of the rings. The joy in showing them to each other, to the photographer. To the witnesses. I could almost feel the sting of her hair against my cheeks as the wind whipped through the temple gardens that day.

Sol raised his brow. I glanced at my hand and saw there was no ring. It was with my gold-button uniform, my shiny shoes, and GEM-issued rello.

"Leaving the desert would be like abandoning a life-long love."

"Hmm," I said with a nod. "So, you've never left?"

"I go where I'm needed. I take things from one place, put them in another. But the desert is where I live. And where I plan to die."

"What about the Common Goal?" I asked between bites.

Sol grabbed a snack and shrugged. "What about it?"

I chuckled, confused by his lack of interest. "Well, I mean, the goal to leave Earth."

"When?" he asked.

"Once the Novi Dom is located."

"When is that? You would to spy it yet?"

"Not yet, but—"

"Wake my bones when you do." He tore a chunk of meat and gnawed on it.

"You don't think we'll find it?"

He shrugged again. "It doesn't matter to me if you do or don't."

I remarked, "I didn't take you for a pessimist, Sol."

His baritone laugh boomed around us, bounced off some distance ridges. "You mistake me, Dr. Morant!" He slapped my shoulder. I winced in pain. "Not everyone is a leaf. Some of us are trees. We have roots."

"I —," I started, then stopped.

He giggled, like a giant child. "Something to think about, huh?"

"Huh," I grunted, tearing off a piece of meat.

The Common Goal had been around since before I was born. According to Sam it was a reactionary solution to a much deeper problem. What that problem was, as far as I understood it to be, was that Earth was spent and humanity was doomed if we didn't leave. The Common Goal, like Sam's student said, had united the global community. Finally. The grand exodus was something all the peoples could agree upon.

Whole economies pivoted in the direction of achieving the Common Goal. Vast amounts of funding that had previously been used for war and destruction was shunted toward research, design, and space exploration. Humanity was, at an instant, relatively speaking, united. It gave everyone a purpose to strive toward. A vision. A hope. A reason to keep going despite the suffering. My parents believed in it. They saw the beauty in it. They raised me to see it, too. And I did. I saw it when I saw those five thousand people board those thirty ships and blast off toward Mars. I saw unity, humility, and courage. I saw heroes. I saw sacrifice. Then I was sent to a school that taught the Common Goal doctrine. My skills and talents were nurtured and made useful by it. The Common Goal became more personal when Itzel revealed her first pregnancy. And it gave me purpose when we lost our babies. The Common Goal employed me, housed me and my family. Why would I question it? It would be like questioning what my father taught me. "All things in God's time." Maybe it wasn't happening in my lifetime, but I was sure The Common Goal would be achieved in Mai's. That's all I could strive for. That's all I knew.

But the problem wasn't Earth. Not according to Sol. The problem was that people forgot their purpose. "Once you forget your history, you forget your purpose."

***

Darkness moved over us. Sol lit the fire then rolled into sleep. It was just me and the night. It felt like a lifetime had passed since I'd seen the night sky. Bare-faced with no telescopes or satellites. No light-filtering dome to give the illusion of stars when it was cloudy. The first time was when I was little. Four or five. My father woke me in the night, helped me to get dressed and led me outside. I felt a little scared but excited.

We rode the skyrail past the city lights halo. South down the coast, then transferred to go inland, before the next city's halo got too bright. When we got off the skyrail, we walked a ways, silent. I remember having no fear because he was with me. And when we reached the darkest, most set back corner of a grass field, my father turned me around and pointed up. I gasped when I saw the Milky Way. I remember thinking it was a magical secret just between my father and I. One that no one else could see.

I sat up, facing away from the firesticks that Sol lit. Their small flames warmed my back as I stared into the Milky Way. It was just as breathtaking as the first time I saw it. Just as boundless and forever. Still cradling the promise of a new home.

I dreamt of Itzel that night. Her warmth surrounded me. I saw her sweet cherub face so clearly. Her lips. Her smile. Her bright, black eyes. She was within reach. She was waiting for me.

***

We set out at first light, before the heat stretched our way. My body was exhausted, stiff, blistered where the boots rubbed. But my heart burned for Itzel. I figured if Shakina could break me out of prison, then she'd be able to find Itzel, too. Wherever I needed to go, whatever I needed to endure, I was determined to do it. To find her and my dear, sweet Mai.

The last stretch, Sol said, was a little easier, but he insisted I take the last dose of myogen. I did once we rested behind a weather worn rock. It shielded us from the morning sun, but the heat was already blurring the sand.

Sol pulled out the compass and displayed the map. We were so close. One more ridge, two kilometers out, then another ten kilometers to go. I grabbed one of the water bottles. There wasn't much left.

"Don't worry, amico! Past this ridge, it'll get better. I promise."

I licked my cracked lips and nodded. "Ok, let's go."

As we crested the ridge, I saw a vein of trees. The closest were short, mostly just branches and dried needles. But the further they stretched from us, the fuller and larger they became.

"Almost there, amico. Almost there," Sol said when I bent over to catch my breath.

I heard birds. Saw some pose in the wind. Not circling vultures this time. Smaller, more agile. Hawks maybe. But then there were even small ones as we stepped under the canopy. They darted from branch to branch. Trilling loudly at each other.

The air cooled the deeper we went. Soon there were more branches and foliage than there was sky. The sun could only peek at us. The trees swayed as wind worked through them. A creek gurgled alongside our path.

"I'll refill the bottles," Sol said, motioning me to sit. He dropped capsules in each one, then sat them in the stream. "Beautiful, right?" he asked.

I was speechless. I mean I didn't want to speak. There were so many sounds, soft, small, bright, and brittle. Coming from all sides. I was overcome but wanted to take it all in.

Sol returned and sat down beside me. He handed over a full bottle. "This part of the forest is a couple hundred years old. A small rancher started planting trees and here we are." He waved a hand around.

"They had plans like this for Mars. Make a forest out of a desert," I said watching all the life overhead.

"Heard you need water to do that," Sol said.

I turned to him, quick to defend the Common Goal. But he was busy, watching life in the canopy, too.

"Yeah," I said thinking about deserted greenhouses, "hard to do without an atmosphere." I shook loose those memories before they welled up. "Ready to go?" I asked.

It was not easier, not in the way I expected. The closer we got to Spot-245, the more obstacles were in the way. Fallen trees, tumbled boulders. Uncleared brush. A swarm of wasps who stripped me of every ounce of courage. But then the trees began to clear. A pebbled path appeared. Human voices blended with the birds.

"Follow the path, Dr. Morant. They'll take care of you down there."

"You're not coming?" I asked, surprised and saddened to part so soon.

Sol smiled, and gave a soft chuckle. "Can't stay this time. Maryene needs me back. You'll be fine."

I extended my hand to shake his, but he was already wrapping his arms around me. I'd never felt small before that moment.

"Thank you," I said.

"We've got history now. Don't you forget!" He patted my shoulder, still making me wince.

He left, walking as though a sixty-kilometer trek was nothing.

"Say *thank you and goodbye* to Maryene for me!" I shouted.

He let loose a laugh and shouted back, "She'll be glad you said so!" A mountain of a man strolling into the trees, hardly making a sound as he went. I kept watching until I couldn't see him anymore. That moment still grips my chest. Sol was– is– a good one.

I turned to the path ahead of me. About fifty meters from where Sol left me was a booth. Two people were inside, talking. A low-cut hedge lined the path, boasting small white flowers. I wasn't sure what was ahead of me, but somehow I knew I was headed in the right direction.

"Welcome!" the woman cheerfully said as I approached.

"Transfer or visiting?" the man asked, looking between me and the small tablet he held.

I stuttered, "I– I don't know."

The two exchanged glances.

"Well, what's your name?" the woman asked, still smiling.

"Tah–" I stopped. I looked back to where Sol disappeared, then back to the waiting duo. "Tolulopé Ayodege Hudu-Morant," I said.

"Oh! Welcome!" they chimed, excitedly. The young man rattled out, "we've been expecting you!" while the woman raced out of the booth and down the path toward a tall, arched hedge.

"Mai is going to be overjoyed! She has been talking–"

"Mai?" I said, breathless, "She's here? They're here?"

Before he could answer, my knees gave way.

Part III

35

I woke to a fan slowly swirling from a curved ceiling. Sunlight angled along a teal wall with a red door left half open. The window to my left framed a thick bush and a cloud-streaked sky. Stiff and sore, I moved to sit up.

"Daddy?"

I turned to see Mai's big brown eyes.

"Oh my sweet baby," I cried. "My sweet, sweet Mai."

She crawled into my arms, pressed her face into my neck. She cried against me. All my pain left as I held her. Her hair, her warmth, her tiny arms around my neck. I brushed her curls back and kissed her forehead, praying this was not a dream.

The door slowly opened wider.

My heart burst when I saw Itzel.

She fell into me and we found each other again.

When she pulled back, I saw the worry as she looked me over. She traced her fingers over my brows and raised cheekbones. She kissed my forehead, my lips, my cheeks, my lips, my hands. My lips. And when she was satisfied that I was well enough, she pressed my hand to her chest and silently cried.

Mai crawled over me and wrapped her arms around Itzel's neck. "It's okay to cry, Mommy. Daddy and I cried, too. We're okay now," she said, eager to soothe Itzel the same way we eased her through tantrums.

Itzel let out a laugh and wiped her cheeks. "I know, baby girl. And I am so grateful. These are happy tears."

Gradually, we made our way out of the bedroom, on Mai's insistence, into the living room where she had flowers to show me. We moved slowly, careful not to lose sight or contact with each other. Mai pulled my left hand. Itzel looped my arm over her shoulders and let me lean against her for the short walk into the next room.

Sun poured through skylights and the eastern windows, brightening the yellow-brown walls. An archway led from the living room to a small kitchen on the other side of the round-walled cabin. The living room had minimal furniture and nothing matched.

Our condo in GEM City touted GEM colors— mostly white with black, blue and gold accents. It made decorating difficult for Itzel. In this new living room, everything had color: blue couch, green lamp, teal pillows, red loveseat, yellow walls.

"See Daddy, I picked them for you!" Mai said, producing a small purple vase of yellow-orange flowers.

I lowered onto the couch to get a better view. The small, bell-shaped blooms had surprise-red centers. "Oh, they are magnificent!" I said, "I love them! Thank you."

Mai swelled with pride as I handed them back to her. She gingerly placed them on the table and crawled into my lap, curling herself tight against me. She placed a hand on my chest and tapped a finger along with my heart beat.

I turned to see Itzel crying again. She shook her head and smiled, then rested her head on my shoulder. She worked her fingers through my overgrown hair, pressed into my scalp, relieving another pain that I hadn't noticed.

She whispered, "I have missed you, every moment of every day."

We rested together, adjusting until we were side lying spoons, stacked smallest to biggest. Mai curled against Itzel, who wiggled her feet between my calves. I wedged my feet against the sun-warmed armrest and draped my arm over my family. Every inch of me wanted to stay that way forever.

"Where did you go, Daddy?" Mai asked.

"Prison," I said. Why lie?

Mai adjusted against Itzel and asked, "What was it like?"

How do you describe torture and abuse to a seven-year-old? I decided on, "Lonely."

"Did you make friends?" she asked.

I chuckled recalling Sam. "Yeah, I made a friend."

"Did you miss us?" she asked, softly.

"You have no idea, Mai." I pulled them tighter against me.

Mai laid still as long as she could. She wiggled free and invited me to go outside with her. As much as I wanted to, my body was too exhausted.

"I think I need another day to rest, my love," I said.

She wasn't disappointed. She pivoted and asked to play with her neighbor friend, Marteen. I was hesitant to say yes, too nervous that if she left, she'd be gone. But Itzel said it was okay.

"Just stay where we can see you," she said, stroking Mai's cheek.

I asked for another kiss before Mai skipped out of the cabin.

After the quiet settled back into the room, Itzel and I arranged ourselves so we could see each other. She sat where the sun drenched her. I sat in awe. We didn't talk much at first. Conversation was led by touch and tears. Fingers tangled in hair, palms pressed against stained cheeks. Words shared with lip and tongue. I could have died there, enveloped by her.

The sun climbed toward noon before either of us spoke.

"How was it, really?" she asked, lying against me.

"It was brutal," I said, looking down at her. "Just brutal." I wasn't ready to hold those memories so I couldn't give them to her. Not in that moment. So I left it at that.

Itzel took one of my hands and kissed my palm. Then she laced her fingers into mine and said, "Shakina said it would be." She paused. "She did a lot for us."

"Like what?" I asked.

"Like asking the Council to let us stay here. Let you stay here."

I propped myself up at the distinction. "What does that mean?"

She let out a sigh. "This place isn't like GEM," she said.

I joked, looking around, "Well I can see that."

She nudged me gently in the ribs. "More than that, Tah. The people here. . . they don't acknowledge the Common Goal. Not like everyone else does."

Instinctually, I got nervous when she said that. Afraid the haum system would record and report. I looked around the room and saw there were no screens, no touchtech. No keypads to program. No speakers built into every surface.

Relieved, I asked, "What do they acknowledge?"

"That Earth has everything we need."

I was going to ask what that had to do with me staying there, but I understood. I represented everything opposite of that notion. I built the damn engine to escape Earth. I was a mascot for the Common Goal. And now, I was a fugitive.

"Shakina convinced them we could stay?" I asked.

"She asked that you could stay."

I shrank from her a little.

"I'm not saying that to hurt you, Tah, but you need to understand the circumstances. They're risking a lot with you here."

"Right," I said. Anger wanted to argue the fact that I didn't ask to be at the Spot, but I didn't have the energy. What difference would that make? Where else would I have gone?

"They're okay with you being here, right?" I asked.

"Yes. A lot of my research has assisted and been inspired by the efforts here and the other Spots."

"How many are there?"

"Thousands, all over the world."

"Did Shakina tell you to come here?"

"No. But I knew I could. I was surprised when I saw her. And I knew she'd get you here if I asked."

I wrapped my arms tighter around her. Drank in her scent. "Thank you, my love," I said.

That night, Itzel drew a bath for me. I asked her to step out while I undressed. I didn't want her to see all that they did or didn't do. Neglect was their main form of torture, I realized. But she said she needed to see, to know the truth. I was embarrassed to show her, all the scars, the wounds. How my skin stretched over bones, how frail I'd become. But she didn't flinch. She cupped my thinned face and kissed me.

She helped me as I lowered into the steaming water. My legs shook as I went but I didn't fall.

"Stay as long as you need to. I'm going to put Mai down for bed," she said as she kissed me again, then left.

The bathroom was small, like everything else in the cabin. The tub didn't fit my legs and torso at the same time but I was too tired to care. I was too tired to care that if I were to have showered, the stream would only hit my chest. I was just grateful to be there.

Steam rose and fogged the mirror over the sink. The faucet let slip occasional drips. I heard Mai singing a prayer that sounded far off but familiar. And then it was quiet. Just the lapping of water against me.

I thought back to the last time I soaked in a tub. It was before the Mars disaster, before water became a chore. Showers were spaced out over days. Then it was bucket baths when the water towers were destroyed. I recalled how grateful I was for the timed-shower stalls in high school. Beau hated them and always complained eight minutes wasn't long enough. I was just glad I didn't have to walk to get the water and wait to warm it up. Eight minutes felt like heaven. But by the time I was at GEM, I whittled showering to a three-minute step in my morning routine. Even on the weekends. It wasn't something to indulge in, it was necessary. But I did enjoy the luxury of an overhead spigot. I didn't have to bend over to wash my head, neck and shoulders as I had in college and in Chicago. In prison, bathing was what it was– a small hunk of soap, a cloth, and my sink when there was water. And then nothing. Two weeks of lying in my own filth.

I shut that memory off as soon as it started to rise. I was clean, warm, and safe. My family was on the other side of the door. I didn't want misery fogging up my gratitude. I sank deeper into the water. Stayed long enough to prune. And thanked God for it.

I eased into bed next to Itzel. I melted with warmth and comfort. Nothing settled my spirit like Itzel right next to me. Being apart felt like a frost-bitten forever, though it had only been five weeks since we fought. *Never again*, I thought. I drifted off to the sound of Mai and Itzel's soft breathing, like a whispered rhythmic lullaby.

36

"You are going to do great things,** Lopé," my father said, low and warm. His thin face rounded into a smile when I looked up. He nodded toward my booklet. "The past will guide you. Without it, many get lost on their way to greatness."

"Yes, father," I said, steadied by his words and his gentle tone.

He turned his attention back to his work and said, "Now stay focused. A person always breaking from work never finishes anything."

"Yes, father."

I sat up, his words clinging to me. "I'm late for work," I said, throwing off the covers.

Itzel rolled over, reaching for me. "Hmm? What?"

It took a moment to realize I wasn't home. There were no amber lights seeping from the floorboards. "Sorry," I said, "I forgot where I was." I lowered back into bed.

Itzel nestled against me and said, "That's okay. We'll go for a walk when it's light out. Help you get settled."

I didn't fall back to sleep. I heard the first birds of morning. I watched dawn break. I heard Mai stir on the other side of Itzel. All sights and sounds of paradise. But my mind was bent on work. I stared at the brightening ceiling, working out my plan to get back to my files, find the data, and finally prove that my outburst toward Beau wasn't anything more than a misunderstanding, an overreaction by me *and* the system. I just needed access to my files.

Itzel took me to the rose garden after Mai ran off with her neighbor friend, Marteen, and a few other children. I wasn't keen on letting her go, but Itzel said this was part of their weekend routine. "Her age group sets the dining hall tables, while the older kids prep and serve the food." Itzel waved and smiled as the children ran off. She nudged me, "She's safe, Tah. And she's happy!"

I couldn't argue with that. Mai was happy.

Itzel walked slowly while I limped along. Forty-eight years old, moving like a crypt-dweller, stiff, wincing, and off-balance. Every joint ached, my leg muscles twitched and jerked. I had to stop a few times to let my calves relax.

"I don't know how you climbed all that way, Tah!" Itzel remarked at the second break.

I bent forward and said, "Sol knew Shakina–"

"Kin."

"Right. Kin. Sol knew Kin. I figured Kin could find you. That's what kept me going."

Itzel rubbed my low back, right where I needed it most. "I'm so grateful to her," she whispered.

"Me, too." I said.

As we approached the garden old memories were dusted clean.

"My mother grew hibiscus," I said, taken by the red and pink blooms. "She called them her big and lovely ladies. She'd say, 'they just open up, like *POW!* You have to admire them for that!'" I smiled at the memory, but that was quickly interrupted by the bees. The garden hummed with them, grating my nerves.

"They won't hurt you, Tah! They're busy with their work," Itzel assured me.

It seemed like everyone at the Spot was busy with work. That morning, Mai went with the neighbors and their son, Marteen, to set tables for breakfast in the dining hall. On our way to the garden, we passed folks digging, pulling, planting. Measuring the wind or fixing a sign post. They were covered in dirt and unfazed by it. Even Itzel had plans to help some teenagers with a crop proposal. Everyone had a job to do while I was in a rose garden, doing nothing but dodging bees.

"I should be working," I said.

Itzel sighed from a bench. "How about taking some time to adjust?"

From the middle of the path, I told her, "I've rested enough, Izzie. I've done nothing for over a month." I tried to make it sound benign, funny even.

She closed her eyes. "That was not rest, Tah. You were in a prison."

"I was scrubbing floors and transporting trash." I heard the sharpness in my tone and softened it. "Idleness isn't good for me. I need to get back to work. I need to finish investigating that anomaly."

Her face bent in concern. "You will, Tah, but you need to rest."

"Itzel, I can't! Beau is hell-bent on hiding the anomaly I found. He has full access to the data. If I wait any longer, who knows what will happen to it."

She dropped her gaze and nodded. "I understand. That would worry me as well."

"My father would always say a person who is always breaking from work never finishes. I need to finish my work."

She looked up, pained. "Do you remember how I was after the miscarriage?"

I sat next to her. "Itzel—"

She raised her hand to stop me. "I know outwardly, I was a mess—like hell sued for murder, as my mom would say." She softly chuckled. "But inwardly, I found a deeper understanding. I learned all the pain that comes with grief is a way the body shows the depth of love. Of truth." She looked up with a sad smile. "I'm not sure I would have learned that if I kept working."

I tried hard to listen and not shut myself off. But those weeks of watching her come undone crippled me. I felt worthless. Work gave me purpose. Without the engine, I would have gone mad. Mad like I did in the prison pit. I wasn't ready to go through that again. I needed to work.

She cupped my hands in hers. "I know the work is important, Tah. It held you together while I was suffering. And I am forever grateful for your strength." Her eyes darted between mine. "But you have a universe within to explore."

I closed my eyes and turned away.

"Just consider it, Tah. You have time here. You can rest."

I shook my head. "You're probably right, Itzel, but I can't. Not yet. Not yet."

For the rest of that day her words sat on one shoulder, my father's on the other. I couldn't appease either one. So I swept the cabin, wiped the counters and ledges. I fluffed the couch pillows. I found task after task to fill the time. When Itzel left for her work and Mai took a nap, I paced the perimeter of the cabin, looking for any distraction. She didn't understand. Sitting too long and letting all the thoughts and memories fill my head felt like torture. Too much fury came with it. And I never wanted her to witness that. Our argument still haunted me and I feared exploding again.

I stepped into the bedroom where Mai napped and watched her. Silence filled my head. All there was to hear was her soft breathing. No birds, no voices, or branches tapping at the walls and windows. Just my sweet Mai soundly sleeping. I sat on the edge of the bed and closed my eyes. Breathed slowly in time with Mai and tried to open myself up to Itzel's suggestion. But something alerted me. An unnatural scratching from the living room. I looked out the window, and saw someone walk away. I hobbled out of the bedroom, ready to run them off. I opened the door. A note slipped down, floated to my feet.

"See you tomorrow. Kin"

37

Dr. Shakina Hakim arrived at GEM in the planning period for Umoja-16, seven years before Umoja-19 launched. We'd all heard of her— a rising star in the astrometer field with a background in archaeology. Odd, but intriguing. Most of us spent our entire academic and post-doctoral training looking away from Earth and toward the future. Her opposite background ruffled some feathers. There was some bitterness in the Novi Dom Locator team about giving the lead position to a new hire. Her predecessor got dismissed because of one too many red code violations. I only learned that after the fact. GEM was good at compartmentalizing.

I first met her just after lunch one day when Beau came to my office followed by an unsmiling, small, brown woman with shoulder length locs. I don't know why, but I had imagined her taller than her 150 cm stature. I didn't expect blue eyes with black specks. Nor did I expect her firm grip and lower than average voice. To be honest, she was nothing that I expected. Nothing any of us expected, least of all Beau.

"Welcome to GEM," I said, shaking her hand.

"Thank you, Dr. Morant. Pleased to meet you."

I quickly learned we had some similarities in that brief interaction. Neither of us liked small talk and we both preferred work to pleasantries.

"She's a little stiff, don't you think?" Beau said that evening, on our walk to the tram. "Icy, really."

"It's her first day, Beau. Besides, we're not all like you."

He nudged me. "I'd encourage you to try. It's more fun on the sunny side."

The working relationship between Shakina and I, without intention, eased into a quiet friendship over the next couple months. Work lunches and work dinners gave way to brief conversations about our hopes. Hopes for success, for the future. She peppered in how she hoped the future wouldn't reflect the past. Not the ugly parts, anyway.

When Shakina left GEM we were ramping up for Umoja-19. I assumed it was some in-team bickering that pushed her out. Even that was a need-to-know basis. Once she was gone, there was no need to know why.

***

I stayed up all night thinking about her note. I was up before Itzel and Mai, full of vigor and cheer. At least that's how Itzel described me. I was anxious, ticking between impatient and excited. I was impatient to see Shakina. Or Kin as Sol and Itzel kept reminding me. "Kin's patience is like the hair on my head," he had said as we climbed through the cave. I remarked that he was bald. He winked at me and said, "exactly, it won't last forever."

I was excited to get back to work, get my mind straightened out, tightened up.

After Itzel and Mai left, I paced. From the bedroom door to the bathroom door, seven strides to, and seven strides from. I wrung my hands and fussed with my shirt. The sleeves were too short, so I rolled them up, unrolled them, and rolled again.

Her knock spun me.

I yanked the door open and there she was. Almost half my height, bronze skinned with black-speckled blue eyes. Her locs half up on top of her head, the rest halfway down her back. They'd grown so much since I'd seen her. And seeing her meant I was closer to my files.

"Dr. Morant," she said in her monotone voice. She extended a hand, forever the professional.

I shook my head in disbelief. "Dr. Hakim. Good to see you again."

Had I been stronger, the four kilometer walk from the cabin to her office would have been no problem. Long legs make short walks! But as it was, I struggled the whole forty-minute limp-along. Shakina was kind enough to walk slowly. I apologized for my snail's pace over cracked earth and gnarled roots. She ignored my self-pity. The only thing keeping me moving forward was the hope of finding the data.

The research center sat in a large, open field with no shield from the sun. It stretched three stories up and a city block long, and just as deep. From a distance, it looked like a typical research and design facility. Signal towers stuck out, staking the sky. But as I got closer, my heart sank. It was welded-together shipping containers and looked like scrap. I doubted that there would be anything useful inside.

"I set you up in my office," she said as she opened a door along the west wall.

"I'm honored!" I joked, masking my growing disappointment. At GEM, she'd never shared her space. Not even with me. Sharing an office sounded like there wasn't enough room for the both of us.

Inside the building didn't inspire hope either. Every door, desk, and lampshade looked well used or piecemealed together. I peeked into offices and labs as we passed and tried not to frown.

She slowed in front of a door halfway down a southern hall. "It's nothing special, but it does what I need."

I silently sighed, thinking there couldn't be much for her to do. To be polite I asked, "What have you been working on?"

She entered a pass code into a panel by the door. "The moon."

"The moon?" I asked, tipping my voice out of condescension a little too late, but studying the most pedestrian object in our sky seemed beneath her.

She turned before entering the room. "Yes, the moon!"

I followed her in, rolling my eyes. "What's happening on the moon, Kin?"

"You'd be surprised," she said, flatly.

I doubted it. And I started to really doubt her. A top astrometer reduced to a lunar looker.

Her office made me itch. It was too narrow. Too full of things that begged for their own space. One half was a bank of displays and system docks, wires bulging out like diseased veins. The other wall was overstuffed shelves. Aged mementos from her archaeology days. At the far end of the office was a small fridge, sink, and two cabinets.

"Coffee?" she asked.

I nodded, "Yes, please," as I looked for a holodisplay, a touchdesk, or vizport. I saw nothing but doubt. How was I going to access the data in a cramped office full of relics?

She ground beans and set up the coffee maker, showing me the how-tos of everything. I tried to show patience but I was there to work, not measure out beans and water.

While we waited for it to brew, she finally showed me the hodge-podge configuration of screens and keyboards. I listened with skepticism.

"I had another engineer set this up. It's CGULS v14.29.4," she said.

My shoulders sagged in defeat. I hadn't heard of that operating system in years.

Kin tapped a command key. Three screens woke up. "She was able to patch a back door into GEM."

And just like that, my doubt vanished. Everything I needed was there. Simple but effective. I felt giddy. I dropped into one of the old chairs, feeling like a camel who made it to the oasis. "This is perfect, Kin! Thank you!"

She handed me a steaming mug and opened the door. "I have to check on something. I'll be back in thirty. Get acquainted with your new setup."

Before she stepped out, I said, "It's good to be working together again, Shakina– Kin. Really good." I didn't expect a response but I was surprised to see a smile.

My eagerness was met with clumsy mistakes. The tactile keyboard sprawled wider than I was used to and the letters were organized all wrong. The laggy touchtech frustrated my fingers. It took twenty minutes before I got the feel for the system and the hardware. Even then, I found myself stumbling through it. The damn system couldn't find 'umoja-19' anywhere. It had to be spelled without a dash. And it wouldn't take 'no' for an answer. Had to be 0 for no, 1 for yes or a dash for help. *Who the hell ever found that intuitive?* I finally figured out how to ask in exactly the right way and suddenly:

Mission retrieved.

My chest expanded with relief as the screens filled with the Umoja craft specs, the crew members' profiles. My engine. All of it.

At once, I was a fish tossed back into the pond! I rushed through the logs and found the preliminary note I wrote about the anomaly. Seeing it gave me hope that I'd find the visual data to support it.

I opened the prox scanner logs and took a breath to steady myself. "Replay prox scan at point five sec intervals."

Replaying sequence.

I had to shake my hands out. Anticipation tingled along each finger. I chewed my bottom lip as I watched the same footage I studied weeks ago.

Coordinates locked. Deuteron engaged. My eyes darted between the data log and the footage.

I held my breath.

But I missed it.

"CGUL replay last five samples at zero point two five rate."

This time I kept my eyes trained on the footage. Everything was the same except the substance.

"No, no, no, no, no."

I repeated the process over and over, twisting my insides tighter around what was missing. Each time the substance didn't appear I pounded my fist on the desk. The screens flinched.

"This can't be happening," I growled.

I was ready to throw the keyboard through one of the screens when I heard the door unlatch. I turned to see Kin sliding into the office.

"How's it going in here?" she asked, pulling over a chair.

I huffed, embarrassed and upset. "Not great."

She scooted closer. "Is it the system?"

"No, no, it's something in the data," I said.

"What are we looking for?"

I explained how I searched through all the system files and came across a prox sensor warning with each attempt. "The prox sensor flagged it, but it wasn't enough to disengage the engine."

"Atmospheric disturbance?" she asked.

"That's what I thought, too. But it didn't interact with our scanners as we'd expect. I ran a NeutSig analysis. Came back with— get this— no neutrinic signature."

Kin turned to me, stone faced. "No neutrinic signature?"

"I ran the scans three times. It kept coming back with no neutrinic signature." She squinted harder at me. I held up three fingers like I was making a promise and said, "three times."

"Pull it up again. I'll put it on the big screen. I want to see the whole sky, not the nose of the ship."

I did as she said. The Dragon filled the larger display between us. I heard her take a breath and realized she probably hadn't seen the Dragon since she left. Not this view anyway. But just as quickly as she was swept up in it, she was back to business.

She played the sequence at normal speed, then again at half rate. She zoomed into the center left portion of the Dragon. She requested the system assess the angular velocity of three stars in the background that I hadn't noticed. The image sharpened and she reset the footage and played it back. I didn't see what she was looking for but then she paused it and said, "There," pointing to the frozen display.

I looked on in confusion.

She stood and pointed more directly at the top left of the screen. "These three stars have been in each mission that I worked on. But this. . ." She pointed to a faint, hazy streak just right of the star cluster. "That's a comet. Keep your eye on it."

She requested CGUL to restart the footage. I watched the comet stretch right to left. Then it froze. For several frames. Then skipped further left.

"Looks like someone doctored the record."

Her words made my stomach churn. I clenched my fists, and felt like breaking bones and teeth.

38

After the success of Umoja-18 where Jingles the Chimpanzee passed through the Dragon's Gate and returned unscathed, GEM hosted an extravagant gala in the GEM City ballroom. Black tie and gown required. It was the most elaborate gala in the years I'd been there. The ceiling was draped in silk sheets onto which was projected an open Dragon's Gate. The Milky Way looked down from the center and highest point of the ceiling. The walls were decorated with holograms of distant stars and nebulas. Orchestral music played. Long tables dressed with fine cutlery, and high back chairs bordered an open space that, as the night wore on, became a dance floor. Waitstaff carried large trays of hors d'oeuvres, and drinks. Dinner was served from the right, empty dishes taken from the left. All food and beverage provided by the good folks at GEM Farms.

"I can't believe she didn't show up," Beau grumbled. He finished the rest of his champagne and signaled for a refresher.

"Dr. Hakim never attends these kinds of things, Beau. Hell, I wouldn't be here if it weren't for you," I said. That was partially true. Itzel encouraged me to attend as always.

A waiter approached with a tray for champagne. Beau grabbed two and offered one to me. I declined and watched him knock back one glass and return it to the tray. Then he waved off the server without saying thank you.

"Yeah, but this is important, Doc. It is important for the team to support each other. She doesn't work like a team player."

"Beau," I said, stepping in front of him. He was flushed pink and sweaty already. "She does excellent work—"

"I know that!" he spat. "It'd just be nice if she showed some appreciation for everyone else's work! It's not that fucking hard!" He loosened his tie and took another swig.

I fixed his collar. "She's just introverted—"

"*You're* introverted, Tah! *She's* a fucking vacuum! She sucks the fun out of everything!"

I frowned at him. "That's uncalled for, Beau."

He rolled his eyes and took another gulp.

I didn't say anything after that. What was the use? He would only get more inflamed if I kept trying. I didn't want to ruin a decent evening. I just didn't understand why he was so bothered by her absence. And why he couldn't let it go.

When Itzel returned from the ladies' room Beau left, barely acknowledging her.

"What was that about?" she asked.

I shrugged and watched him huff away. "He's upset that Shakina isn't here."

"She's never liked events like this," Itzel said. "She told me she never attended any of her five graduations."

I chuckled and turned to her. "It's Beau. You know how he is about this sort of thing. Optics." I shrugged again.

Itzel nodded and hummed. "It's curious how some of us need a spotlight, and some prefer to stay in the wings. Neither is wrong, just different."

"He's always been a showman, that's for sure," I said. "Good thing he's the director."

"And what a lovely show he's put on tonight," Itzel said, smiling up at me.

I looked around at the two-hundred or so GEM employees. All of them dressed up, chatting and laughing, toasting to a job well done, *"Forever onward!" "Onward toward the goal!"*

"Yeah, I suppose," I said.

I was envious of Shakina's stubbornness, or whatever it was that kept her home that night, and all the other galas she skipped. I was only there to avoid Beau's tantrum.

***

I angrily rocked in the office chair. Recalled the back of Beau's head work through the crowd in the underground transit system. The memory played on loop, repeating inside me: *Beau, you snake! You fucking snake!*

Kin stood and asked, "More coffee?"

I blurted, "Why would Beau do this?"

She gave me a blank stare before turning away.

I rattled on, "I get it. He didn't want me to share it. He thought it was too minuscule of a finding to report, but why delete it?"

She poured the beans and pressed the grinder.

I glared in her direction, annoyed by the interruption. When it stopped, I started again, "Why would someone delete something that they said didn't matter? If it doesn't matter so much, leave it alone!"

She filled the water pitcher and poured it into the back of the coffee maker.

I stood and started pacing. "What difference would it make? If it's a timeline thing, we've postponed missions before— why would this be any different?" I was boiling over in frustration. Her silence didn't help. "He left me right as I stepped on the transit pod. I looked up and he was gone!" I threw my hands up. "He did it right behind my back!"

The coffee maker gurgled. The bittersweet filled the small office. And she just watched me.

I paced back and forth, one hand on my hip, one finger against my teeth. One cuticle chewed up in anger.

Finally, she spoke up. "Umoja-18 was more successful than what was reported."

I stopped. "What do you mean?" I searched her face.

She took a deep breath and closed her eyes. "When I got the footage from the q-scopes. . ." she paused. Time slowed down. The room tightened around us.

"I found it," she said.

The skin on my arms prickled. "Found what?"

She paused so long I felt like I was tipping forward. She shook her head then finally met my gaze. "The Novi Dom."

At first it didn't register. Her words didn't make sense. But then it slammed together. "You what?!" I shouted, then quickly apologized. "I'm sorry— you found the—" I was out of breath like the marathon was finally over. Like victory was won. "Shakina— Kin, that's, that's," I looked around the room, trying to stabilize myself. "That's amazing!"

I rushed toward her but her face stopped me. A steely coldness was in her eyes. I stuttered through questions, "why didn't you — this is huge — what happened?"

Her lips and brow tightened like she was disgusted by my excitement.

I took a step back, careful not to press for more than she was willing to give. "Shakina— you achieved the biggest step toward the Common Goal— why didn't you. . .?"

She cocked her head to the side. "Do you know how many people have been slaughtered for gold?"

The question startled me. "Kin, what are you talking about? What does this have to do with anything?"

"Do you know how long slavery has existed?" Another bewildering question, asked like a dagger. Her eyes and nose flared. I tried to answer but she wouldn't let me. Her voice sharpened, "Since the beginning of human history, every kingdom and empire. All of them had slaves. All of them!"

"Shakina—"

"It's in our DNA," she growled, "like a disease we can't breed out. You think we wouldn't do the same on a new planet?"

"Shakina — slavery hasn't existed for nearly two-hundred years," I pleaded.

"It didn't stop!" She shouted and threw a hand in the air, "They just hide it better!"

I stared at her. Silent. The computers hummed. The coffee spluttered. I felt trapped.

She spoke first, voice low and razored. "How did you feel when you first saw Mai?"

I shook my head, confused. "Shakina, what does this—"

"How did you feel when Mai was born?" she asked again, cutting for an answer.

"Cured," I blurted.

She stepped toward me. "Happy? Joyful?"

"Yes," I said, stepping back.

Her eyes narrowed. "And then what did you feel?"

"I don't know," I said, anxious for her to stop asking.

"Yes you do. What did you feel after the joy?"

Mai was perfect when she was born. All twenty toes, twenty fingers, two big, dark brown eyes, a head full of slicked back, black hair. She was soft and warm, delicate and real. I held her for hours as Itzel rested. I laid down to hold Mai's tiny warm body skin to skin against my chest, and memorized every curve of her face, her coiling hair, each tiny nail, and every wrinkle in the palm of her hands and bottoms of her feet. There was silence in my head as I held her, ease in my chest. It felt like breathing under water. Only one thing undid that sense of relief:

"Fear," I admitted.

Kin asked, "Fear of what?"

"Fear that I'd hurt her. Fail her. That someone else would hurt her. Or take her from me."

"Did you know enslaved women in the North American slave states smothered their infants? Did you know that?"

Horrified, I shouted, "Shakina!"

"Listen to me!" She charged toward me, jabbed a finger in my face. "They birthed babies with no relief or comfort. Then they smothered them!" Her eyes pierced through me. Sharp and violent. "Do you know why?"

I shook my head.

"To save them!" she hissed. "Save them from slavery. Save them from beatings. Save them from the humiliation waiting for them." Tears sat on the edge of falling, but she turned away before I could see her cry.

I didn't know what to do. I didn't know what to say. I didn't fully understand her reasoning— the Novi Dom was a planet, not a person. Not a child. She had no authority to hide it. It didn't belong to her.

"Not a single civilization got it right," she said, softly, like she was talking to herself. "Over six thousand years of human history we always find a way to ruin everything." She let out a sigh. "I couldn't let us do it again."

I let some time pass before I asked, "What does this have to do with Beau?"

"I was in my office, reviewing the composite data. I thought everyone had gone home— I should have locked my door but I thought I was alone. Then he was there, and I didn't have time to hide it," she said. "And the way Beau looked at it, like a fiend. . . this perfect planet, he looked at it like. . ." she trailed off.

I knew the look she saw. I saw it the day of the Umoja-19 launch. That unblinking stare with a too wide smile.

I motioned for her to sit and went to pour more coffee.

"Hiding it wasn't enough."

Something in her voice sent a chill through me. "What do you mean?" I asked, making sure to not spill the hot liquid. I glanced over my shoulder at her.

She had her back to me when she finally replied. "I planned to do something about it."

I put the pitcher down and turned. "What?"

"It's why I had to leave." She studied her hands, opening and closing them slowly.

"What'd you do, Shakina?" I whispered.

She wiped at her face and turned to me. Her eyes were red and dry. "I planned to kill him."

39

I've known Beau longer than anyone else. I knew him before he grew facial hair, before he hit his second and third growth spurt. I knew the glinting eye and smirk that lit up his face when he snagged a girl's attention. She, one of however many, never knew that there were many. He had a way of making a girl feel like that first star in the night sky, shiny, sparkly, and brand new. He'd spread them out so they all thought they were the first and only light in his dark sky.

I'd recognize that hungry stare and almost smile he'd toss my way during a party or hang out where the boy-to-girl ratio almost matched. He'd throw that look at me before he'd disappear into another room like it was a set of keys and I was his chauffeur. He'd need about an hour and I better be ready to go when he was.

"My little heartbreaker," his mom would say, sweeping back his hair with a saccharine sense of pride. "Just a handsome little devil."

My mother never would have called me a little devil. And never so affectionately. It felt icky hearing and watching how proud she was of her son and his ability to break hearts. Like stepping barefoot into a pile of chewed up and spat out gum.

I sat quietly in our dorm room, letting myself disappear into my bed linens when the Soncals first visited. They fussed about Beau, his grades, his dust of a mustache. His casual conquests. Eventually they noticed me.

I liked the Soncals. They were inviting and adventurous. More importantly, they were parents.

Mr. Soncal, Beau's father, was a huntsman as well as a businessman. He prided himself on his kill count, "Twenty chimera and climbing," and funded that pride with military contracts. "Peace keeping contracts," he assured me when we first met. I hadn't required assurance, but he gave it freely. "Unified Nation contracts, son. Peace requires patrol. We patrol to keep the peace." The Soncal Company built shatter-proof all-terrain vehicles, capable of storming through any climate, peaceful or not. But all I heard was, "son."

When Mr. Soncal took me hunting for the first time with Beau and a few men from the Soncal company— owned and operated by the Soncal family for four generations—I had a hard time raising the rifle. It got heavy and my hands got sweaty as I aimed it at the winged jackal chimera. The man-made crossbreed sat lopsided and too heavy on a low hanging branch some fifty meters away. The snow silenced the forest. Crisped the air. Compacted beneath my stomach and elbows and thighs. Mr. Soncal clapped me on the back and said, "Don't worry, son, chimera were made to be hunted. Made by man to be killed by man!" That didn't help. All I saw was the malformed spine and fogged eyes when I looked through the sight again. I feigned a stomach ache and marched through the snow back to their log-beam lodge at the base of the mountain range they owned. Fourteen generations of owning mountains and all that came with them.

Mrs. Soncal, Beau's mother, made a cup of tea for me. She was a skier. The skill ran in her family. Twelve generations of lean, long-legged, tucking and weaving champions. She retired from the competing side of the sport when she married Mr. Soncal. Not because he asked her to, although he had asked her to.

"I quit because I was done with it. I was bored. I skied my whole life. I was ready to do more!" she said with her back to me. We were in the kitchen part of the log-beam lodge. I thought it would be rude if I sat somewhere else. She was busy fixing a bouquet of flowers in the bathtub-sized kitchen sink. Snipping stems and popping off dead flower heads. It was warm enough to remove my parka but not my parka pants. From the waist down I looked half chimera, too fat to move with thin, socked feet.

I held the steaming cup of tea between my hands. "What do you do now?" I asked. The tea was still too hot to drink and there was no one else to ask her this.

She turned and looked at me with the same stare and almost smile that her son liked to throw around. "Whatever I want!"

I got nervous and looked down. Took a sip of tea and burned my tongue.

The Soncal family gatherings were vastly different from my own. There was alcohol at the lodge and tea in our reading room. There were rifle sightings and headshots at the lodge and evening devotions in our home. There was big, sweaty laughing in the lodge. And police tape running across our courtyard.

I liked pretending to be their other son. I liked taking pictures with Beau's parents during our award ceremonies and our graduation celebration. I liked having sets of arms around me, all three of us smiling at the camera. Me, a Mother, and a Father. I liked having a brother in Beau. I liked not being alone. I liked it all so much I ignored the smirks and dead chimera, and forgot all about devotions and courtyards.

I ignored a lot of Beau's manners. When he invited me to meet some of his college buddies he brought back to the lodge one winter break, I ignored his retelling of his most recent heartbreaking tendencies. I tried to ignore how all his buddies had their own breaking tendencies. I hoped they ignored my lack of them.

I told Beau about Itzel that visit. He nudged and asked for details. Details I knew weren't meant for sharing. He lost interest when I told him: "She's beautiful!" "Mmmm, nice!" "She's smart!" "Yeah?" "She's kind." That bored him, and I think that's where our paths diverged. He pursued excitement and shiny new things. I ventured toward creating my own family.

We kept in touch but with no urgency. He'd been too busy to attend our wedding. He'd been too busy to send an invite to his. But then my research popped up on the Common Goal circuit. My engine proved useful. And suddenly we were brothers again. Grown and married. Meeting Sarathi and witnessing Beau gush over her, led me to believe he changed. That his tendencies had mended.

∗∗∗

I felt dizzy, unsure of Kin. She sat between me and the door. I hadn't noticed until that moment how strong Kin looked. Her bare arms were sinewy and toned. I knew I wasn't fit enough to fight her. I'd have to pretend my way around her.

I finished pouring the coffees and cautiously approached her. Placed her mug down like a peace offering. In return, she handed an envelope to me. It was plain white, no writing on either side. "Read it," she said. "Then I'll explain."

Inside was a single piece of paper, printed front and back. It was addressed to the GEM Employee Relations Officer, dated two years ago. I scanned through the introductory paragraph: Shakina Hakim, formal complaints, Aristide 'Beau' Soncal.

That sticky gum feeling returned. I shuffled my feet with no relief.

The complaints started with compliments. He liked her eyes. He liked them a lot. He liked her hair. He suggested she smile more. He said she was too pretty to scowl. I could imagine the look on his face with each "compliment." I heard the half laughs he gave even when no joke was told. I knew this Beau well.

Next came unnecessary touch— hand against hand, hand on shoulder, a hand moving down her back. After the fourth incident of unnecessary touch, she requested a personal safety sensor. She set a meter radius around her when she was alone. In her office. In the hallways. In the lounge. In the atrium. In her lab. On the tram. She wrote that he ignored the yellow warning the sensor produced when he stepped inside that radius. And he did so seven times over the course of her first three months at GEM. She listed each activation. He knew better than to touch her and set off the red-light warning. That would have been automatically reported to GEM Security and his face would pop up on their watch list. Two red-light violations would have resulted in expulsion from GEM and a tarnished work and social record. As far as I know, there is no such punishment for yellow warnings.

Slight relief came when I saw the dates between complaints spread out. In those four years, spanning between Umoja-17 planning and Umoja-18's completion, Shakina became a work-sister for me, a home-sister for Itzel and an Aunty for Mai.

But then Umoja-18 ended in success and the complaints sprang up again. The yellow-light activation data accumulated. Seventeen in two months.

My hands became hardened knots as I read my own name as a witness to his disdain. The time he bumped into her as we walked down a hall filled my mind. His snide remark was spelled out on page two: "Wear a bell, Shakina! I can't always be looking down to see you." His words stuck out like gravel in dirty pink gum.

I tried not to be angry at her but I wanted to ask *Why didn't you tell me? Or Itzel?* But the answers were in the questions. She couldn't have told either of us. She knew as well as anyone that Itzel didn't fit in at GEM. Telling Itzel would have jeopardized Shakina's legitimacy.

And Beau was my pretend-brother.

In the six months following the Umoja-18 mission, she went through three job reviews, four unannounced office searches. Beau rejected her reports calling them inadequate and "error riddled." Her recommendations and requests were denied. Her budget was slashed. Her team was reduced. Her work load increased.

And all that time, I hadn't noticed. Or maybe I had and just ignored it.

Itzel noticed. We were cleaning up after dinner. It was the fifth dinner Shakina had declined to attend when Itzel asked, "Have you talked to Shakina lately?"

I placed a sealed dish of leftovers in the fridge and shrugged, "No. She's been pretty busy. Why?"

There was a pause and a worried look on Itzel's face. "It just seems strange that she hasn't come over in a while."

I let out a sigh. "It's been busy. Lots of changes and planning. I'm sure she's just feeling the pressure like all of us."

"If that's all it is, fine. But. . ."

"But what?" I asked.

"I don't know. I just miss her, I guess."

"I'll stop by her office tomorrow. Check in on her."

I tried to recall if I followed through. I looked down at the complaint and accepted that I probably hadn't.

I put the paper back in the envelope. I slid it back to her and asked, "Is this why you tried to . . ."

"Kill him? No. This was just a reason to quit GEM, not kill him." She grabbed the envelope and put it back in her filing cabinet. "I wanted to stop him from getting access to the Novi Dom."

I sat up, stunned. "Kin, that's—" I didn't know what to say.

She finished for me. "Crazy? I know. But I figured since he and I were the only ones who knew about it, eliminating him would keep it hidden."

"You made that conclusion based on how he treated you? I don't mean to belittle this at all, Kin, but that's extreme."

She drew in a slow breath. "People have to wear personal protection sensors at GEM. One of the most secure and monitored places in the world. It's not just him."

I had to look away from her for a moment. How I had not questioned their presence at GEM was beyond me.

"There's plenty of people who feel entitled to everything. They're greedy, hell bent on dominating. They act like that's what they were placed on Earth to do, like it's their sacred right. Subdue and dominate." She rocked back in her chair. "They've been using that line for thousands of years. . . I'm sure they'd do it again on the Novi Dom."

"You would have gone to prison, Kin," I said, eyeing her.

"I know. But he'd be dead. I'd be as close to dead. . ."

"What stopped you?" I asked.

She rocked back to sitting. With a sigh, she said, "I saw him with his family." She sounded relieved and defeated over it. She shook her head, studying the floor. "I was right there, finger on the trigger. Timed his whole schedule. He came out of his house, right on time. With his daughter."

She paused and I could see it. I could see Beau flutter his hand into the sky and playfully coax his daughter to catch-the-butterfly. I could almost hear her squealing as she skipped and jumped, her fingers nicking his just as he lifted his hand higher. He'd play this game with Mai, too. Two little butterfly catchers, trying to hold his hands.

"Then his wife and their son raced to catch up," she said, voice tempered, eyes focused. "I had a clean shot." She stared into my torso, like she saw him there. I wanted to turn away but then she blinked. Something softened in her. "I couldn't play God." She raised her gaze to mine. "As much of a menace as he was— as he is," she said, "he's a good father."

I nodded. I knew that Beau too.

40

I **didn't know this woman sitting** next to me— this Kin with Shakina's mannerisms. After several minutes of studying her profile, I asked, "Why'd you change your name?"

"Shakina didn't fit anymore," was all she said.

I was reminded of how willingly I let Beau rename me. It wasn't just because everyone at the school said Tolulopé as if they had marbles in their mouths. But I wanted to leave Tolulopé, and Lopé, back home, dead with his parents. I didn't want to be that version of me as quickly as possible. A new country, a new school, a new family— it felt like the perfect time to escape the past.

When she didn't offer another reason, I told her I needed a break. I didn't look at her when I said that. I just got up and left. As the door closed behind me, I heard her say she'd be looking for the anomaly and that lunch was being served if I was hungry.

I wasn't hungry. I was uneasy. I was unsure of this moon-monitoring Kin who confessed treason and murder plots. I was unsure if I could, or should, trust her.

I forced myself to smile and nod at people until I was outside again. The sun was hot and high. I shielded my eyes and looked around for a sign post to point the way to the dining hall. Maybe Itzel and Mai would be there. Maybe seeing them would help me settle.

I plodded along the path, fighting through the thick fog of everything Shakina said. The Novi Dom. The harassment. The thought of her, hiding in bushes, sighting Beau. I didn't understand that line of thinking, how she'd been driven to that. The Shakina I knew was logical. Rational. *Where did she get a gun?*

A voice pulled me out of my thoughts. Its familiar and deliberate cadence stopped me. I looked around, searching for its source, but all

I saw was tall grass on either side of the path. Trees and bushes in the distance. I tipped my head side to side until the words came clear.

"A recent report from Great Brazil has indicated a rise in waterborne illnesses. Scientists are still unable to determine the cause." The voice moved along my left, but there was no one there. I leaned in its direction, listening harder. "The number of deaths reported has reached twenty-thousand. The coastal leaders have called for martial law. However, the fishing community has pushed back, citing economic decline and record reports of starvation."

I closed my eyes and had to steady myself. I'd forgotten the world in less than two months.

"In the Mid-Eurasian regions, the male population continues to decline. Radio-nuclear researchers have correlated the shortened lifespan to the soil rehabilitation efforts of the 130s. One in three men who participated in the decades' old effort—" The source moved again, further from the path. I strained to find it. "—live past sixty-five. Violence broke out in Toronto this week as the domestic terrorist group, the Doomsdayers, continue to clash with the Canadian Armed Forces. Several hundred have been arrested. Canada's Spokesperson has released a comment stating the Dominion wishes to prevent further violence and destruction of property. The terrorist group's leader has called for more transparency in government spending, specifically for the Galaxy Exploration Mission—"

I needed to know more. I trod through the waist-high grass, following the voice. The stiff reeds pushed back. Their edges cut at my hands.

"In Portugal, UN soldiers have been deployed. . ."

That halted me. UN soldiers were last ditch efforts before subduing an aggressive nation. Two months and the world was falling apart.

I pressed another meter in the direction of the news when a man popped up. I stumbled backward. He grabbed my arm to steady me.

"You okay?" he asked. "Lost the path?" He tapped his pants pocket and the broadcast stopped.

"I... I... hadn't heard world news in a while," I admitted. "I didn't mean to sneak up on you."

He waved me off. "I returned the favor by the looks of it. We're evenly matched." He removed a dirt caked glove and extended his hand. "Quamy."

"Tah," I said, giving his thick-skinned hand a shake.

He squinted at me for a moment. "Dr. Morant's husband, yeah?"

I relaxed a little. "Yeah."

His face widened into a smile. "Welcome!"

"Thank you," I said, relieved by his enthusiasm.

"Really hope you all plan on staying. Her work has contributed a lot here." He swept his calloused hand behind him. A wind worked through the grass as if on cue. "It would be great to have her here permanently."

I tensed at the word *permanently* but quickly smiled when he turned back around. "We're taking it one day at a time. But she and my daughter have enjoyed being here. I'm grateful for that."

"We're glad to have them, Tah."

He was busy working his glove back on when I remarked about the last thing reported. About Portugal and the U.N. "I didn't realize tensions had worsened."

He looked around and leaned in, lowering his voice. "I was a news junkie before I got here. Old habits are hard to shake."

I nodded to hide my frustration. I wanted to know more about the world. Not him. I asked if there were more radios. "It'd be nice to know what's going on."

"Oh sure," he said, "you can borrow them from the visitor center. But," he leaned in again. "Just between you and me, it doesn't help."

I frowned. "Doesn't help what?"

He took a breath and shrugged. "It doesn't help. Knowing everything doesn't help."

I shook my head, bothered, and said, "I don't understand what you're saying. It doesn't help who? You?"

He raised both hands and leaned back. "I've been here eight years. I've seen this place thrive. And I've seen the world shrivel. I can't help what's happening in Brazil, South Africa, India— I can't help the rest of the world."

I cut him off, "So why listen?"

He studied me for a moment. "Knowing what's going on out there motivates me here. Confirms a lot for me."

I let his words hang between us before I asked if I was on the path to the dining hall.

He smiled and said, "Yeah, half a kilometer. Can't miss it."

I thanked him and pushed my way out of the grass and back to the lumpy path. I glanced back and waited for him to duck back into his work before I started walking again. I limped my way back to the lab. Back to this new Kin. Back to find the anomaly. I needed to figure it out, so that we–everyone on Earth–could get out. Shakina found the Novi Dom. Maybe I could convince this Kin to find it again.

41

Kin was on a call when I returned to her office. I listened as the person on the other end patched us into SOL3 satellites. The satellites are stationed closer to the edge of the Oort cloud, monitoring activity near the Dragon's Gate.

How quickly would they find the hack? I couldn't help my paranoia. I didn't know who she was dealing with, I felt like I hardly knew her. When did she become so covert?

I watched and listened, fidgeted nervously as they talked. Plenty of orbital racers slingshot their hyperdrive crafts around Neptune. Some with hopes of sneaking past the Unified Nations' security fleet for added notoriety. Only a few got away with it. Most flyers unknowingly triggered the securities' signal sweep. It would hit them with an EMR, knocking out their power and slapping on a twelve-year flying ban— a lifetime in space travel. What would be the punishment for an alleged dissenter turned fugitive, and now a hacker? I'd lose everything, but I had no other choice. And I believed none of us did.

Kin gave me a thumbs up an hour later. Whoever was on the other end of the call said she owed him. Big time. "As always, I don't know you, you don't know—"

She hung up before they finished and turned to me. "We're in."

My nervousness turned to excitement as I watched an elaborate data tree branch across her screen. We were one step closer to escape.

Kin slid through one back channel after another until she found the logs corresponding to the Umoja-19 leap. The visual rendering of the mission sent a rush of relief through me. It was there, untouched. I almost cried.

We copied and down flowed the file. Saved it in four separate data vaults. I didn't want to lose any of it, ever again. I wasn't sure how I was going to study it further from this ramshackle of a building with outdated systems. But at least I had the data. I promised myself I'd figure the rest out later.

Once secured, I played the entire three attempts to show Kin. I told her she could run a NeutSig scan herself if she didn't believe me. She waved me off and focused on the footage. As we watched it I saw nothing different, but Kin kept rubbing her eyes. I asked her if something was wrong, she said, "I don't know. Something about it makes my eyes hurt. Let me try something."

I nodded and she went to work, proving her patchwork system was more than capable. It was impressive. She isolated the darkweave distortion and inverted the wavelength, turning the black of space blue. Then she slowed the playback to a quarter speed and turned off the overhead lights.

I hit play when she was ready. The expected sequence of events happened in their expected order: the Umoja craft emitted its transposition beam, the beam pierced the Dragon, a pause. But then something unexpected happened. Ripples appeared. Slowly moving away from the craft. Spreading out and out as if the craft tapped a pool of water.

My mouth went dry. My heart thundered in my chest.

Kin paused the video as the ripples reached the edge of the Dragon.

"What the hell is that?" she asked, quietly.

"I have no idea," I whispered back.

"You said you ran a neut scan, right?"

I didn't answer immediately. My mind flipped between bewilderment and wonder. I'd never seen anything like it. What I saw as just droplets was a whole ocean of something unknown.

"Um, yeah," I said, "when I first found it. No neutrinic sig."

"What about a signal sweep?" she asked.

I couldn't look away from the screen. "Okay," I said.

She moved cautiously. Tapped slowly and quietly at the keys. CGUL analyzed the paused frame. As it worked, Kin asked, "Do you think it's a signal net?"

I didn't know so I didn't respond. But a signal net, like what the UN security fleet used to monitor activity, wouldn't distort the space around it. Far as I or anyone understood. And it wouldn't stop a transposition beam. At least not the ones we used.

We waited in silence, both locked on the image. There was an edge of fear in me the longer I stared at it. The same kind of fear a child has in the dark. There's a terrifying mystery to it.

I jumped when Kin spoke again. "I've never seen one this big. Who do you think— you think ALN did this?"

"No." I shook my head. "They don't have the tech for something this big."

"China?"

"No," I said. "Why would anyone block a mission?" I thought about the UN soldiers deploying to Portugal. There'd be no befitting punishment for a whole nation sabotaging the Common Goal. Then I thought the only people trying to stay on Earth were people like Sol and Kin. . . and Itzel. I shook the thought loose and twisted my attention back to the frozen image while CGULs analyzed it.

I wondered if it had always been there? This. . . veil? Dr. Dragonimassi never wrote about it in all her articles and books, and diary entries. Six crafts successfully crossed through the Dragon's Gate before Umoja-19. Where'd it come from? And if it had always been there, what activated it this time?

CGULs chimed. The analysis finished. We both leaned in, surprised by the report.

"It has a modulation sequence. . ." Kin said, almost as a question. "It's faint. And brief." She got up and turned the lights back on. "It doesn't make sense— a signal net would have a longer modulation sequence, especially for something this big. And an origin signature. This doesn't make sense, Tah."

Nothing makes sense! I thought. I pinched the bridge of my nose trying to piece things together. "What if we ping it?" I suggested. I didn't know what else to do.

She raised an eyebrow. "With what?"

I sat up. "Well, like you said, there'd be an origin signature. What if we echoed the signal back? A reply might offer more information." I shrugged when I heard myself. I was throwing anything and hoping for something to stick.

She was quiet for a moment, mulled it over. "We could use the SOL3 satellite maintenance transmitter."

"Are you sure that's wise?" I asked, wary of another charge on my record.

She shrugged. "They only get checked if something goes wrong. And if someone does see the sequence, it's so brief it'll look like background noise."

I considered the risk-benefit ratio. Seemed low enough. "Okay, but we'll need a channel for the reply."

Kin was already tapping her way into the SOL3 maintenance channel. "Tah, whatever this is, it stopped us from crossing over. We have to accept that *that* might be the response."

I leaned back, she was right. Why would anyone answer the door they just slammed shut? How do we convince them to?

When I was in grade school, I had a hard time making friends. The majority of the children were locals. They lived well enough but not safeguarded like my family and the handful of ALN children like me. They kept their friendships closed and locked me out. They made sure I knew I wasn't welcome. They hurled insults if I sat too close, or stood too close. Or walked too close. While my mother eased my pain when the kids made fun of me, it was my father who had helped me do something about it.

"Everyone wants to prove two things in life, Lopé: one– that they are good and, two– that they are smart. Give them the opportunity to do so." He patted my shoulder and said, "Ask one of them for help, or give them a puzzle."

"What about a riddle?" I asked.

Kin turned to me again, questions gathering between her brows.

"What about Tinget's paradox?" I said. I looked at the display. The frozen veil stared back. "If anyone can solve that, it would be whoever did this."

42

Five days passed since we set up the signal and sent it out. Five days that I woke before dawn, plodded through damp grass to the lab. I put the coffee maker to work over and over again. Five days I waved off Kin when she asked if I'd eaten or taken a break. Five days of Itzel and Mai visiting the office to coax me home in the evenings. I knew we'd get an answer. And I wanted to be there when we did.

Over the course of those five days, I assured Itzel everything was fine. I was just excited. But that was a lie.

At GEM I focused on the Common Goal. I knew the role I played and I did it to my best ability. When the failure occurred, I did my job and found what could have caused it. And then I was stopped from doing my job. Forced into submission. When finally able to resume my work, I found out that the Novi Dom had been located and that the person who found it hid it. All of that on top of the reported forest fires in sixty-two countries. And floods in twenty. And tornadoes all over. And hurricanes everywhere. And earthquakes underneath it all. And famines. And outbreaks. And riots. And all of it happening all over the world. All at once. And I was sitting easy, in a glorified eco-commune, waiting for an answer to a paradox.

Nothing was fine. I felt worthless. And I was furious.

In the dining hall on the fifth night, the tables were full. Live music played just beneath the happy sounds of people enjoying themselves. I sat between Mai and Itzel and did my best to stay sweet. I laughed when everyone else did. Nodded at just about everything said. I passed the salt and pepper when they were passed to me. But all I wanted was a reply.

I watched the sky just past the hall's entrance and hoped to see a morse code signal flashing the solution. I wanted the heavens to crack open and the face of someone's God tell me to knock it off and leave Them alone. I would have settled for anything.

I looked at all the people sitting at our table. I wanted to yell at them. Ask them how they could be so selfish. How could they just sit and eat and garden all damn day when the world was falling apart. I couldn't sit there any longer pretending like everything was fine.

"Izzie," I whispered when I noticed a lull in the conversation.

"Yes, hon?" Worry took over her face when she saw me.

"Can we talk?"

"Ok."

She moved around me, and crouched between Mai, Marteen and his parents. They quickly agreed to watch our daughter and even suggested a sleepover. We thanked them and kissed Mai goodnight.

There was a sliver of a moon that night. The air was damp and cold. A breeze carried the smell of earth and manure. Frogs and crickets crooned their nightly racket. Our footsteps crunched over gravel and twigs. Everything grated against me.

When we couldn't hear the dining hall anymore, she asked, "What's wrong, dear?"

I tried to be vague at first. "Everything," I said. "Everything is wrong, Izzie."

"What is bothering you, specifically?" she asked.

I scoffed. "I am having a hard time here, Izzie. I don't see how this is helping."

She stopped midstride. "What do you mean?"

I bit my lip then said, "I want to go back to GEM. I think I can be of better use there."

She stared at me. Silently. Mouth slightly agape. The last bit of sun showed the furrowed lines in her face.

"I can patch things up with Beau. We can—"

"We?"

"Yes, you, me, Mai. We, us. We can go back and—"

"And do what?" she asked, tight in tone.

I expected resistance. "If you don't want to go back with me, that's fine," I lied.

"You'd leave Mai?"

"She'll come with me!"

Itzel huffed out a laugh. "Have you asked her about this? Have you considered what she wants to do?"

"Izzie, she's a child," I said, confused by her reasoning.

"Yes, a child who is becoming her own self here. She's learning a lot. She's making friends."

"She had friends at GEM!"

"Abby? Beau's daughter? When was the last time they had a playdate?" I couldn't recall. "That's not fair, Itzel."

"It's not fair to make decisions without considering her well-being, my dear. You're a fugitive. You think they'll just accept you with open arms? No harm done? What happens to Mai if they aren't so forgiving?"

I snapped at her, full of anger. "What isn't fair is that everyone here acts like everything will be okay! As if the rest of the world doesn't matter! There are starving and dying children all over the world. This spot hasn't solved anything. This isn't solving the pandemics, or world hunger. All these crops can't feed more than a couple thousand people. You all haven't helped anyone but yourselves!"

I didn't need the sun to show me I'd gone too far. Again. That I'd said enough to put space between us. Again. That I'd broken promises again.

A foul silence hung between us, too thick for an apology to cut. I didn't even realize we stood almost two meters from each other. Could have been a hundred for how far away she felt.

She spoke with a soft voice in the darkening night. "I don't understand, Tah. The man I married always searched for the truth." Her voice wavered. "I think you could find some here."

My heart broke, but my anger hardened against it. "The truth is there's only 85 years left on the clock, Itzel! None of the Spots will be here in 85 years!"

I heard the gravel as she stepped toward me. "You might be right, Tah. Eighty-five years is not a long time. But there are millions of people working on solutions to allow us to stay. If a billion people focused their energy and generated communities like this in their regions, great things could happen." She was toe to toe with me now. "At GEM, it's less than a thousand people making decisions for everyone else. I'll take my chances here." She gently touched my arm then started back toward the dining hall.

My heart raced in rage. "I'm going back to GEM," I said loud enough to silence the insects and frogs.

I heard her pause. "If you go back, you're going back alone."

My ribs cracked as she walked away. "You're leaving me?" I asked.

She didn't even turn around to answer. "No, my love. You're leaving us."

Night sounds swallowed the rhythm of her steps. Her words echoed within me. I stumbled when I tried to follow her like even the night knew I wasn't worthy.

Seventeen years. I put seventeen years toward the Common Goal.

Forever Onward!

It was all I'd known. I was raised up believing that it was the only solution.

Onward Toward the Goal!

She tried to tell me on my first day at the Spot, and encouraged me to look inward. To rest. To take time to understand what I'd just been through. But I was never trained to look inward. I always focused out there, where the sun can't quite reach.

As I stood there, alone in the night, I had nowhere else to look but at myself.

43

I walked, sat, stood, and slept on eggshells the whole twenty-four hours after that fight. Itzel and I moved around each other like moons on different orbits, circling Mai's needs and wants. We crossed paths a few times and my whole body bent in Itzel's direction. Then she'd leave the room or go outside, or strike up a conversation with someone she knew. I'd spin away in agony, waiting for the next time.

She said she wanted me to find truth at the Spot. So I made that my duty. Instead of spiraling out in the lab hoping for a response, I started attending meetings around the Spot. If this was where Itzel and Mai were going to be, then I made it my business to understand it better.

The rain collection meeting had been reasonably interesting. Its opening devotions started slow with some drums, a prayer asking for inspiration, followed by some brief and uplifting readings. That brought back childhood memories, in the family courtyard. Mom and dad, uncles and aunties. Cousins and neighbor kids. I hadn't thought of devotions in decades. I never thought to apply them to meetings.

Then there was a presentation of the year's rainfall, the successes and failures. Then they opened it up for discussion. I was surprised there was a time limit for each person. Pleased that after someone spoke they didn't speak again until everyone else with something to say said it. The facilitator even asked me if I had thoughts. I was so busy observing, I turned around to see who she was pointing at. I politely declined and went about predicting who would speak next. As interesting as it was, it didn't hold my attention after the first hour. I chose the back wall or the corner closest to the exit for the next three meetings.

The last one I attended was intolerable. I shifted left to right and kept my arms crossed as I half listened. The speaker in the thatch-roofed, two walled hut, kept pausing halfway through his sentences. I wasn't sure if it was for dramatic effect or that everything seemed to move slower at the Spot.

I looked around the squat space, expecting to see others stretching their necks or taking deep breaths, wanting the meeting to be over. But the fifty-some people, old and young, sat poised, thoroughly engrossed in the subject: compost! A stomach-turning discussion on precisely how much dung should be mixed with which pile of chicken bones and corn husks.

The presentation was nearing its second hour. *Just leave* I told myself each time I blinked to hide a yawn or an eye roll. I could have left, but the suspicious smiles I'd get on my way out kept me in place. People stood along the open sides of the hut like thick bars blocking the way.

It wasn't like this at GEM. GEM was built on the efficiency model. Not everyone needed to know everything, just what their duties were. The decisions were made based on the goal of getting out. It was the minutiae of getting the right bolt in the right hole that took the most time. Not the decision-making. If someone wasn't an expert they didn't give their ideas. What would their ideas be based on? A feeling? A notion? There was none of that at GEM.

"And now, we have Dr. Julian, who will answer some questions."

My God, the hands that shot into the air, like toys on a timer. Thirty of them waved to the presenter. I took a deep breath and tried my best to not look annoyed. I missed GEM. I missed the need-to-know basis of decision making. The only thing keeping me in the meetings was what Itzel said: If I left, I'd be leaving alone.

Honestly, I just wanted to be in the lab. I wanted to refresh the screens, ensure the signal was strong, that the random echo was still rebounding off the veil. I just wanted to be there when the answer was received.

I promptly left the meeting when it was over. Three hours and forty-eight minutes listening to the how and why behind different piles of waste and dung. I passed the signage for it a little ways up the path, I rolled my eyes and kept moving. I cringed at the idea of Dr. Jones or Commander Bierdot seeing me attend a presentation on literal shit.

***

In the two weeks of being at the Spot, I'd learned my way from our round-faced cottage to the dining hall, the visitor center, and the lab. These meetings and presentations opened up new routes to take, new plots to see, new people to meet. And each time, I felt Itzel and I drawing closer to each other. But there was something about all of it that still made my skin crawl. The slow motion of everything— like which particular material of which particular pail to catch the water should be used in which neighborhood for the permanent residents. Or the homey pride in making everything by hand. Handmade blankets on handmade benches, sat on by people in handmade garments, talking about their handmade baskets to carry their handmade candles to their handmade mud huts that housed their handmade hopes and dreams.

Or maybe it was the dirt. The different kinds of dirt and the way each kind of dirt elicited a holy expression of interest and gratitude. Maybe it was GEM's lingering influence on me, but I looked at dirt as something that should be removed and banished from living spaces. At the Spot, a pile of dirt held the same importance as a moon rock rich in astrydium. They couldn't travel between stars with dirt! But by the way the people who worked in the dirt talked about dirt, they made space travel sound frivolous.

Maybe it was the pleasantness in everyone. The regard for each person and every animal. The wonderment in their eyes when a butterfly landed, or a bird took flight. Or when a gnat farted! Saying 'hello' or 'hi' or 'good morning', 'good afternoon', 'good evening' to every single person, felt like punishment. Like writing the same sentences over and over and there wasn't really a lesson to learn. Having to regard everyone that crossed my path made me want to be in the lab all the more.

I entered the visitor center and gave my regards to all the Greeters with a well-practiced "Hello, just looking, thank you." Then I made my way to the list of activities for the day. There were nature walks which made me laugh because all there was was nature. Nature threatened to break through the cracks in our cabin. And at some point, I came to the realization that I'd never been in nature so thoroughly. Not in my whole life. I went from compound to private school, to college labs, to a domed city. Being *in* nature felt like a fish flopping in the forest.

I wanted to enjoy the Spot. I wanted to ease into it like a warm bath. Let all its slow-motion essence swallow me up and emerge refreshed and calm. I wanted to love it like Itzel loved it. I wanted to come home in the hot afternoon, smudged all over with plant dyes, and dirt, and maybe even a little manure, beaming at the fruits of my labor.

Maybe that was it. The immediate reward in everything they did. I spent seventeen years working toward getting a ship through the Dragon's Gate. And even when that was achieved, we needed to get humans across and then we needed to make sure we found a planet and we needed to make sure a living organism could survive on that planet. How many years or decades were we from completing the Common Goal? How many generations until we could grip the soil on the Novi Dom and brag about its mineral composition?

That's what it was: I resented the Spot. I resented how right and humble they all were. And if they were right, then I had to accept everything I'd been taught my entire life was a lie.

44

I don't know who started the lie. I don't know if anyone does. Sam tried his best to tip my scales in his direction about the Common Goal. "A reactionary solution for a reaction system!" He said that so many times, I stopped reacting. If he was a bigger man, less frail with better balance, I think he would have beat it into me. Not that Sam was a violent man, just passionate.

Sol laughed at the Common Goal despite his suffering. Kin came undone when she found the Novi Dom. They all knew a lot about the past. Maybe too much. That was the basis of all their concerns about the legitimacy of the Goal. But the words that stirred me the most were Itzel's: "The man I married always searched for the truth. I think you could find some here."

***

I stood in front of the events' infoscreen in the visitors' center, trying to find my next informational to attend. By then, I'd gotten used to the routine of devotions, presentation, consultation, and possible resolution. I admit, I was impressed by the commitment everyone showed to carry out the group's resolution, when there was one. Even if people felt differently in the beginning, and they often clashed, when a decision was made everyone supported it. I don't think that's how the Common Goal was established. But like I said, I'm not sure who started it.

Just as the screen refreshed, a man approached me from the side. At first I thought he had bad vision and needed to get closer to the information. But each time I stepped away, he inched closer to me.

"Can I help you?" I asked, finally looking at him. I was surprised to see him staring at me.

"You're Dr. Morant's husband, right? The uh—" he snapped his fingers while he searched for the right words. "The chief scientist at GEM, right?"

His tone startled me more than the question, but I wasn't sure how to answer. Technically, I hadn't been fired. "In a manner of speaking, yes."

"So what do you think of all these talks?" he asked, sharpening his gaze.

I glanced around but no one was paying attention to this man or me. I felt that maybe someone should. He didn't have the inviting attitude everyone else at the Spot had mastered.

I hesitantly smiled and said, "They've been informative." And most of them had been. I learned that I didn't care much about composting or collecting rainwater. I didn't say that out loud. He didn't seem like the type to take a joke.

"You're pretty eager to leave a lot of them," he said, stepping close enough that I felt heat coming off him.

"I'm sorry, who are you?" I asked, feeling uneasy that he'd been watching me.

"I'm a resident of the Spot. Have been for ten years now."

I glanced around again, hoping one of the greeters would stop greeting and help me. A guard would have, or at least barked out a warning. But here, I was on my own.

"Ten years is a significant amount of time," I said, taking steps toward the door.

He stepped in front of me. He was short and sturdy, carrying danger in his eyes. "I hope you can appreciate how much Dr. Morant has contributed here, and around the world."

I wanted to get away, but not cause a scene. "Yes, I do," I said, "I'm constantly humbled by her impact. Now, excuse me, I am trying to—"

He cut me off. "What have you done?" His whole face and body flared.

"Excuse me?" I asked, taking a step back.

"What's your contribution? You've been attending all these meetings, last one in, first one out. What are you giving in return? What are you leaving behind when it's time for you to go?"

"*What?*" I asked, feeling my anger rise.

"What is *your contribution*?" he said, slowly, exaggerating the sounds as if I didn't understand.

"I'm a Global Contributor," I said with Warden Nattle's gravel in my voice.

The man cackled at my response only making me more inflamed.

"You think your little engine was a contribution to humanity?"

I clenched my jaw and took several steps back. I couldn't lose control there. I spoke slowly, trying to keep my calm. "I am only trying to learn about the Spot and–"

"And take it for your precious Novi Dom!" he jabbed. "That's all you are! A taker! Just take, take, take!"

Finally, a staff member approached and asked us to leave. I was glad for it. I apologized as I went. But outside didn't give me any relief. He was like a fly on food.

"You think because you're married to Dr. Morant you get a free pass, huh?"

I should have kept my mouth shut. But I stupidly replied, loudly with knotted fists, "I never said that!"

"You don't have to say it. It's the way you don't appreciate anything! I've been watching you at the meetings. The eye rolls, the yawns. You don't appreciate being here!"

"Jax!"

We turned to see Kin standing behind us.

"Oh, Kin! What perfect timing! I expect you're going to defend him," the man, Jax, said, arms folded across his wide chest.

"I'm not defending anyone," she said coolly.

Jax let out another cackle. "No, but you sure did a good job getting the Council to agree to let him stay."

A shadow moved across Kin's face. "If you are suggesting that as a Council member I persuaded the other members to allow Dr. Morant to stay here, I would advise you to read the Community Covenant again. The insinuation that any individual has sway over the institution of the Council denigrates the foundation on which the Spot was built. Need I remind you, we operate in accordance with our shared Covenant. And if it assures you, I stepped out when the Council decided the matter."

She did not look in my direction as she spoke, reminding me that I had no say in any of this. "However," she continued, "if you have a problem with the decision made based on the principles outlined in the Council's Code of Conduct, then I suggest you submit an appeal and wait for a response."

I looked back to Jax. His bull posture tamed. His chin tipped down. "I apologize for the insult, Kin. But some of us are concerned about his presence. He is a Dominion fugitive. If they want, they can come with force to take him."

The skin around my neck stung. The scabs from the collar only recently shed.

Kin eased. "Your concern is valid, Jax. The Council consulted at length." She paused and closed her eyes. Her voice was soft when she spoke again. "We aren't infallible. Collective decisions do not keep us impervious to mistakes. However, mistakes are future lessons. Should Dr. Morant's presence pose an actual threat to the Spot, not an assumed one, I'm sure the Council will adapt accordingly."

Jax turned to me, a gentler man. "I apologize, Dr. Morant. I may be a long-term resident, but old habits die hard." He extended a hand and a sincere smile.

I received both with some hesitation. Then he shook Kin's hand and was gone. Just like that. No guards. No Auxen. No batons cracking at the backs of his knees.

I had assumed over the weeks I'd been at the Spot that arguments, fights, disagreements, skirmishes didn't happen. That somehow, everyone there just learned to suppress that side of themselves. Maybe they learned how to tie their anger up with a smile, then bury it somewhere in the Spot's ninety-three thousand square kilometers— a fact I learned in one of the informationals. After that surprise confrontation, I learned a little more about the Spot.

Kin motioned me to follow her toward a shady path with benches. We sat silently for a moment. A cluster of teenagers passed before I asked, "People are allowed to get angry here?"

She smirked. "Everyone gets angry. Some people have a hard time letting go of their anger."

I quietly chuckled and shifted the conversation away from me. "So, you're a Council member? You didn't mention that before."

She closed her eyes and nodded.

I stared at her until she peeked at me. "*You* ran for council?"

Like an annoyed older sister, she glared at me with fake annoyance then rolled her eyes. "No one *runs* for anything here. The Council is elected by secret ballot. Permanent residents only."

"How do they know who to vote for?"

"They vote for whomever they wish."

"And everyone is okay with the results?" I asked.

She leaned back and talked at the drying leaves overhead. "The community has an annual conference, a few days to go over the issues and the accomplishments and goals for the future. A day of prayer and meditation. Then there is a day to vote."

I thought back to the last time I voted. It was for President Cooper, his pre-approved cabinet and his trillion hheq investment in GEM. All I had to do was submit my vote with a thumb print through my rello. It took all of twenty seconds on the tram heading into work.

"That sounds really. . . special," I said.

"It is," she clasped her hands in her lap and nodded to herself. "It's an honor to be trusted with the well-being of the community. But it is a lot. It is taxing. It is exhausting. A lot of responsibility to serve thirty-five-hundred people."

"Did you even want to be on the Council?" I asked.

She let out a laugh that played up the path. "Heavens no! I was shocked! I hadn't even been here long. Sixteen months, maybe. But it's a sacred process here, so I was, and am, honored to serve."

"How'd it feel?" I asked.

"What? Getting voted on?"

"No..." I looked around, making sure no one was within earshot. Old paranoias are hard to shake. "How'd it feel when you first got here?"

"Oh. . ." She took a deep breath. "That was hard." We met each other's gaze and she repeated herself, nodding. "That was really hard."

I found myself choked up and looked at the ground. "I didn't know what to expect when Sol told me about this place. I just figured it'd be like GEM, maybe a little dirtier," I said with a sad laugh. "I mean, not really.

But I didn't know how different it'd be." I paused to let a young family pass, watched as their children chased falling leaves. "I'm learning so much and I'm so grateful to be here. And everyone, well almost everyone, is so nice, but it just feels. . . feels like. . ."

"Like what?" she asked.

"Like the bottom will fall out," I said. "Like this won't last. And truthfully, it feels like I'm just twiddling my thumbs while the world burns. People are really suffering out there and I'm going to meetings about rain water, compost, and whatever else." I let out a defeated sigh. "I just need something to do so I don't lose my mind."

"I felt the same way when I got here."

"Yeah?"

"Yeah. We came from GEM culture. It is hard for those two to mix. One is hell-bent on leaving. The other is bent on staying." She looked at me, a little sad behind her eyes. "I don't remember exactly how long it took for me to accept this culture, but it took time."

I heard a low rumble and looked past her to the west. In the distance, a bruise of clouds formed.

"Do you ever miss GEM?" I asked.

She studied the sky too, then said, "Not at all."

A gust of wind pulled leaves from branches and swept them further down the path. The orange and brown ones clattered as they went. We were the only ones there as far as I could tell. Just us and birds.

"Tah, places like GEM are for people like Beau."

I chewed on that for a moment, not sure what she meant. "People with boundary issues?" I asked, glancing at her.

"No. People who define themselves by what they have, can achieve, or can acquire. People who can be bought. Manipulated and controlled."

Suddenly I recalled that dream I had in prison when my family sat across from Beau and his family. And Beau was unwell, rotting from the inside. And a woman drank my blood. Dream interpretation always seemed like nonsense to me. I figured it was just my brain trying to make sense of the nonsensical turn of events. But there was something pathetically hungry about the way Beau stared at the woman who whispered like gold in my ear.

"All this time, I thought of Beau as the manipulator," I said, sheepishly. "I blamed him for everything that went wrong."

"He's a mess, but I would bet that somebody helped make him that way," she said. Her attention wandered with the wind.

I thought about Beau's parents, how they used high reward and humiliating punishment to counter his spoiled upbringing. How obsessed he was about being better than his father. How much his looks, prestige, and pedigree meant to him. The way he had to impress his superiors and name drop the powerful. Who was he talking to when I went to his office? Felix Santigo? She'd been to his house on several occasions. Were they friends? Lovers? Or did she offer him something better? Her company, Dyastryde, expedited astrydium harvesting and production on the moon. The same astrydium used to fuel the Umoja crafts. Maybe he was just doing his job.

"GEM felt too political," Kin said. "The Common Goal shouldn't be political."

"Do you think the Spot is the answer?" I asked.

She stared into the distance for a moment as the storm rolled closer. Then she turned and placed a hand on my shoulder. "Time will tell."

I was surprised by how much she sounded like my father, comforting and assured. She even patted my shoulder like he used to. She left, letting me know this storm was going to be a big one and I should head home soon. I thanked her, but stayed a little while longer. I hadn't seen or felt a storm in a long time. I marveled at the size of the clouds and how fast they moved. How swollen and dark they got. The sheet of rain in the distance looked like a tunnel between ground and sky. GEM kept us protected from the elements so well that I forgot what rain smelled like. I took a deep breath and could almost taste it. The trees were full of warning birds. The wind thrashed at the tallest branches, then swooped down and swept the fallen leaves up again. It was chaos and fury, things GEM would never allow.

45

Lightning shattered the sky that night, releasing an amount of rain I'd never witnessed. The Spot transformed into a series of rivers. I raced home as quickly as I could. Paths flooded, moats formed around clusters of cabins. Crops that stood up to my armpit were beaten flat. Itzel ran out to greet me, with a wool blanket canopied over her head. Mai put down towels inside, leading me straight to the bathroom to remove my clothes and put on the robe hanging on the wall. When I came back out, I had to pause. Itzel and Mai were curled into each other and Itzel was telling her about the Cloud Chasers.

"They are nomadic Spot residents that go into the desert toward the end of summer and convince the sky to cry."

Mai whispered, "How?"

"It's ancient wisdom," Itzel said. "Almost forgotten over the centuries-"

Lightning sparked. Thunder cracked. We all jumped silent. Then Mai fell to giggles.

By the time the storm passed, Mai fell asleep on the couch, I sat on the floor. Slowly, Itzel joined me.

"Are you still planning on leaving?" she asked. I want to say there was sadness and longing in her voice, but she was stoic as she waited for my answer.

"No," I said.

"What changed your mind?"

I inched closer to her. "You gave me a lot to think about. What's true, what's false. What role I want to play in Mai's life. . . I'm so sorry for what I said, Itzel, and how I said it. I'm so sorry."

She let out a sigh and moved her hand toward mine. "I've noticed you trying to understand the Spot and getting more involved. I know it's a big change for you. I appreciate your efforts."

"I've been thinking about what you said in the rose garden, about looking inward," I began, clasping her fingers.

"Oh yeah?"

"Yeah, and as usual, you bring wonderful insight into my narrowly focused life."

"And what have you discovered?"

"That looking inward is difficult."

She softly laughed and moved her legs against mine. Relief flooded me.

"And I'm impatient for results. Things move a lot slower here, but they've built a self-sufficient community in the desert. That's pretty impressive."

"Any news from space?" she asked, playing loop-de-loop with our fingers.

"Not yet," I said. I was surprised by how detached I felt when I said it. "I'm starting to come around to the reality that we won't get a response."

"You're okay with that?" she asked, turning onto her side and making a round hill with her hip, one my hand couldn't resist.

"Yeah, I think so." I slid fingers down her soft slope. "Kin and I talked about how different the Spot is compared to GEM."

She raised her brows at that but didn't say anything.

I asked, "Do you think Beau would like it here?"

"Ha ha ha!" She laughed loud enough to wake up Mai, but she melted back to sleep. Itzel dropped her volume. "Are you planning on inviting him?"

I glanced from her hip to her face. A frown flicked quick, showing a glimpse of how she really felt. I laughed and said, "No. . . Kin said GEM is for people like Beau. People easily manipulated. I never thought of him like that."

She let out a sigh, scooched closer and rolled onto her back. My hand didn't know what to do with itself.

"It doesn't take much effort to go with the flow, especially if prestige is promised."

I laid down beside her and asked, "Did I go with the flow?"

She took a while to answer, which made me nervous. Was she trying to find the nicest way to say yes? Or was she compiling her inventory of evidence to back up that yes? Neither matched Itzel's personality but a man can't help but worry when his wife takes her time to answer a simple question. My brain filled with my defense and objections.

"You went where your heart led you," she said softly. "You've always loved space and that's the difference between you and Beau."

We turned our heads and stared at each other. She'd gotten so brown. Smile lines played up her eyes. She looked like a woman baked with joy.

The last of the rain and a distant roll of thunder filled the silence that eased between us.

"Izzie, do you think I'd fit in here?" I asked.

She looked down at our interlocked hands. "Do you want to?"

I wanted to be with her and Mai, wherever that was. That's all I knew. And I told her that much.

The next day, I half expected to open the door to a wall of water and drifting trees. Roots and all. Instead, a tall, thin faced greeter stood on our porch, grinning, with a different kind of storm in tow.

His hand shot out soon as I opened the door.

"Tah Morant, I'm Seung Jae, Jae for short. Pleasure to meet you. Would you please follow me? You have a guest." He shook as he spoke, and he spoke fast. Too much caffeine? Maybe. But as we started trudging through the mud, I started to suspect it was something he couldn't help. For how young he was, he moved like a much older man.

Everywhere looked beaten up. Tree limbs laid in places they shouldn't be, at angles that didn't make sense. The pathways were clear of water, but were thick with mud and slick with leaves. It looked like "Hell sued for murder" as Itzel's mother would say. But the people weren't mourning. They were gathering supplies to fix what was broken and making quick work of it.

"Who am I meeting with?" I asked. My gut knotted up at the possibilities.

"Oh!" Jae abruptly stopped and handed me a note. "I am just all over the place today!"

"I think everyone is a little out of sorts after that storm," I said before looking down.

My heart stopped.

You're hard to find. But not impossible. ~ T. Laine

I slipped the note in my pocket and motioned for Jae to continue on. I felt as torn apart as the Spot looked, not knowing if I should be honored or worried.

We passed the visitor center and the informational halls, the turn off for the dining hall and the permanent residences. The whole time Jae chattered about Ms. Laine.

"I used to be the manager at the flagship Meridian— the *original* ten-star skytel! Served for 8 years! That's why I walk like this— you get rickets living up there so long. Anyway, Ms. Tessa Laine could be an absolute *bitch!* But she was always nice to me and tipped very, very well! I just adore her."

I tuned in and out as he talked. Partially because he never stopped talking and partially because I kept replaying the last time she and I met.

"I was speechless when I saw her arrive! I hardly recognized her. She had her hair covered, wearing the biggest visor over her face and the *least* flattering jumpsuit I've ever seen!"

How did she find me?

I thought back to how desperate Maryene and Sol were to get me out of their bar before too many people saw me. And then that wild eyed man did see me. Called me a murderer. Maybe he dropped a clue and Ms. Laine picked it up.

"And for you! I mean it makes sense. You're all over the news." Jae gasped and stopped. I nearly walked into him. "I am so sorry! I promised myself I wouldn't say anything about all of that. Blame it on the storm!" He kissed two fingers and flung them up at the sky, turned and carried on. "I am so excited to put this in my journal tonight! This is just fabulous. Do you think she'll take a picture with me?"

I had been studying the ground for answers to my own questions when I realized he was actually asking me about that picture.

"Would that be inappropriate?" he asked, face scrunched up.

I blinked hard at him. "You never took one with her before?"

"Oh, pfft! And lose the one break I had? Not worth it!"

I shrugged. "I'm sure she'll say yes since you two know each other so well."

Jae smiled like a flattered, much younger man. "You're right! She and I do go way back! One time I saved her life. Well not really, but almost!"

We turned left at a sign that read Administrative Halls. Jae was spinning off about sneaking into her hotel room and I was wondering why I'd followed him in the first place. What did Tessa Laine need with me? Why hadn't I declined the invite? And how in the world did she find me?

"Dr. Morant?" Jae said, startling me out of my head. He held a door open and motioned for me to enter.

The admin building was simple. Open and clear hallways, rooms that lit up as we passed and dimmed behind us.

"She's in the last room on the right," Jae said, quieter. I imagined that's how he sounded as manager on the Meridian. "I'll be waiting right here if you need anything." He gave me a warm, professional smile— not too big and with a slow blink.

I thanked him and prepared myself. I wasn't the same man she'd met before. Whatever mess she brought, I was ready for it.

She stood when I entered the conference room. Sunlight and a breeze snuck through honeycomb vents spaced high on the walls. Her sharp features softened into a smile. Her hair hung in shoulder length twists softened her angles further. She offered me some water from a pitcher sitting in the middle of the table. I declined and thanked her as she poured a glass for herself.

"GNN thinks I'm on vacation in Mexico," she said. "In case you're curious if anyone knows I'm here."

"I'm more curious about how you found me," I said, still standing.

She adjusted in her chair. "I have my sources."

That didn't settle my unease. Nor did it incline me to stay.

"I've been worried about you," she said. "Worried that I'd offended you when I asked about your parents."

I stayed silent, unwilling to give anything away.

"I couldn't help but look into it." She pushed a folder toward me.

"Into what?" I asked.

"Your parents. Their death." She tapped the folder with a sharp red nail. "I'm not sure what you already know, but you might find some of it interesting."

I glanced between her and the folder. I did my best to keep it together. Inside I was a mix of fear, anger, and curiosity. "Is this why you came here? To give me this?" I asked.

"I tried to follow up with you the day after the mission but everyone I spoke with said you were indisposed."

"Is that all?"

She smirked and said, "No."

We played chicken for a minute. Staring at each other, daring the other one to speak first. I won.

She leaned back in her chair and crossed her legs. "As you probably know, a commission has been appointed to investigate the mission failure."

I nodded. The government convened a commission any time a mission failed.

"Well, they want you to testify."

That did surprise me.

She smiled and watched me. Then quickly sat up. "Word is, Director Soncal keeps delaying the information hand-off. Something about a recording in a conference room and keeps coming up with excuses like data breaches and security issues."

I made a note to tell Kin about that later. Even if Beau was lying, she'd want to cover all traces. Her mention of the conference room wasn't lost on me; I didn't have much faith it would work in my favor.

"But the commission isn't playing around. They set a date. Twentieth of October."

Five weeks, I thought. *What about my disciplinary martial?*

"I just think it's curious that you, of all people, ended up at a detention center. . ." She leaned back again and studied me. "That doesn't make any sense. You're one of the Dominions best and brightest. You built *the* engine!"

"What do you want, Ms. Laine?" I asked, unflattered and ready to leave.

She sat forward and rested her elbows on the table. "I want to know your side of the story. For nearly two months, it's been speculation after speculation." She tapped at the folder. "But you come from a good family. You went to the best schools. You have always stayed in line. Something happened after that mission. And I think you're the only one who won't lie about it."

"Is this a trade off? You give me my family story, and I give you mine? It was a robbery, gone wrong. What more do I need to know?"

She looked at me, pierced through to my core. "I'm giving you an opportunity to know the truth. And to tell your own, Dr. Morant."

I didn't respond.

She abruptly stood. "Or you can have everyone else tell it. Lies and all. It's up to you." She took a sip of water. "I leave tomorrow morning. I hope I see you before then."

She left me this time. I heard Jae's shrill laugh and a thank you. He got his picture. I got a folder of things I wanted to forget.

46

I asked Jae to find Kin and send her to my cabin, then I rushed home, folder in hand. Itzel sensed my unease when I returned. I told her everything was fine, but Mai needed to go next door. She didn't put up a fight, but Mai eyed me like she knew something was wrong. After Mai was gone, I told Itzel about Tessa Laine and showed her the folder but not its contents. Itzel's eyes widened with worry. I told her we had to stay calm. We, including Kin needed to talk with reason about Ms. Laine and the implications of her being at the Spot.

When Kin arrived, the three of us sat around the table, with the folder in the middle.

Kin asked the logical question, "How'd she find you?" I knew she was asking with concern for the Spot.

"She said she has her sources," I said.

Itzel and Kin shared skeptical glances.

"What does she want?" Itzel asked.

I shrugged. "A story."

I was surprised when Kin asked, "What are the risks of talking to her?"

We glanced at each other. Itzel spoke first, "I'd be worried about Tah's safety." She gripped my forearm. "And his freedom."

I squeezed her hand to calm her.

Kin nodded in agreement. "I'm worried about her presence in general. People are already in a frenzy about her being here. . . for you."

Itzel moved her hand to my knee that had started bouncing under the table.

Kin rubbed her temples. "She could bring the wrong kind of attention."

"This could be an opportunity," I said, interrupting their back-and-forth.

They went silent and stared at me.

"How about this," I said, "we limit what we tell her. Keep it focused on the mission, the anomaly and what we found."

"I'd rather not be mentioned," Kin said, firmly.

"Fine, no mention of you," I said.

"What about the Novi Dom?" Itzel asked.

Kin answered for the both of us. "Absolutely not!" She had her personal reasons, but I knew mentioning it would set off an international crisis.

"What about our signal?" Kin asked, anxiously tapping the table.

She and I went back and forth. She was reluctant at first but saw the necessity of telling Ms. Laine when I mentioned my notes with the initial findings. "I'll tell her we haven't received a response yet."

"You haven't received a response," Kin corrected me.

"Right. I haven't." I stood and turned to leave.

"What about the folder, Tah?" Itzel asked.

I stared at it.

I wanted to believe it was a robbery, but there was a detail that never left me: the gold bracelet my mother wore. The one I'd picked out for her.

I grabbed the folder and said, "Tessa can tell us what she found. And if it sounds right, I'll tell her what Kin and I found."

"Us?" Itzel asked, slowly standing.

"Yes, Izzie. I want you with me. I want you to know the truth, too."

Three glasses, a full pitcher, and Ms. Laine sat ready for us. She stood as we entered. Itzel greeted her warmly. "I admire your work, Ms. Laine. You have always had a voice of truth and we both admire that. It is essential in times like these."

There was a pause before Ms. Laine thanked her then quickly motioned for us to sit. "If you're both ready, I can share what I found about Dr. Morant's parents."

Itzel and I exchanged nervous glances. "I'm ready," I said. Inside, I was vibrating, eager to know the truth, but terrified for little-me and how loudly he might scream.

Tessa sat tall and spoke plainly. "It appears the ALN targeted your father. To silence him."

I closed my eyes, my stomach churned. I felt hot.

"He knew of a crucial failure point in the Mars-bound crafts."

I heard them, my parents, whispering behind his office door. My father, shrinking. My mother, reminding him to pray.

"According to his reports, he found that the radars were vulnerable to x-class solar flares. Prior to the launch date he saw evidence of one developing, that was off the charts and likely to erupt during the voyage."

He didn't want me to talk to my MarsPals. He knew a catastrophe was coming.

"Had his supervisors taken his warnings into consideration, the Mars ships would have likely completed their journey."

Scattered debris and frozen bodies flashed before me.

"He wrote a series of internal reports and memos but—"

"Nobody listened," I said, cutting her off. "He would yell that all of the time." I looked over to Itzel. She looked devastated, hand over her mouth, tears ready to fall. I squeezed her hand as Tessa continued.

"He was persistent though. Very dedicated to telling the truth. He got in contact with a local media station." She opened the folder and slid a piece of paper to me. Handwritten correspondence between my father and the station producer.

"He was going public?" I said, taking in my father's scrawled desperation.

"Yes. And to keep him from going public, I suspect the ALN bribed someone to break into your home."

"Do you know who did it? Who shot them?" I asked, anger growing inside.

Ms. Laine shook her head. "No, but it looks as though whoever did it was looking for something." She reached to open the folder again. To show us something.

"Are there crime scene photos in here?" I asked.

Tessa nodded.

I shook my head. "I don't need to see them."

She let out a slow breath. "Dr. Morant, your father never saw the bullet coming."

"What about my mother?" My voice cracked. "Why'd they shoot my mother?"

She looked at me, an apology in her eyes. "They probably didn't expect her to be up."

I felt sick. I gripped Itzel's hand to keep from cracking open. I wanted to scream. I wanted to destroy something. I looked to my wife and saw only sorrow. Tears fell as she mouthed, "I'm so sorry."

"Dr. Morant," Tessa said softly. Her eyes were sharp when I met them. "When I couldn't reach you, I knew something was wrong. I tried every avenue to find out what happened with the mission and with you. GEM gave me the run around. It was weeks before I knew you were detained."

The news report. The guards' breakroom. Mai on the balcony. My body tensed as I recalled the pain that followed.

"Someone will be looking for you. And if I can find you, someone from GEM will, too. They tried to silence you once." She paused. "They will try again."

I pulled Itzel in, held her face close to mine. I wiped her cheeks, but the tears kept falling. I whispered, "I should have listened to you sooner. What a mess I've made." She shook her head but I needed her to understand. "No matter what happens, stay with Kin. Everything will be okay. You and Mai will be okay." I kissed her forehead, folded her into me, and rocked the both of us.

Tessa stepped out to give us time. "I'll be ready when you are," she said, and closed the door behind her.

Once we'd collected ourselves enough, I invited Tessa back in. I told her about the anomaly and how Beau tried to hide it. How the record was doctored. And how I found an alternate view through another telescope and found it was immensely bigger than a few unknown particles. I told her about the echo-signal and how long I've been waiting for a response. "Sixteen days and counting."

She looked like she'd struck gold, wide-eyed and beaming at her notes. "This is incredible," she repeatedly whispered. "Absolutely incredible!"

"So what now?" I asked, relieved to have gotten it all out.

Her elation simmered. She took on a much more serious tone. "Lay low. Wait for the summons."

Itzel nervously asked, "How will they know where to send it?"

"I've got some back channels through the government. I'll call in some favors."

"What about my charges?"

Ms. Laine leaned forward and smirked. "A commissioner got hold of some footage showing a little spat between you and Beau."

I shifted forward, eager to know more.

"Well, a majority of them felt that you were unduly handled and think there may be some fishy business happening at GEM."

"What does that mean?" Itzel asked.

"It means that they're dropping all charges."

Itzel clapped, relieved.

Tessa cooled the room with, "But he has to testify."

"Done." I said. "That's all I've been wanting to do. But how will I get there? GEM's cherootzim doesn't run this far," I joked.

Ms. Laine scribbled down another note. "Leave that to me, too. I have to do my due diligence but if all of this checks out, Dr. Morant, this is the story of the century! I'm going to have every newstream at that hearing!"

I shot her a nervous look.

"It is better that everyone sees your face, hears your voice, knows your name! Not to be morbid, but if anything happens—"

"I get it," I said, raising a hand to stop her.

Ms. Laine said she'd be in touch and wished us all the best. We said we'd keep an eye out for the summons and wished her safe travels. After she left, Itzel and I slow-talked a while.

"I'm afraid, Tah."

I saw that fear weighing down her face and shoulders. I wrapped my arms around her. "Me, too."

We fell apart, together.

It was early evening when we left the administration building. The sun pressed into the western horizon. We decided to check the dining hall for Mai first. It would be dinner time soon enough. But as we started down the path, we saw someone moving fast in our direction. Itzel gripped my arm as we watched. The person waved their hands over head, yelling something.

I squinted. "Is that Kin?"

The person got closer, shouting but I only caught half of what they said, "—SPONSE!"

Then Itzel slapped my arm. "Tah, she's saying—"

"WE GOT A RESPONSE!"

Part IV

47

The summons arrived almost two weeks after Ms. Laine's visit. I read and reread it, making sure the charges were dropped. They had been. Just like Tessa said, it was the recording of my outburst that saved me. The commissioners' wording warned that GEM's disciplinary practices far outweighed the offense. They recommended an investigation be done to improve and prevent future incidents. I took some comfort in knowing my suffering was not in vain, that maybe some good would come of it.

I sighed in relief that I was officially a free man. One they wanted to hear from.

"What will you wear?" Itzel asked from our cabin's kitchen.

The kettle pipped up then reduced. I heard the water pour. I knew she was waiting for a reply but I couldn't answer immediately. My head was full.

So much had changed before the summons arrived. Or rather, I'd changed. I cried more. I cried often. I cried watching Mai sleep, or watching the sun set. I cried each time I was reminded of my parents. My throat tightened in gardens where I'd think of my mother. My eyes stung in mirrors when I saw my father. I dreamt of them. Alive and living, laughing with me over some silly thing. I missed them. And I shared that with Itzel and Mai.

I understood more– about myself and about that part of Itzel that needed to share grief. I apologized many times for leaving her on her own after we lost our babies. I'd been put to shame for showing pain or grief early. I guess I'd learned to hide it. But now, all that grief broke free. Memories, warming and terrifying ones, bubbled to the surface, showing me more than I'd ever thought was inside.

But the response. . . learning the truth behind the anomaly. . . that transformed me.

"I don't know," I said, finally looking up to answer her. "I haven't thought about it."

So much of my life had been in uniform. I wore uniforms to primary and secondary school. Full body safety gear in university when I was a student and when I was hired on as an adjunct. When not in safety suits, I wore the same slacks and button-ups every professor wore. No need to impress. At GEM, even the casual wear was branded with its initials, lest we forget what and where we were. Prison was a yellow top and bottom, blue shoes, and defeat. The Spot was the first place in my life where I had to choose what to wear.

Itzel joked about what I was wearing, a muddy green robe over a stone brown shirt and gray pants. "You'd make the headlines for sure! *Missing Scientist turned Messiah on the Mount!*" Her laugh filled the cabin, and sent a bird into flight.

I stood and modeled the loose garments, turning side-to-side. "You don't think this will send the right message?"

She chuckled, "If you're taking on a vow of silence!"

"Hmm, maybe not then," I said, returning to the chair.

She joined me with two cups of tea. She stroked my beard and twisted her fingers through my kinked-up hair. I closed my eyes and melted with her touch.

She kissed my forehead, sat, and asked again, "Seriously, though. What will you wear?"

I looked down at the drab colors. Everything I wore at the Spot looked about the same: loose, wrinkled, faded by the sun when it was hung to dry. I knew I couldn't arrive at the Dominion's capitol, present my testimony dressed as though I'd just rolled out of bed. I looked at Itzel in her marigold sundress.

"What would you suggest?" I asked.

"Something new. Very new!"

***

The sky was black turning blue the morning of our departure. Tessa Laine fulfilled her second promise. A mid-sized skyvan whirred in waiting. Its mirrored, windowless shell gave the illusion of dark water, like it wasn't really there. The secure van had no demarcation, signage, or decals. Just a chameleon surface, blending with its surroundings.

Mai sagged against Itzel, whimpering about how tired she was. Itzel quieted her with, "You can sleep on the way." I held our luggage as they boarded the van.

Kin, in a rare moment of sentimentality, said she was proud of me and told me not to lose face. "You have gone through a lot, Tah." She gripped my arm for emphasis. "Don't let anyone, and I mean *anyone,* undo the man you've become." Then she hugged me tightly, like she was afraid to lose me.

"I hear you, Kin. Thank you for all that you've done."

I thanked the others who'd gathered to say farewell then joined my family. The door sealed shut. The lights dimmed. Mai sprawled across one of the cushioned benches. Itzel, sitting opposite Mai, patted the space next to her for me.

The van's comm system welcomed us, instructed that we remain seated and secured with the safety harnesses. It informed us there would be no stops along the two-hour journey. A latrine was behind the bench Itzel and I shared. Food and drinks were available above the bench Mai claimed. Entertainment was accessible upon request, including a scenic drone-view of the trip.

My stomach dropped as it lifted into the air.

"How are you feeling?" Itzel asked, quietly. She laced our fingers together.

I searched myself, waited to hear screams or feel a souring in my gut. Surprised by their absence, I answered, "Fine. . . Great, actually."

Itzel smiled and leaned into me. "Good. You feel strong."

To Mai's delight the benches folded out to small beds. She stretched, starfishing herself with room to grow. It didn't take long before she drifted into sleep. Itzel and I watched her limbs gradually curl inward, her belly evenly rose and fell.

"She's going to be tall like you," Itzel whispered.

"Her body is catching up with her personality," I jokingly agreed.

"Hmm, she has grown more confident, too. So have you darling. I appreciate it."

"You think so?" I asked, wrapping an arm around her shoulder.

She nestled into my side. "I do. Don't you?"

I chuckled softly. "Oh, I suppose," I said. "I pray it's for the better."

Not long after Mai's dip into slumber, Itzel joined her. She kissed me then curled around our daughter. I watched them for a while. They bent and entangled their arms and legs, breathed in waves together. My everything, at peace, before me.

I tried my best to sleep. The bed was not long enough in any direction. Too much of my lower legs hung off the edge, putting pressure on my back. Despite the soft cushion, too much of it reminded me of the dungeon. I folded myself to fit, but stiffness grew in my bones and I had to stand to stretch it out. There was not enough room in the craft to pace, two strides this way, two strides that way, but my mind needed more. I requested a visual of the journey. A view of the desert had eased me for so long, I figured why not now? It was early but we were nearly a half hour into flight which was plenty of time for the sun to light up the desert.

A screen lowered from the ceiling like a divider between the benches. I immediately recognized the bordering rock wall separating Mexico and Texas from Canada. From where we hovered, the four-meter-thick wall looked like a crumpled zipper over sun dried animal hide. I saw the tramline running parallel to it. The white, pill sized car crawled its way west. I saw the mountain range shadows that used to greet me each morning as I headed into work. They stretched long and dark in the rising sun.

I didn't see the GEM City dome but I didn't need to. Nor did I want to.

I let out a shocked laugh when I saw Umoja Village rebuilt. No evidence of the destruction I saw months ago. I wondered how quickly they reassembled it. How much Beau had to beg, if at all, to get it back to usable standards.

Beau. My chest tightened at the thought of him.

"You're grieving," Kin had said when she heard me gnawing on what he'd done to me for the umpteenth time.

"Grieving what? He's an as—he's an idiot," I growled.

"Fine. But he's been your best friend for a long time. Your brother even."

I didn't respond to her when she said that. She didn't say anything more. She had left me in the office to chew on his name as long as I needed.

As I watched the desert roll under us, that grief settled around me. Beau had buoyed my boyhood, kept me from slipping into dark spaces no child should be left to drown in. He'd done his best to keep me lifted even while at GEM. I came to understand that what I had called *parading* was his showboat way to elevate me. Parts of me miss that friendship, still.

I'd like to believe that if he weren't being dragged down by whatever, or whomever it was, he'd have made better decisions. I pitied him. He could have been great, greater than his father even. He had always been more charismatic, less rough around the edges. If it was glory he was after, Beau could have reported finding the Novi Dom. He could have claimed a mountain range all his own, bigger and better than his family's. Hell, he could have named a whole continent after himself. But he didn't. I'll never fully understand why.

I hadn't seen or spoken to him in the three months since he visited me in prison. While I sat across from Mai and Itzel, I could say he'd have no effect on me. But what would happen when I saw him? When I heard his voice climb over everyone else's? I wondered if enough time had gone by to truly forgive him and not let old habits reignite. I wasn't going to inflict the same suffering he put me through. What good would come of that? Besides, I promised Itzel I'd keep cool in the fire. I promised Kin I'd stay dry in the rain.

I must have dozed off. Itzel's voice shook me awake. An urgency sharpened her whisper, "Tah! Tah!"

"Yes, what is it?"

"Look!" She pointed to the screen between us.

I hardly recognized my GEM employee picture. My tight fade. My fresh shave with a forced smile, and tired, sunken eyes. Had I always looked so extinguished?

"Sources claim that Chief Scientist of GEM's Umoja Program, Tah Morant, will testify at the Commission hearing. This comes following his recent detention at a Threat Protection Center. It is unclear at this time what his Dominion status is—"

"Izzie, why are you watching this?" I asked, shifting my gaze away from the screen.

"I want to know what we— you— are heading into." Uneasiness crept across her face as she looked at me. "I am not worried about you, Tah. It's everyone else. We're walking into the lion's den. I think it's best that we be prepared."

I nodded at her concern, but I felt prepared. I knew what I was going to say– the truth. What the Woven told me.

***

After Ms. Laine left, and Kin came running to tell me that we'd received a response, my world expanded to the universe.

I stuttered, "What— what, what do you mean?"

Kin frantically asked, "What do you mean *what do you mean*? A response! We got a *response*!"

I took off. I ran as fast as I could. Dodged residents. Skipped over rocks and roots. Furious excitement carried me through the research center into our office. I crashed into my chair, trembling too much to tap a key. Kin stumbled in soon after, out of breath but laughing.

I grabbed my head, dizzy and exhilarated. "What do we do?" I asked, giggling like a child— a child whose wildest dreams just came true. "What do we do?"

"Take a breath!" Kin said, lowering into her chair next to me. I did. She and I breathed together, eyes locked on each other. In. And out. "Again," she said. Slower, we breathed in and out.

"Ok," I said. "I'm ready."

The first transmission read, "Tingret's answer would render infinite possibilities in your understanding. Nineteen in ours."

My whole body tingled. I looked to Kin. "They really answered?"

Kin's face was wide with glee.

"Did you respond?" I asked.

She shook her head. "I wanted you to be here."

It took everything in me not to hug her.

"What do we say?" I asked.

She shrugged again, looking just as perplexed and thrilled as I was. "Thank them?"

I nodded and slowly turned back to the screen. I clenched and released my fists before I typed, "Thank you for your response. My name is Tah Morant. I am greeting you from Earth."

It was probably only seconds before they replied. But it felt like life stopped. The humming servers, the occasional beeps, the sounds outside. My heart. My thoughts. All of it stopped.

And then, "We know who you are. Greetings."

Kin squeaked. I jumped. She grabbed my wrist. "They know who you are!"

"How?" I typed. I hit send and held my breath. Sweat beaded along my forehead and under my arms.

Kin rocked, nervously.

"Your thoughts led to the vessels that have journeyed beyond what you call Oort cloud. We thought we should learn about you."

I snatched my hands from the keys. *My thoughts?*

Kin grabbed my wrist tighter. "Tah, is this real?"

My mouth was too dry to answer. My body too rigid to move.

"Ask them who they are," she said, finally releasing her grip.

Sweaty palmed, I did.

They replied, "It is not a phrase you will be able to say, nor fully understand."

I asked what they meant.

"You think in unitary minds. We are like your understanding of cloth: many threads, each unique and necessary. But all one cloth."

My head tingled at the thought. A hive mind, but not.

I asked what we should call them.

"You may choose," they replied.

I looked at Kin. She stared at the screen, unblinking.

I typed, "How about The Woven?"

"That is respectful and not inaccurate. We accept."

Fixating on the screen, Kin repeated it, "The Woven," quietly to herself.

"What should I ask next?" I whispered to her.

She didn't answer. She was bewitched. Kept re-reading their words. I watched her eyes search the transmission as if she'd find them staring back.

"Kin? What do I ask?"

She pulled back into herself, looked around the desk then to me. "What? Ask about the failure!"

How insignificant it became at that moment. But I quickly typed, "Our engine failed on our most recent journey. Do you know why?"

"Yes."

Kin and I exchanged looks. My skin tightened along my forearms. A chill crept through the air.

I asked, "Why?"

Their response was swift. And startling.

"We intervened."

48

It had been years since I was in Chicago. The last time was for a hearing regarding the Umoja-15 failure. That was a decade ago. Since then, Itzel had journeyed back for conferences a handful of times. Ever since funding for her research dried up, she had no reason to return either.

The hearing was held at the same building, sitting along Michigan Ave, looking over Lake Michigan. It hadn't changed. From a half block away, I saw the bronze lions bookend the stairs to the entrance. Sam told me the building used to be an art museum, but was looted two hundred years ago. Canada rebuilt the entrance to face mostly north so most Americans would, too. I couldn't imagine it facing any other direction. Lake Michigan looked beautiful in the early morning.

I had hoped to get there before the media. I didn't expect a crowd to be there before me. Newscasters were already checking their angles and volume. Protestors, separated from the media by barricades and Auxen, were pulling out their banners and noise makers. A few were arguing with guards about their right to be there, their right to speech.

A month ago, all of this would have disrupted me. But since our conversation with The Woven, everything else was just noise.

I had asked them, The Woven, if I could share what they told me. They said, "Of course if you think it would be useful". I chuckled thinking about that. Useful? Ha! More like quintessential. I had stumbled out of Kin's office, seeing every door, window, blade of grass and bird in the sky as meaningless and meaningful all at once. Everything and everyone was almost permeable, like I could touch its essence if I stood still and listened long enough. I realized, more than ever— more solidly than before— that I had spent my entire life looking for the facts and never seeing the truth.

I gave a sharp tug at my new suit jacket as I rounded the side of the building. I wasn't sure about the suit at first. The thin, gold stitching felt too opulent. The six beveled gold buttons dotting my torso shone too beautifully. The diamond-weave deep, green fabric moved like a second layer of skin, smooth and breathable. No catching at the cuffs or bunching where I bent. Itzel suggested the color based on my undertones. Like my father, she said, I had cherry in my skin. She said the green lifted it nicely.

In the hotel, Itzel told me to stand in front of the mirror and see myself. Graying, coiled hair, tapered at the sides. Big, black eyes, heavy lids, wide nostrils that pinched at the bridge. A beard with silver in the mix. I saw my father's pride smiling back.

Itzel whispered into my ear, "That's the man I married." She moved in front of me. One hand grazed the back of my neck, the other pressed against my chest. "I'm so glad he's back."

If Mai hadn't been in the hotel room, I might not have left when I did.

"Looking sharp, Dr. Morant!"

I looked up and saw Tessa Laine pass along my right. I wanted to thank her for all that she had done, but she didn't stop. Just tossed a wink at me and followed the herd of reporters into the building. They barreled past, nearly trampling each other. But not Ms. Laine. She seemed to glide, untouched. Unperturbed.

Loud voices snatched my attention east.

TICK TOCK GOES THE DOOMSDAY CLOCK. The scrawled red letters were on every banner and across every shirt. There were always demonstrations and protests at these hearings. Everything GEM did pulled out their chants and banners, calling GEM scammers and parasites. As I watched them collide with security guards and armed Auxen, I saw more than just the angry faces they made. I heard more than their accusations of greed and exploitation. I saw their fear. Fear that time *was* running out and that they would be left behind. Fear that each time GEM failed, another second was lost on their clock. Their fear didn't quiet them, though. It made them louder, and in that way, less afraid of the consequences. I could admire that much.

I was glad to see Major Bierdot alone in the waiting room. Instead of GEM's cobalt blue, gold, and black, she wore the rifle green duty uniform of Canada's Armed Services. Her rank pinned to her chest. Her hat folded neatly on the table. She didn't look up when I entered. She was occupied with notes I'm sure she had memorized weeks prior.

"Major," I said, softly.

Her confusion switched to warm recognition. "Dr. Morant! My goodness!" She stood and stretched out a hand.

"Good to see you, Major," I said, cupping her hand in mine. "It has been a long time."

We were about to sit down and catch up when the door opened.

"Holy shit! Tah Morant!"

I took a breath and turned. Beau, hair slicked to perfection, grinned at me. His smile stretched too wide. His eyes shimmied. His hand couldn't stop reaching for his hair, which had not moved. Three young, eager-eyed men flanked him. They shared his mannerisms and styled themselves in his image. It tickled me.

Bierdot and I stood. Beau pulled me in for a hug.

"I can't imagine what you've been through." He slapped my back as he whispered, "I did everything I could!"

I heard his apology even though he never said it.

"That's the past, Beau. There's nothing to forgive," I said, patting his back.

He released me with a quick, confused laugh. "Well, uh, look at you! You look good, man! Great suit! What is that? Raylon?" He pinched at my lapel, eyes darting everywhere but at mine. "And this beard! Didn't know you had it in you!"

"Well, there's a lot you don't know, Beau," I said.

He took a deep breath and clapped his hands loudly. "Hopefully not too much!" He chuckled to his three look-a-likes. They quickly laughed in unison before he looked back at me. "They've got our statements so this shouldn't last too long. My guess: we'll be out by lunch." Beau glanced between Beirdot and I. "We're checking out this new Indian spot later. Care to join us?"

I declined, "I have plans with Itzel and Mai."

I saw relief and worry mix in his face. He recovered with a hand through his hair, the other punched my shoulder. "You brought the family? Why didn't I think of that!" Another round of chuckles. "GNN got it right: Chief Scientist Tah Morant, family man through and through! I'm going to have to take lessons from you!"

When he asked Beirdot directly, she declined as well. He shifted and combed through his hair. He looked relieved when an aid entered the waiting room and asked if we were ready. Beau rubbed his hands together and whispered, "Show time!"

The swarm of voices on the other side of the Chamber Hall doors quieted once we entered. I paused at all the faces. Previous hearings garnered only a few newstreams, governmental aids, and curious onlookers, but this time every seat was filled. The walls were lined. The mezzanine, where no one ever sat, leaned forward with hundreds of people, stretching to get a look at us. At me. Ms. Laine's reach was a powerful thing.

I spied Mai and Itzel in the mezzanine. From the front row, Mai waved excitedly and Itzel blew me a kiss. I waved and kissed back, emboldened by their presence.

The aid led us to our seats. Bierdot sat between Beau and me. We faced a bay of cameras that separated us from the seven commissioners, who sat behind their elevated, wooden bench. They nodded at each of us. Then Commissioner Yang, in the middle, called the hearing to order, banged her gavel, and it began.

Beau first.

"Thank you, Madame Chairwoman, and thank you to the entire Commission for your time and attention today. I believe the final incident report you have received highlights the major findings of our team.

"As indicated on our postmortem analysis and assessment, both of which are included in the official report for your perusal, there was a procedural error preventing transposition through the Dragon's Gate."

Some of the commissioners swiped through the provided report, nodding in agreement.

"It says here," a commissioner to the right of Chairwoman Yang started, "that a new recruit caused a coding error."

I saw Bierdot wince at that. She shifted in her chair and quietly cleared her throat.

"Yes, and he has been terminated. That kind of mistake cannot and will not be tolerated at GEM. Even small errors are very costly and put our brave astronauts in danger."

Another commissioner asked if there was any damage to the Umoja-19 craft or the engine. Beau quickly assured them, "Per our select engineering team, no damage has been detected, furthering our conclusion that it was a human error and should not delay future missions."

Future missions, I thought. *Like dead flies on a window sill. How long would we exhaust ourselves trying to escape?*

As Beau answered questions about the multi-trillion hheq budget spent on Umoja-19, I thought about how much was lost over the past decades. The babies Itzel and I lost. The marriage I lost sight of. The parts of my past I lost. Sam lost his mind.

When a commissioner asked about the launch site and the explosion, I thought about Sol and Maryene, motherless because of rocket debris. I thought about that wild-eyed man screaming at me, scarred by debris. Lost his love at the launch. How many others were impacted by our missions, regardless if they were deemed a success or failure?

Beau downplayed the explosion. He actually blamed it on the increased sand and dirt in the air caused by the million people GEM invited to the launch. Never mind it was his idea to invite a million people that day.

I waited for someone to inquire about Beau's lack of forethought, or challenge his audacity to hold no responsibility. But they didn't. Instead Chairwoman Yang thanked him for his testimony and moved on.

49

Commander Bierdot was called next.

"Thank you, Chairwoman Yang. My full account is included in the incident report. I have nothing to add. I would be happy to answer any questions you may have."

"Commander. What is your official title?" a commissioner at the left end of the bench asked.

"I served as Commander of the Umoja-19 crew, my service title is Major."

"Ah, thank you, Major. How many times have you flown deuteron-powered missions?"

"I don't have the exact number but I would estimate several dozen," Bierdot replied.

"Your service record shows sixty-three training flights, four missions as navigator, three as pilot and the last five, you served as commander."

"That sounds about right," Bierdot chuckled softly.

The commissioners warmed with looks of impress, all except the one questioning her. "So in terms of first-hand experience, you would be the most experienced, correct?"

"I leave that judgement to you, Commissioners."

"Thank you, Major. That is precisely why you have been called to testify." The commissioner gave a brief sneer then resumed. "Do you agree with Director Soncal's conclusion regarding the cause of the engine failure?"

Taut silence gripped the room. Stiffened backs lifted out of chairs.

Bierdot took a breath and gave a well weighed response, "Commissioner, I am not an engineer and I was not present at the postmortem disassembly and inspection. That being said, the crew and I did not witness any system warnings."

The commissioner pressed on. "To be clear, you've never experienced *this* sort of malfunction in previous missions?"

"In previous missions, there were failures. And those were well documented, but there were system warnings and evidence of component or system malfunctions. So, no, I have not experienced any similar failures."

There was a long pause as the Commissioner glanced down at his notes. The other commissioners watched on, curious but silent.

"Major Bierdot, as your crew prepared to transpose through the Gate, you state that you did not see any system warnings and there were no visual abnormalities?"

Out of the corner of my eye, I saw Beau shifting in his chair. I didn't have to look to know the gripped-jaw face he was making, the red working up his neck.

"That is correct, Commissioner. We fly by instrument and as I stated in my account, there were no warnings or disturbances that I, or the other crew members, noted."

"I see," the commissioner said. "So you are unaware of Section 23, Addendums A through F provided by Dr. Morant?"

I did my best not to react. Bierdot pulled slightly back from the table. "No, I am not familiar with that portion of the report."

Murmurs kicked up behind us. Cameras lifted and focused on Bierdot.

"It is rather enlightening, Major. I would suggest you and your crew read it. There was one part in particular that caught my attention. On—"

"Excuse me, Commissioner!" Beau interrupted.

The whole chamber turned in surprise. The commissioners exchanged glances.

He stood and said, "I don't believe that section is part of the vetted, formal incident report. Several statements in it are anecdotal and cannot be corroborated."

I fought the urge to reach behind Bierdot, pull Beau back to his senses.

"Director," the commissioner sighed, "we are a commission of inquiry, not a rubber stamp. We inquire into all matters regardless of who signed off." He turned to Chairwoman Yang. "Madame Chair, may I proceed?"

Beau sat down, rigidly. He knew what was coming. I knew what was coming. But Bierdot was blindsided. I wanted to lean over to apologize, but that would only make matters worse.

"As I was saying, Major Bierdot, on page fifty-two, there is a table providing environmental conditions at the time of the deuteron engagement. At the bottom of the table, there is an entry that references a vaporous, perhaps plasmic anomaly which failed to register a neutrinic signature. Are you aware of this anomaly?"

I heard Beau grinding his teeth.

"No, sir. I was not and am not aware of any plasmic anomaly."

"You didn't see *anything* matching this description?"

"No, sir. Again we fly by instrument. So—"

"So, you don't concur with Dr. Morant's findings, either?"

Bierdot flinched at the question. "I didn't say that, Commissioner. I said there were no system warnings—"

"Wouldn't such anomalies put your crew in danger?"

Bierdot straightened against the accusation. "I would never put my crew in danger, regardless of a mission. I stand by that and I am confident in my judgement." A razor sharpened in her voice, "I would defer the answers to your questions to Dr. Morant, whom you stated provided the addendums to which you refer."

The commissioner stared at Bierdot, smirked, then said, "Thank you for your service, Major. I have no further questions. I yield back, Madame Chairwoman."

Yang called for a recess, cracked her gavel. The chamber filled with noise. I looked at Bierdot. She looked back at me with stark confusion in her eyes.

The three of us sat in forced silence for the ten-minute recess. Bierdot cut glances between Beau and I. Beau was coming undone. He yanked loose his tie, unbuttoned his shirt. Reddened in his throat and face. I felt him radiating from across the table as we sat there, not talking. He tried, though. He tapped for my attention. Mouthed and mimed at me. When he started coughing words into his fist the supervising aid offered him water. I chuckled at her polite way of quieting him.

He fumed as we were escorted back to the Chamber Hall. Bierdot and the aid were a few strides ahead of me. Beau was hissing up my side.

"For all our sake, keep it simple, Tah. Don't make a fool of yourself," he whispered.

"This isn't my first time testifying. I'll be okay," I said, veering away from him.

He stayed on me. "That's not what I'm talking about and you know it!" he growled. "I'm talking about your damn anomaly!"

The aid and Bierdot looked back at us. I motioned that everything was fine and whispered to him, "I'm only going to share what I learned."

"*What you learned*? About what? About this plasma shit you can't even identify? You'll look like an idiot!"

I rolled my eyes to dull the spark I felt and kept walking.

The Chamber doors opened. I saw most people were already seated. The aid motioned for us to hurry. I picked up my pace. Beau followed intensely.

Three meters from the threshold, he hissed, "Just keep your mouth shut!"

Heat rushed through me. I twisted around at him. Anger burst out my mouth before I could catch it. "I'm not here as part of your fucking dog and pony show, Beau! This isn't about you!"

He flinched.

For a moment, I savored his fear. Let it feed the broiling inside me. But then Kin's words rushed in: *Don't let anyone, anyone, change the man you've become.*

"Beau," I said, letting a breath cool my insides. "I haven't been moping around for the last two months. I've gone over every detail of what went down, even the facts you tried to hide." He started to speak but I kept going. "I figured out what happened and I'm going to tell them— all of them. Everyone. I'm going to tell them what I found. And you won't like it. But it's the truth."

His face contorted like I'd stabbed him.

I put a hand on his shoulder, tried to ease my own anger. "It's just my observations, Beau. No extrapolations. Just the science."

He jerked away.

The aid warned, "You two are holding up proceedings."

I turned and continued toward the aid waving us in. As I neared the Chamber door, Beau tried me again, whispering angrily, "If you fuck this up, I'm not going to help you. You're on your own."

I was struck by how small he became in that moment. How juvenile he'd remained. Aristide 'Beau' Soncal was still a frightened child, like I used to be.

I ignored the aid coming toward us and lowered my volume. "We're not children anymore, Beau. It's time you grew up."

He snapped back, breaking past a whisper, "Is this about *self-improvement* now? I *love* self-improvement. Always have!" He slicked back his hair, stretched an angry grin across his face. "Tell you what, don't bring up this wisp shit, and I'll take all the self-help classes you want!"

"What is wrong with you, Beau?" I asked, motioning for him to keep his volume down.

"What's wrong with me? What the fuck in wrong with you!" He yanked at my suit jacket. "You and this bullshit!"

I took a step back.

"Excuse me, but the commissioners are waiting," the aid warned, reaching for the both of us.

I held up a hand to stop him. "Beau, I can't do this with you anymore. I thought I needed you. But I don't. And I've done alright without you." I straightened my jacket and left him there. I was ready to testify.

50

Leading up to the hearing, Kin helped compile the data. We rendered and spliced visuals, documenting every step to ensure the integrity of what we found and how. We saved our conversation with the Woven, metadata and all. Made hard copies and read them aloud to each other to make sure we saw the same thing.

She asked, "You understand the consequences of this, don't you?"

I nodded, eyes still on the transcript.

"I mean, the personal consequences," she said, shifting to serious concern.

I looked up at her. Felt the weight in her stare.

"Yeah," I said, "I understand."

And I did. I knew the moment I showed the expanse of the anomaly, and what it meant, that it would challenge everything. Especially the Common Goal. In doing so— despite my immunity— I was laying my head on a guillotine.

***

When Yang called me to testify, I introduced myself, "Tolulopé Ayodege Hudu-Morant. Served as Chief Scientist for GEM's Umoja missions for seventeen years." Then I started with the anomaly comparing the doctored footage to what we pulled from the SOL3 scopes.

"As you can see, the footage on the right shows the comet moving constantly, right to left. However, in the video on the left, it stops, then leaps forward, uncharacteristic of any non-self-propelled object in space."

The crowded gallery and mezzanine hummed with curious murmurs. The commissioners exchanged glances. Bierdot looked on, wide eyed, mouth slightly open. Beau avoided me completely, finding his finger nails and shirt sleeves more interesting.

I continued, "Due to the altered state of the original data, I have submitted the SOL3-Scope renderings to the Umoja archive for a more complete record."

"Is there evidence of who—" Yang started but commotion in the mezzanine interrupted her.

I searched for the cause. Across from where I stood, I watched as bodies shuffled out of the way for two people to sit in the front row.

A sickening feeling wormed around my stomach when I saw her. That dark presence that purred in my ear, promising to fulfill all my holy and hellish desires from my dream, suddenly took shape. A silver bob, green eyes, red lips. Felix Santigo.

Next to her sat her ever present and always silent pilot.

I shook the nightmare loose and scanned the room. I saw Beau shrink in his seat. I glanced between the two, Felix Santigo and Beau. She sat, poised, somehow floating in her seat, eyeing her prey beneath her. Beau looked pathetic, slumping forward in his chair, unable to hide.

It finally dawned on me. It was Felix who'd gripped him, fed him, housed him, revitalized his youth. For what? What did he have that would interest her? The Novi Dom?

The thought knocked the wind out of me. *Beau, what have you done?*

"Doctor, do you have any evidence as to how the record was altered?" Yang asked once the chamber quieted.

I returned my attention to the commissioner, but I felt Beau watching me. I shook my head. I had no doubt he was responsible, but I had no proof. Not even a data signature. "I do not, but will leave that up to your investigators, Chairwoman."

"Very well," Yang said with a sigh as she made note of my response. "Please continue with your presentation, Dr. Morant."

"Thank you, Madame. Upon further inspection of the footage pulled from the SOL3-scopes, I was able to gain a more comprehensive view of the anomaly."

A distant vantage point of the Dragon's Gate replaced the split screen videos. The Umoja was a speck compared to the red opening that filled two-thirds of the display.

"This three-second video will be played at a quarter rate. We begin immediately prior to the deuteron engine engaging and end immediately after."

I pressed play. The room leaned forward in silence.

As the first second stretched into four, I worried that nothing would happen, that history would repeat itself despite the efforts made. But there it was. The veil, rippling out in front of the craft. Undulating across the Dragon's Gate like the thinnest pool of water, tapped by a fly.

The whole chamber gasped. *Finally*, I thought. *Finally, everyone will see the truth!*

"ENOUGH!" Beau leapt out of his chair, hands raised like talons. "ENOUGH!" he yelled. Spit flew. "This is nonsense! Absolute nonsense, Commissioners! How can you sit here and listen to this!"

Yang cracked her gavel, demanding his removal. Security moved in. I had to do something. I refused to see someone else suffer the way I did. Not even him.

In three strides, I was in his face, gripping his arm.

"Don't do this to yourself!" I whispered.

He tried to pull away but I held firm.

"You won't last a day in detention!"

We met eyes. His anger flinched, then twisted his face into a snarl. He looked like an animal caught in a trap. Furious and afraid.

I growled, "When they find out what you've been hiding, everything you know and love will vanish. *Everything.*"

Beau looked past me and saw the guards surrounding us.

"I know about the Novi Dom," I whispered through gritted teeth. He scowled and tried to pull away. I didn't let go. "I haven't told anyone, but keep this up and everyone will know. And they'll bury you. Your father will see you fail."

His eyes flicked back to me, panic tightening his pupils.

I pulled away enough to see his whole face. I moved my hand to his shoulder and pressed him back to his seat. "Just sit down and listen. It's your only way out."

I watched as reality shook him, forced him to consider his next move. His jaw tightened. His eyes darted around then came back to me.

"Fine," he whispered.

I let go and backed away.

He fixed his unmoving hair. "I apologize to the commission for my outburst," he said to the commissioners. "It will not happen again."

The seven members conferred with each other before Yang spoke. "Your reaction to Dr. Morant's findings is curious, Director Soncal. But your friend and colleague seems to have convinced you to not make a spectacle of our proceedings. This is the seat of the Dominion where respectful decorum is expected. One more outburst and you will be removed."

The air was thick. Reporters squirmed in the chairs. Aids and assistants eagerly tapped at their comms devices. Spectators looked on, unblinking.

Chairwoman Yang motioned for me to continue.

"Thank you, Madame." But before I could continue the stern-faced commissioner who'd grilled Bierdot started.

"Uh, Dr. Morant?"

"Yes, Commissioner?"

"Are you suggesting this *anomaly* botched your mission?"

"Coincidence is not causation," I said. "But I was intrigued. Upon further analysis, I found that it emitted a very faint signal. One that was not picked up by the Umoja system because it did not surpass the expected background noise from surrounding SOL3-scopes. I was able to set up a system to reflect the signal back, to see if I could pinpoint the source."

"And were you able to?" he asked.

"Yes, I was."

"Well?" he pressed.

My heart kicked in my chest. "I received a response."

The room tightened at my words. Yang beat back the slightest noise that seeped from the mezzanine.

"You're implying you made contact with the anomaly?" the commissioner asked with ridicule.

"No." I swallowed to wet my mouth. "I am stating that I made contact with the ones who created it."

The crowd surged again, drowning my words. The gavel cracked for silence.

The commissioner flung his hands up, impatient. "The ones who created it, Dr, Morant? Who? Who created this anomaly, Dr. Morant?"

"The Woven," I said, loudly.

A mix of disbelief and mockery filled the chamber. The commissioner shouted over the crowd and drew them to yield. "And what did they tell you?"

My heart was in my throat, thundering for me to keep going. "They told me that they intervened. They won't allow us to leave our solar system."

Chaos uncorked. People jumped out of their chairs. Gnashed at me. Beat their fists in the air. Screamed, "Lunatic!" "Heretic!" "Liar!" The whole room turned against me. The ones standing along the walls ripped off their jackets. Revealed their red stained shirts. Others pulled rocks from their pockets, and cocked their arms to throw them. Security pushed through, grabbed the aiming assaulters. Dragged them out while they kicked and screamed, "You're killing us! You're killing us!"

I searched for Itzel. I saw her, worried, cradling Mai in her lap. I gave her a nod and small smile to assure her everything was going to be okay.

My gaze was drawn several seats to her right. To Felix Santigo. She was smirking, chin resting on one hand. Her smile widened when she caught me looking.

The lights flashed. A siren blared. Santigo didn't flinch.

Chairwoman Yang stood, shouted everyone be removed. The guards doubled in number. Auxen marched in, automatically began grabbing and removing the loudest objectors.

"Madame! Please!" I yelled, running in front of the bench, hands raised. I pleaded, "Please, they need to hear this!"

She glared at me, unconvinced.

"This is a public hearing!" I shouted, breaking over the noise. "The public should be here!"

She measured my words. Then she rapped her gavel and ordered the guards to remain alert. She demanded people stay seated and silent for the remainder of the proceeding. "This is my final warning!" she said, sweeping her gaze over the entire room.

"Thank you, Madame Chair. And thank you to all the commissioners." I bowed, ready to resume my testimony.

A commissioner asked, "How do you explain previous successes and this mission's failure? By my count, the last four went through without issue."

"Umoja-19 was our first *manned* mission," I said.

That got eye rolls from several commissioners and a choked groan from the gallery.

"You're saying four astronauts were blocked from crossing the Dragon's Gate, Dr. Morant? Do you hear how silly that sounds?"

"No, sir. I'm not saying four astronauts were blocked. I'm saying humans, in general. Humans are not allowed outside of our Oort cloud. We can't leave our solar system until—"

"You solve Fermi's Paradox only to tell us we can't leave! You're making a mockery of the Common Goal! Is this a joke to you, Dr. Morant?"

The whole room turned against me. The commissioners. The crowd. They groaned and tossed their hands in the air. Beau held his head in his hands. Bierdot looked utterly bewildered.

"No," I said, determined to make them understand. "The Common Goal unites humanity. It has given everyone a purpose."

The crowd settled a fraction. The commissioners straightened in their chairs.

I continued, "All I am saying is that we need to change the goal. New information requires us to take new action."

"Change the Common Goal? Did your Woven friend tell you what we should change it to?" another commissioner asked.

"Not specifically. . . They just said we have all the guidance we need to figure it out," I answered, unsure how to summarize all that the Woven had told me.

"Did they say when we can leave?" another asked.

"When we can be trusted to regard life– *all life*– as sacred. Ours and all life surrounding us."

Quiet settled and lingered. All I could hear was my heart pounding.

"What if they're lying to you?" Yang asked.

"I have considered that. I've asked myself what would they gain from watching us suffer to extinction. . . If they are powerful enough to stop us from leaving, then surely they are powerful enough to destroy us. But they haven't. They've quarantined us. And until we heal from within, we can't leave."

Another commissioner, one who'd been silent up until that moment, asked, "So what do you propose we do?"

I cleared my throat. "As a scientist, I say test it. Send two ships. One manned, the other operated remotely. As Commander Bierdot testified, there was no danger to the crew. And Director Soncal testified no damage to the craft or the engine." I paused and watched three of the commissioners soak up my words. To reach the other four, I offered, "To remove bias, I relinquish my position at GEM."

I turned to Beau. He looked shocked. "And perhaps Director Soncal will take a leave of absence as well, thereby removing our bias and influence on the matter."

"And what do you think of this, Director Soncal?" Yang asked,

Beau stood, buttoned his jacket and said, "I support this plan and will remove myself from the next mission."

I exhaled, surprised that he listened to me.

51

After my testimony, Chairwoman Yang adjourned the hearing for the day. The chamber was thick with worry, anger, and suspicion. She ordered that Bierdot, Beau, and I be escorted by security to the waiting room while the chamber emptied. I was first to leave and felt a gap around me. Neither Bierdot or Beau, or any of the guards, were within an arm's length.

In the waiting room, I felt seventeen years of focus and toil roll away from me and leave me stranded. Bierdot made no eye contact as she took a seat a few chairs away from me. Beau stood at the far end of the room, feverishly messaging someone.

I didn't try to bridge our gaps. Instead I focused on our family plan to take Mai to our favorite park by the water, where Izzie and I had our first date. I closed my eyes to recall every detail of that day, but the noise from the hallway pulled me back. There was a lot of anger. I understood the anger. It welled up from the most common source. Fear.

When the aid returned to let us go, Bierdot gave me a firm handshake and best wishes for my future. There was a detachment in her farewell, as if we were on opposite teams now.

Beau left without a word. Or a look. He was just gone.

I found Itzel waiting where we'd planned to meet. Mai ran to me with tears in her eyes.

"I'm scared, Daddy!" she whimpered as I squatted to her level. I wrapped my arms around her and sighed. I felt awful. She was so young, and the only other time she'd witnessed such upheaval was the day of launch.

"It's okay, sweet pea. It was a scary day, but it's over now. Ready for our walk?" I leaned back to wipe her cheeks, but Itzel caught my eye.

She cut a look toward the entrance and shook her head. I frowned, not understanding.

"It looks *busy* out there," she said.

"Oh, well. Change of plans," I said, trying to loosen the tension I felt in my chest. I smiled as Mai searched my face. "We'll just head to the van and figure out what we should do from there." I kissed her forehead and stood.

From behind me, a woman softly spoke. "We're heading to the roof as well."

I turned. Mai squeezed my hand and tucked behind my leg when we saw Felix Santigo standing a short distance from us. Itzel moved to my side.

"It looks a tad dangerous out there," Felix said with a hint of pleasure. "Better we stick together. There's safety in numbers."

I looked to Itzel who only raised her brows. It was my decision to make.

"Please lead the way," I said, swallowing my hesitation. She was the last person I wanted to share a small space with, but I wanted to get Mai out of the city as soon as possible.

Mrs. Santigo looked pleased with my acceptance and turned. We followed her to the elevator where her pilot was waiting. He wore all black; a black cowboy hat, black shirt and jeans, black boots. And black belt with a shining silver buckle. He tipped his head and said nothing. The elevator opened. Mrs. Santigo stepped in first. Then Itzel and Mai. Her pilot motioned for me to step in next and followed in after. He stood next to Felix, across from me.

"Orbital racer?" I remarked, pointing toward his belt buckle.

"Orbital champion," Felix answered for him. She swept at his shoulder, dusting at something I couldn't see. "Nigel is a world-class pilot, retired orbital racer, and three-time champion." She brightened suddenly. "We'd be more than happy to fly you back to. . ." She trailed off, waiting for me to fill in the blank.

"No, thank you," Itzel said. She stepped closer, shielding Mai behind both of us. "We've already made arrangements."

Mrs. Santigo waved Itzel's decline away. "I insist!" She pulled a scarf out of her bag and covered her hair with it. "My craft has plenty of room for all three of you."

"We have our own means, but thank you for the generous offer," Itzel said, more firmly this time.

I saw curiosity work across Felix's face, but she hid it with a grin. "No need to share a rootzi with the riff-raff." She slid her gaze between Itzel and I.

"A friend arranged our transportation," I said.

She smirked, "Nice friend," then moved on. "Dr. Morant, I was very intrigued by your testimony. What a spectacular experience that must have been! What did you call them? The Woven?"

I hesitated to answer. "Yes. The Woven."

She let out a breathy laugh. "I imagine that must have been life-changing!"

I broke into a smile thinking about that day. And couldn't stop smiling. "It absolutely has been."

She tipped her head, letting some silver hairs fall across her face. "And what a profound statement: That we won't be able to explore the galaxy until we mend our ways? I'm curious if they gave specific instructions on how we can do better?" She covered her mouth and let out a soft chuckle. "I feel so silly asking that. *Of course* we can do better! We can always *do* better. But I'm sure if people *knew* what steps we could take that would give them some comfort."

"We have to pay attention to the exigencies of the day. They said we have entered a new phase but are trying to live by the rules of an outdated era. They didn't elaborate, but I think we all know what they meant."

Her eyes widened. "So you know what we need to do?"

"The Woven pointed out that we have all the information we need. It's simply a matter of collective will." That set her back. "But Mrs. Santigo, please don't take my word for it. The transcript and encounter are part of the public record. Study it for yourself."

The elevator chimed. The doors opened and a strong gust of damp air swept in.

"I see," she said.

I couldn't tell if she was annoyed or calculating. I was just happy that the ride was over.

Nigel stepped out first and motioned for us to proceed while he held the doors open.

The city stretched out around us. It was not the beautiful view I recalled. The trees were too manicured. The grass cropped too short. The buildings blocked the sky, each one built to out-reach another. The rootzi traffic added to the angry crowd swarming the building and two security copters darting overhead. They blasted commands to disperse and threatened arrest from their loudspeakers. Mai flinched and hid behind Itzel's dress. I nudged Itzel to hurry as Mrs. Santigo hung back to walk on my other side.

"Have you thought about being their liaison? Their global ambassador?" she asked loudly.

I slowed and looked at her.

I had thought about it.

I had tried to reach out to them on several occasions. I wanted more information, more understanding. For a moment, I admit that I thought Felix Santigo could help. She had money, connections. More than what Tessa Laine had. Santigo had power. She could make things happen. Then I remembered that nightmare and the maggots eating Beau from the inside out. I remembered how freely blood flowed from me and how quickly my family left.

I jokingly said, "That would be something, but I don't think they're hiring," and picked up my pace.

"Well, if they aren't going to utilize such a brilliant mind, I would be honored to have you join my company." She pursed her lips into a tight, puckered smile then chuckled at my surprise. "There aren't too many companies that can afford to sacrifice their image by hiring a counter-culture maverick like yourself, Dr. Morant."

I laughed hard enough to startle Itzel ahead of me. She turned around, looking confused. I held up a hand to assure her everything was fine and to continue on to the van.

Felix placed a hand on my chest to stop me. I pulled back, alarmed by how casual she was.

"Dr. Morant, you would be a perfect addition to Dyastryde."

"The mining company?" I asked. "What could I do for a lunar mining company?" I stepped around her, determined to get to my family and away from all of this.

"Oh, you'd be surprised, Dr. Morant!" Santigo nearly shouted to be heard. "Many great things are happening on the moon!"

That stopped me.

Her words took me back to Kin's office. We were desperately trying to maintain contact with the Woven. But they went quiet after our first, and only, conversation. I felt rejected, like maybe I'd offended them. Like maybe they saw through me, thought I wasn't sincere.

"Maybe this is all we get," Kin said. "It's more than what Dr. Dragonomassi got, and she died a happy woman."

I frowned at her. "She nearly lost her mind trying to understand the Dragon's Gate. I wouldn't consider that happy." I sagged in my chair.

"You've never read her journals?" Kin asked.

I scrunched my face in confusion. "What do you mean? She was quoted in every text since I was in secondary school. I've read all of her biographies and articles."

Kin stood up and walked over to her bookshelves. "No, I mean *her* journals. No editor, no censorship." She ran a finger over the worn spines of her old books.

"I didn't know there were unpublished writings." My curiosity grew as she plucked a thin, wax-cover book from the second from the top shelf.

"*She* published them, but by then, she was old news." Kin turned to a page and handed the delicate book to me with reverence. "I think about this when I watch the moon."

I remarked under my breath, "I still can't believe you're studying the moon, Kin."

"Just read it!" she snapped.

The pages were yellowed and thin. The cover was rough in my hands. There was an earthy musk to it. But the words were poetry.

> *As I ponder the magnificence of this portal to eternity, I*
> *find myself unworthy. Not in a way that diminishes me,*
> *but in a way that inspires willing submission to the truth:*
> *This is not our way out. This is God looking in.*

I smiled at Mrs. Santigo. "I'm sure many things are happening on the moon, but that's not my interest. Thank you." I climbed into the van, waved and closed the door before she said anything more. I was done with looking so far away.

Our spirits rose as the van lifted off and banked its wide turn over Lake Michigan. It climbed higher to carry us away from the hearing, from the Dominion capital, from a seventeen-year career obsessed with escape.

Mai folded into my lap. I pulled Izzie close.

"I heard Felix ask you to join Dyastride. To help their lunar mining operation. Are you interested?" she asked.

I had to laugh out loud. "Is that a trick question? Or a test?"

She didn't respond.

"No, I have no interest in that. I think I need to take some time. Pull weeds. Plant seeds. Make you tea. Bring you breakfast in bed. That's the job I want."

"But what about the moon? Aren't you concerned? We shouldn't take it for granted."

I thought about it briefly. "No. Kin can handle that."

Part V

The following transcript is the substantive communications between Dr. Tah Morant, former Chief Scientist, Umoja Program, CGA-0126-U019 and The Woven, an extra-terrestrial being encountered during investigation of Mission Failure Incident 19-0163-07-07-5X. It omits only the antecedent transmissions in which the two parties established their capacity to exchange communications. The full set of transmissions and their signal encodings, including all antecedent transmissions, have been secured by a trusted third party. An exact archive copy may be accessed at common-goal.umoja.19.logs.incident.CGA-0126-U019.

The first transmission occurred on 163-09-15.

Trans-mission Sequence Number	Sender	Message
0	Woven	Tingret's answer would render infinite possibilities in your understanding. 19 in ours. Thank you.
1	Morant	I send you greetings from Earth. I am called Tah Morant.
2	Woven	Greetings. Yes, we know who you are.
3	Morant	How?
4	Woven	Your thoughts led to the vessels that have journeyed beyond your heliosphere. We thought we should learn about you.
5	Morant	Who are you?
8	Woven	That is difficult to state in human terms. Your understanding of identity is primitive.
9	Morant	How so?
10	Woven	You think of unitary minds. We are like your understanding of cloth. Many threads. Each important, unique and respected, but one cloth.
11	Morant	What should I call you?
12	Woven	You may choose.

Trans-mission Sequence Number	Sender	Message
13	Morant	How about The Woven?
14	Woven	Agreed. It is respectful and not inaccurate.
15	Morant	Our engine failed on our recent journey. Do you know why?
16	Woven	Yes. We intervened.
17	Morant	Why?
18	Woven	Are you familiar with your history?
19	Morant	Somewhat.
20	Woven	Then the reason should be apparent.
21	Morant	Please explain.
22	Woven	-862, -493, -425, -282, -235, -167, -118, -45
23	Morant	Those brutalities were a long time ago, before the Global Accord.
24	Woven	Ha ha.
25	Morant	Are you laughing?
26	Woven	Yes, we laugh a lot.
27	Morant	About what?
28	Woven	Anything funny.
29	Morant	Such as?
30	Woven	Here is a good joke. On Earth to please God is very simple. Make a sincere effort and God will be pleased. But to please a human being is impossible. Even God cannot do it.
31	Morant	That is funny. Why did you laugh about the Global Accord?
32	Woven	How old is the universe, as far as you know?
33	Morant	At least 27 billion years.

Trans-mission Sequence Number	Sender	Message
34	Woven	Saying those atrocities are in your distant past. That is funny.
35	Morant	Umoja, our exploratory mission, was for peaceful purposes.
36	Woven	For a chief scientist you are not very observant. That is also funny. Humans do not yet know how to make peace. They have been shown, but so far remain willfully ignorant.
37	Morant	Many of our earlier flights were successful. Why didn't you stop them?
38	Woven	There were no humans on board. You are free to learn everything you can about the universe. But you cannot be allowed to poison the rest of the galaxy with your ego.
39	Morant	How was this decided?
40	Woven	Consensus.
41	Morant	Among whom?
42	Woven	Everyone we know, some trillions of minds.
43	Morant	Would they reconsider, if we agreed to abide by certain conditions that you establish?
44	Woven	We could ask, but it is unlikely.
45	Morant	Please do.
46	Woven	Done. The decision is unchanged.
47	Morant	Already? Did you really ask? How could you get consensus among trillions so fast?
48	Woven	Thought is much faster than light. Looking at the facts the best course is apparent to all.
49	Morant	What facts?

Transmission Sequence Number	Sender	Message
50	Woven	Humans have not yet learned how to work with one another, nor the world they have been gifted, with respect and harmony. Why would you be given other worlds to ruin? If you cannot achieve unity among your own kind, there is no reason to believe you would live in harmony with others.
51	Morant	Some among us feel that the human race will die if we cannot find another habitat.
52	Woven	Escape is not a solution. You would just inflict your ignorant ways on another world.
53	Morant	What then?
54	Woven	Change your paradigm.
55	Morant	Our paradigm?
56	Woven	Yes, you are like a caterpillar that wants to live in the cocoon forever. That will kill the butterfly. You are in a new phase. Trying to continue to live according to the former one will lead to extinction of you and everything you touch.
57	Morant	Do you think there is any hope for us?
58	Woven	Of course, you have been given sufficient guidance and you are intelligent.
59	Morant	Guidance? Why do you say it like that?
60	Woven	It is sacred, relevant, trustworthy.
61	Morant	You mean sacred scripture?
62	Woven	Yes.
63	Morant	Is that how you advanced?
64	Woven	Of course.
65	Morant	You received educators too? Like us?

Trans-mission Sequence Number	Sender	Message
66	Woven	Ha ha. Humans think these great educators came only to you? That is another thing we laugh about. Guidance is given to all. That is the covenant. It is a property of the universe. Study and respect it as you do gravity and DNA. Then the way becomes clear.
67	Morant	So you believe in God?
68	Woven	Not with the anthro-centric warlord connotations you inject into that title. More like the Onlooker sought by all, to use a reference you may be familiar with.
69	Morant	But you do believe in a transcendent being?
70	Woven	Believe? More like certitude.
71	Morant	How do you know?
72	Woven	When you have seen what we have seen, experienced all that we have, you would be unequivocal.
73	Morant	But how do you know?
74	Woven	The same way you do. The truth is manifested by great educators, as you call them. We understand it according to our capacity. As our awareness grows we learn to abide by new truths. That is how we advance.
75	Morant	It is the transition to a new truth where we stumble.
76	Woven	Agreed. Part of you is stuck in the old age where humans are to subdue nature and by inference dominate creation as though your animal existence is all that matters.
77	Morant	Is your guidance different?

Trans-mission Sequence Number	Sender	Message
78	Woven	Only in secondary particulars. The essential truths are the same, eternal. That is why you and us can talk meaningfully.
79	Morant	May I ask a question about the gate that we discovered?
80	Woven	You may, but we may not know the answer.
81	Morant	Did you create it?
82	Woven	It predates us. We believe it was installed by another people before our time who have since moved on to some other part of the universe.
83	Morant	Why do you continue to operate it?
84	Woven	It runs by itself. We do not know how to remove or close it without destroying everything on either side of it. We have chosen to leave it alone.
85	Morant	Thank you. That is helpful to know. Could we meet in person?
86	Woven	That would not be useful now, nor probably within the scope of your mortal frame. No doubt we will see each other in the future state.
87	Morant	You mean after we die?
88	Woven	Yes, when the creator's sign separates from our physical form to be precise. We are friends and friendship continues. You are well aware of that.
89	Morant	Yes, but it is nice to visit with one's friends, elevate conversation, and seek a common cause.
90	Woven	Agreed. But your tasks are not the same as ours. Study the sacred text for your new phase. It will illuminate both your goals and the path to advance which honors them.

Trans-mission Sequence Number	Sender	Message
91	Morant	Do I have your permission to share our conversation with others?
92	Woven	Of course, if you think that is useful.
93	Morant	Thank you. I understand.
94	Woven	Farewell. May you be confirmed in your efforts.
95	Morant	Farewell? Shouldn't we set up another conversation?
96	Morant	Hello. Hello. Woven are you there?
97 163-09-16	Morant	Hello. We got cut off yesterday. Could we continue our conversation?
98 163-09-17	Morant	Woven, please respond. I will need your help to corroborate this communication.
99 163-09-18	Morant	Hello Woven. Would you consider continuing our conversation with others here on earth so that they may hear your thoughts firsthand?
100 163-09-20	Morant	Greetings friends, could we resume our conversation?
101 163-09-22	Morant	Hello Woven, would you be willing to share why you have cut off communication? Have we offended you in any way?
102 163-09-25	Morant	Greetings again. Are you there?
103 163-10-01	Morant	Hello friends. Just out of curiosity, how did you solve Tingrit's paradox?

Trans- mission Sequence Number	Sender	Message
104 163-10-09	Morant	Dear Woven. I miss talking with you. You have been a good friend to us. I realize that your intervention is not out of any sort of animosity. In the end it will be for our own good. We would welcome any further interaction with you. We will continue to monitor this communication channel. Please respond at whatever time suits you.
No further transmissions have been received.		

Acknowledgements

First, we give our thanks to God, the All-Knowing and the Unknowable. We could not have predicted this journey once we started, but what a journey it has been. We owe so much to two women: Aurelia Blake and Linden Qualls. Your words, wisdom, love, support, research, advice, questions, pushes, and patience helped us show up for each other again and again, and without your combined presence, this journey would have ended quickly.

We want to thank our writing coach, Kim Douglas, of Write2Unite, who helped us mine and sculpt this story in ways we never could have done on our own. You challenged us to explore the darker, deeper sides of characters, examine with nuance, ask more questions and listen with curiosity. Tah Morant could not have found himself without your guidance. Our relationship as writers and business partners would be half as strong as it is today without your fountain of compassion and understanding. And thank you for inviting H.E. Wallace into a writing group where she found a wealth of inspiration, creativity, and necessary constructive criticism to keep crafting. Thank you Kim, Kemba, Sharon, Sid, and Masud. Your encouragement and artistic integrity lifted H.E. higher than she knew was possible.

Thank you to Dennis and Denise Stafford of OrganicSol. Without your help, all the work on the other side of writing would have been a long-avoided chore. You both lifted a load that neither of us had the desire or true capacity to do.

To our editor, Brooke Bryan, you served as a fresh pair of eyes when our vision had begun to blur. Your gentle nudges, your strong suggestions, and your willingness to be open to the ideas we wanted to explore gave us the right amount of self-awareness and confidence to solidify this first novel.

We also want to thank our advisors: Nathan Alan Davis, Dr. Lou Strolger, and Rose Croshier. Nathan, thank you for giving H.E. that early boost of confidence and thank you for pointing us in Kim's direction. You have no idea how much that weekend meant to the development of this book.

Dr. Strolger and Rose Croshier– call it luck or a blessing, but knowing two international experts in astrophysics and space policy feels unreal. Your perspectives, insights, and knowledge were desperately needed and we couldn't have found better people to provide it. Thank you for letting us ask our simple questions about complex theories and systems. Thank you for explaining those complexities in ways we could understand. And thank you for being part of this project and witnessing its evolution over time.

We want to thank Asiya Aidarkhan for creating our cover artwork and crafting beautiful images to bring our story to life.

Thank you to our first-draft readers: Barry Wittman, Anisa Kline, Khadija Morang, Bruce Parker, Jane Croshier, Rose Croshier, Linden Qualls, and Kevin Clark. Your feedback on that early draft reshaped this novel tremendously. Thank you for your frank and honest opinions.

And many thanks to our dear friend, Cyprian Sajabi. Your kindness and willingness to share parts of your personal history breathed life into Tah Morant. He would not exist without your story.

We would like to thank George and Laura at Patchwork farms in Dayton, Ohio for showing us how an intentional agriculture community would function. Their ingenuity and analytical approach grounded our understanding of Spot-245.

Thank you to Becky Norwood at Spotlight Publishing House. Your patience, guidance, flexibility, and knowledge made getting this book into the world easy and personal. And finally, we want to thank all of our friends and family, near and far, that listened, critiqued, prayed, advised, consulted, and cheered us on from the sidelines. There is no way two people with no clue about writing a novel could have written this book without all of you. We are honored, humbled, and immeasurably blessed.

Thank you isn't enough.
~ H.E. Wallace & Roi Qualls

About the Authors

~H.E. Wallace

Compelling stories have always captured H.E. Wallace's attention. INTERWOVEN, her debut novel, ties together her love for a good story and the dream of writing one.

Before becoming a writer, she earned her clinical doctorate for physical therapy and worked as a licensed physical therapist. That role gave her a chance to help people in her community, but left little room for creative expression. In 2020, in a leap of faith, she left her job to start over. The years that followed brought their share of uncertainty and underemployment, but they also sparked a deeper understanding: true transformation—both personal and collective—often begins with spirituality and the arts. Together with her co-author, Roi Qualls, she founded Knowetix to explore these themes. Through their work, they hope to inspire others to grow, create, and build stronger communities.

Beyond writing, H.E. Wallace's interests include reading, visual arts; music, audiobooks, and podcasts; threadworks, nature walks, and travel. She currently lives in a seaside Washington town near her mother who was the first to encourage her to write.

~Roi Qualls

Roi Qualls conceived his first novel, INTERWOVEN, in 2013, and it would not leave his mind. A decade later, he retired from his career as a database architect to bring it to life with co-author H.E. Wallace.

Together, they launched Knowetix in 2023—a creative collaborative rooted in storytelling, spirituality, and the vision of a just and unified future.

Roi studied philosophy and education at Earlham College before moving into software development. Over the years, he co-founded several startups—some were successful, others not so much — but all held important life lessons.

Deeply committed to community building, Roi actively supports efforts to advance racial harmony and justice. He lives in beautiful Yellow Springs, Ohio, with Linden, his wife of 45 years. They have two daughters and four grandchildren who bring them daily clarity and joy.

Amid a busy life, Roi finds peace in the company of the wildlife in his backyard and hope in the belief that stories—honest, courageous ones—can move hearts, shift thinking, and give strength in the struggle to shape a better world.

Points of Failure
Extra Materials

On the Knowetix website you will find additional information about the Points of Failure series. There is a Glossary of Terms, color maps and other bonus items. Here's the link:

knowetix.com/points-of-failure/extras

We invite you to post a review!
Please share feedback on our book.
This is the first in our three-part series
and your feedback is vital.

Envision the Future, Together.

Roi Qualls and H.E. Wallace —co-creators of Knowetix and authors of **Points of Failure Vol. 1: *INTERWOVEN*—** are available for talks, panels, and conversations exploring transformation, justice, spiritual insight, and the future of humanity.

Their storytelling bridges imagination and reality, offering fresh perspectives on how we live, what we value, and where we're headed as a global family.

From classrooms and podcasts to book clubs, conferences, and spiritual gatherings, they welcome invitations to spark meaningful dialogue on the forces shaping our inner and outer worlds.

knowetix.com/connect/

www.ingramcontent.com/pod-product-compliance
Lightning Source LLC
Chambersburg PA
CBHW061517020726
47502CB00006B/2117